Praise for Cherry Adair

White

"A gripping and passionate [...] thor Cherry Adair. This bo [...] page one and doesn't let go [...] the hero home with final wo [...]
—Seattle [...]

Hot Ice

"A relentless page-turner with plenty of enticing plot twists and turns."
—*Seattle Post-Intelligencer*

"[A] fast-paced and intricately plotted tale of danger, deception, and desire that is perfect for readers who like their romantic suspense adrenaline-rich and sizzlingly sexy."
—*Booklist*

"Adair has done it again! The chemistry between Hunt and Taylor is red-hot, and the suspension is top-notch."
—*Rendezvous*

"A very sexy adventure that offers nonstop, continent-hopping action from start to finish."
—*Library Journal*

"Get ready to drool, sigh, and simply melt . . . Fascinating characters, danger, passion, intense emotions, and a rush like a roller-coaster ride."
—*Romance Reviews Today*

Also by Cherry Adair

THE EDGE BROTHERS TRILOGY
Edge of Danger
Edge of Fear
Edge of Darkness

OTHER TITLES
White Heat
Hot Ice
On Thin Ice
Out of Sight
In Too Deep
Hide and Seek
Kiss and Tell

Books published by The Random House Publishing Group are available at quantity discounts on bulk purchases for premium, educational, fund-raising, and special sales use. For details, please call 1-800-733-3000.

Night Fall

A Novel

CHERRY ADAIR

BALLANTINE BOOKS • NEW YORK

A Ballantine Books Mass Market Original

Copyright © 2008 by Cherry Adair
Excerpt from *Night Secrets* copyright © 2008 by Cherry Adair

Published in the United States by Ballantine Books, an imprint of The Random House Publishing Group, a division of Random House, Inc., New York.

BALLANTINE and colophon are registered trademarks of Random House, Inc.

This book contains an excerpt from the forthcoming book *Night Secrets* by Cherry Adair. This excerpt has been set for this edition only and may not reflect the final content of the forthcoming edition.

ISBN 978-0-345-49990-5

Cover design: Jae Song
Cover photograph: Age Fotostock

Printed in the United States of America

www.ballantinebooks.com

OPM 9 8 7 6 5 4 3 2 1

To the incredibly brave men and women of the United States armed forces who put their lives on the line every day to serve our country here and overseas. You labor every day to ensure the safety of the people under your protection, risking your lives to preserve the lives and safety of others. Your sacrifices are not forgotten. From the bottom of my heart I thank you.

Night Fall

One

"Morning," Kess Goodall said absently as she and Simon Blackthorne passed in an upstairs hallway of the city offices of Mallaruza's state capitol building. Tear and sweat tracks painted pale lines through the dirt on her sunburned cheeks, and her gray eyes were shadowed. Something was up. She made no effort to hide it; in fact Simon observed that despite the greeting, she was barely aware of those she passed, and probably wasn't even seeing individuals as she speed-walked by.

Intrigued, he turned to watch her retreat.

Cute ass.

She was publicist for Abioyne Bongani, Simon's old college friend and current president of Mallaruza. Goodall had held up well in the past two months, considering that she'd been banished to this tiny country in midwestern Africa. No one wanted to hire her back in Atlanta, Georgia, where she was from. The PR community there had closed ranks on her. Instead of looking for a job anywhere else in the United States, she'd opted for a time-out here in Africa.

She hadn't chosen easy, that was for sure.

Escalating skirmishes on the border between Mallaruza and Huren, an outbreak of some deadly virus, and the upcoming elections were all keeping her out of trouble and on her toes.

As far as Simon could tell, she'd done a pretty decent job of promoting the good Abi was doing for his country. Since Abi was becoming suspiciously more saintlike as the day of his reelection approached, her duties were of the cheerleader variety—exactly what the untidy, yet vivacious, Ms. Goodall excelled at.

She wasn't going to hinder Simon's investigation in any way. Intel divulged that she'd been fired from the PR company she'd worked for. Being phenomenal at her job had saved her cute ass every time she'd pulled some insanely over-the-top stunt. Like attacking one of the other members of the staff, or throwing a vase full of flowers at a client.

She was impulsive, volatile, and unpredictable.

Simon had a wary respect for unpredictable.

His work as a T-FLAC/psi operative made unpredictable the norm. But an unpredictable civilian, right in the middle of what had the potential to be an extremely volatile conflict between two small countries, was *not* good.

His job here was simple. As president, Abi Bongani had called him in because he suspected another wizard might be manipulating the skirmishes on his border with Huren. The Hureni were a violent people, but they usually kept their fighting internal. Recently they'd started sending sorties deeper into Mallaruza.

Pillage, murder, rape, and general mischief. The Hureni were full-service bad neighbors, and bad for Abi's campaign.

As a friend, Abi didn't want Simon doing any more than tracking down the wizard responsible. He had his own ways of finding out *why*.

Simon was happy to have an all-expenses-paid vacation in Africa. The ocean was nearby and he was between ops. Why not? It had been years since he and Abi had tossed back a few beers and caught up on college memories.

Hmm. There'd been a redhead then, too. Or had it been a blonde? Since Goodall was reportedly a magnet for trouble, and wanting to know what the tears meant, he decided to follow her, undetected, into Abi's office. Loose cannons tended to go off in the worst possible situations.

The wide hall was filled with people rushing about. Simon strolled into a nearby public restroom, letting the door swing shut behind him. He checked the stalls, making sure the men's room was deserted.

He shimmered, invisible, back into Abi's opulent

office to hear what she had to say. Of course Abi, being a Half wizard, sensed that he was there. He lifted his head and frowned in Simon's general direction before he waved Goodall to one of the chairs in front of his desk.

"How was the trip?" Abi asked, his deep voice holding only a hint of Africa beneath his American high school and college English. He was an intelligent guy, with a capacity to do good like few people Simon knew.

He and Abi had lost touch over the years, but Simon knew his old friend was an idealist, a champion of lost causes, and had a competitive streak a mile wide. Simon had been intrigued to get the call asking for his help.

Crossing his arms, Simon took up position near a zebrawood bookcase holding leather-bound, foiled, first editions. None read. Just for show. But a classy show.

He considered himself a good study when it came to women. The bedraggled, baseball-cap-wearing redhead, walking to some internal tragedy, would not normally have garnered his attention. He liked women a great deal, but he had an aversion, a *strong* aversion, to sloppy and ill-kempt. When he had time to indulge himself, he usually went for sophisticated, well-educated, well-groomed, brunettes.

Goodall was a bit too straight up and down for

his taste. And her red hair wasn't just red. What he could see of it was wild, grab-your-attention, screaming *orange*. The color matched the bright orange hiking boots on her small feet. Subtle, she wasn't.

What she *was* was hot.

No matter what the hell his eyes conveyed, the message got tangled en route to his brain. Oval face, tender mouth, big eyes, freckles, and long lashes. The small, messy package that was Katie Goodall was sexy as hell, no matter how disheveled.

The president remained standing until his publicist sat in one of two fussy high-backed chairs in front of his mile-wide desk. Abi was an okay-looking guy. Not quite as tall as Simon's six three, and a little paunchy, but attractive enough to get his fair share of the ladies back when they'd attended MIT together. The conservative light gray custom-made suit and white shirt complemented his dark skin.

The somber, businesslike attire was a good choice for his position, but not Abi's usual taste, which ran to garish, flamboyant colors, and in the case of his office, baroque and ostentatious.

Goodall fell more than sat in the chair. Her cheerful bravado had apparently left her at the door. Beneath the dirt and the smell of clean perspiration was the scent of warm woman. For some inexplicable reason, and stunning him to the core,

Simon felt his body tighten. For her? His senses became sharper as he looked beyond the too-baggy khaki pants, the filthy, once-white T-shirt, the baseball cap, and the orange hiking boots.

Now that she was somewhat sedentary—somewhat being the operative word since the woman moved even when she was seated—Simon reevaluated his first impression.

She whipped off the khaki cap and pulled out the elasticized blue fabric tying her hair back. "We were too late," she said morosely, running her fingers through curly, dust-dulled hair and dislodging a shower of sand and debris.

Abi's brow folded into a frown at her words. Like Goodall, he was oblivious to the bits of grass and twigs littering his carpet. He rubbed a broad-palmed hand across his mouth, his black eyes shadowed. "Terrible. How many dead?"

"Five entire villages, all the way upriver." She scooted forward to perch on the edge of the deep seat. "Mr. President, I know you're doing everything you can to help. But I really think we need to ask the World Health Organization to step in. Whatever this virus or disease is, Konrad—Dr. Straus—*none of the doctors* can keep up with it. Thousands of your people are dying every day while they try to figure out how the disease is transmitted. We have to find someone who can get an immediate treatment. And we have to do it now."

"I'm well aware of the situation, Kess," he told her gently, and Simon could tell that the news, while expected, was a blow. Beads of perspiration dotted Abi's forehead, and he absently removed the decorative red silk hankie from his top pocket and wiped his face with it. "Rest assured I'm doing everything in my power to discover the cause and cure." He balled the damp cloth in his fist. "Where is the medical team you traveled with?"

"Still in the last village we came to. It's—God. It's horrific." She rubbed grimy fingers across her eyes as if by doing so she could stave off the vision of what she'd seen. "They're trying to save as many people as they can. I only came back for supplies, and to see if we can get them more help."

"Kess, you know that out of the four million people living in my country, over a million are in need of humanitarian assistance . . . Yes. I know. I know. One group at a time. All right. We'll send them more aid. They'll get as much help as they need," Abi told her, his tone grim as he reached for the phone. "I don't want you going back there. If y—"

"I promised I would. I'm careful, you know I am, but I can't *not* go back with the supplies and do what I can to help. Please?"

"Kess." Abi's tone gentled. Simon could tell how much his friend liked the scruffy woman seated before him. "You're neither a doctor nor a relief worker. Let the professionals do what I pay them to do. Your job was merely to observe."

"Please."

She was as hopeful as a puppy, and apparently Abi wasn't immune to her luminous gray eyes. "All right," he said again, his tone heavy, his face ashy with fatigue. "But you *have* to listen to what Dr. Straus tells you to do. You *must* promise not to jump in headlong to help people just because you want to help. Leave it to the professionals, all right?"

"I promise."

Yeah right. Her eyes, wide and sincere, said it all. This was no look before she leapt kinda woman. Impulsive was her middle name, and damn the torpedoes.

He'd bet his custom Taurus 1911, rosewood grip and all, that she would jump in where angels feared to tread, and get in everyone's way while she was at it. Enthusiasm didn't make up for actual knowledge. He'd better keep a trained eye on her while he was here. Screwing up wasn't a risk he was willing to take.

Abi's government couldn't provide security or services for the millions who needed it. He was doing a herculean job as it was. Added to his own people, whom he had to feed and protect, were millions of refugees he was allowing to cross his borders for protection.

The fighting between government and rebel

forces was resulting in attacks and human rights violations against civilians. The north of Mallaruza was in a state of crisis as civilians were caught between rebels, government forces, and armed bandits.

Abi had his job cut out for him on every front.

The least Simon could do was help him with his small request. Find the wizard tango who thought he could manipulate Abi for his own, as yet unidentified, purposes. Easy enough to do both.

Abi picked up the phone. While he gave his aide instructions to equip Ms. Goodall with everything she'd asked for, Simon ran a critical eye up and down the woman, sitting hands clasped between her knees. She was practically vibrating with impatience. To get out of there? To kiss a boyfriend good-bye before she left? To grab a shower before her hasty departure? he thought dryly.

"All right. Your supply trucks and three doctors will meet you outside in four hours. You can lead them to the village. Then you stay clear while they do what they can."

"Four hours?!" Horrified, she shot to her feet. "That's *way* too long—"

"It's as long as it'll take to gather what you need, and collect the doctors from their various posts."

She stuffed her fists deep into her pockets, then visibly relaxed her shoulders. "I know. Sorry. It's just that . . ." she trailed off, frustrated.

"I know, Kess. I know. Those are my people dying." Abi rose and walked around the edge of his desk to clasp a large hand on her shoulder. He gave it a squeeze, then stepped back, his expression somber. "Be careful."

"I will," she assured him, already striding to the door and her getaway. She hesitated, hand on the ornate brass door handle. "It's a privilege working for you, Mr. President. I hate to think how many more millions of your people would be dead if not for your compassion. Thank you."

Simon barely had time to shimmer across the room and whisper in Abi's ear, "Tell her you want your friend to go back with her. I'll leave Nomis with you." Nomis was Simon's name for his alter persona. Being able to be in two places at once was one of his powers. A good one to have in the counter-terrorist business. T-FLAC frequently got two for the price of one with him.

"Kess, just a minute." Abi halted her before she could pull the door open. "As a precaution I'd like my good friend Simon Blackthorne to go with you. I don't like the idea of you driving back on your own. Especially as the village is so close to the border."

A slight frown pulled Simon's brows together. She hadn't mentioned the location of the village. Unless they were working off of previous intel, which was possible.

"I won't be alone, I'll have—"

"Medical personnel doing their jobs."

She chewed her bottom lip. Simon's gut tightened. Must be indigestion. No way would his libido kick in with "Kess." No way. Hell, he even knew *why*. One of his worst foster mothers had been slovenly, with a mean right hook and a glint in her eye that said if it weren't for CPS knowing where six-year-old Simon was, he'd be dead.

Simon required his women to be fastidious and well groomed, so having his pulses jump, and his libido rise—for *Goodall*, was an aberration. Disconcerting to say the least. Fortunately, it would pass.

"Right," she said, resigned to having a babysitter on the return trip. "Okay. As long as he's ready to go right away."

He was. Because while Abi had told her four hours, he suspected she'd be gone the second she could get out of here.

She was already a pain in his ass.

Simon shimmered outside Abi's office door. A quick glance up and down the wide marble-floored corridors showed him he was alone. He materialized and knocked.

She opened the door, a small frown between her red brows. "I—" she glanced from Simon to Abi and back again.

Abi waved him in. "Kess, meet my friend Simon Blackthorne. Simon, Kess Goodall, my publicist."

"Oh." The guy she'd seen in the hallway. "Hi," Kess managed. Holy crap, he was *gorgeous*. Tall, broad, and tanned, with dark green eyes that seemed to see clear into her brain. She blinked to dispel the notion. Normally she wasn't tongue-tied around a guy, no matter how attractive, well dressed, and suave.

While he was a gift of sartorial splendor, even wearing plain jeans and a bright white T-shirt, she was a mess. After traveling, at breakneck speed, for four hours through the bush in an open jeep, and after spending three nights sleeping on the ground, she needed a shower and change of clothes. Desperately. He'd smiled in the hallway, but he wasn't smiling now.

She probably stunk to high heaven. "I have to go home and change. And shower," she tacked on quickly.

"I'll go with you."

"You'll go w—" Her heart did a little tap dance at the image of this man squeezed into her tiny shower stall with her. Wet skin. Soap. Slippery skin on slippery skin. "*What?* No," she said a little too vehemently. "I mean, no, just wait for me downstairs. I'll be back in an hour." Fifty-six minutes of that scrubbing off bushveldt.

He glanced back at President Bongani. "The backup supply trucks will be here—"

"At three," the president told him.

Kess wasn't waiting another four hours to start back. "Oh, yeah. Okay. I'll meet you downstairs at three. You'll need to bring a sleeping bag and enough supplies for three or four days."

"No problem."

She bet not. The man looked like he could handle just about anything. Good to know, because he was in for a shock when he saw the condition of the villagers. "I hope you have a strong stomach." She wanted to put him off. She really, really didn't want the distraction of him in the medical camp. "It's *really* bad. Lots of blood, people throwing up everywhere. No proper toilets—"

"I get the picture," he said, cutting off her litany of gross things he should anticipate.

"Don't worry, Kess." The president clasped his friend on the shoulder. "Simon can handle anything."

"I'm sure he can." She sounded as gloomy as she felt. It was going to be impossible to concentrate with the guy around. Kess wanted to lean into him just a little, to inhale the dizzying fragrance of his skin. *Damn* he smelled good. There was a faint tang of citrus mixed in with the fresh smell of the sea. He smelled . . . lickable.

Oh, please. Get a grip, she told herself sternly. She was hallucinating. She just wasn't accustomed to people smelling as . . . *clean* as this guy did. The men and women she'd been with for the last couple of weeks had to wash where and when they could. A shower was an unheard-of luxury. Yeah. He smelled clean. She didn't. That was it.

No it wasn't. Everything about him made her want to fling herself into his arms and yell "Take me, take me." She bit back a grin at what his response to *that* would be.

Pulling on her baseball cap, she snugged it down low on her forehead. She hadn't had sex in—three years? No wonder she was salivating. Simon Black-whatever was great-looking and exuded sex appeal. A few days spent at the medical camp would dirty him up some, and she'd be too busy to have lusty thoughts about him. She hoped.

She had to keep her focus when she went back. She wanted every moment of the doctors' struggle documented for the articles she'd write about what a helluva guy the president of Mallaruza was. This was important work. Not to mention she had a lot to prove to her peers back home. She might be on the other side of the world, but since she'd been fired from Wexler, Cross, and Dawson a year ago, she had the feeling that people in the small PR community were watching her every move. And just waiting to see her fall flat on her face. Again.

She didn't doubt that she was good at what she did, but she had an unfortunate history, and people had long memories.

Kess took this presidential campaign seriously.

Abioyne Bongani was a great man, doing incredible things for his country and his people. But this was Africa, where the good stuff went completely unnoticed by the rest of the world. Her well-placed articles and photographs would change all that. By the time she was finished, she'd make sure the world noticed.

"Downstairs? Three?" the president's friend said, verbally snapping his fingers under her nose to bring back her attention.

As if she were a toddler with the memory span of a newt. Considering what tangent she'd just been on, it wasn't exactly unjustified, she admitted. "Bring sunblock, it's hotter than the hobs of hell out there and not a lot of shade."

Kess turned on her heel and strode off down the corridor, not looking back. She kept her footsteps at a reasonable walking speed, and her back straight. But she could *feel* Simon's eyes on her every step of the way.

The only plus side was that she couldn't imagine a guy like *him* being attracted to a woman like her. Which, while an excellent deterrent to any inappropriate lusting on her part, was quite disappointing. She wondered if she could change his mind.

Kess grinned as she got into the antiquated elevator that joltingly carried her, and several other people, to the lobby. The president's friend might be just the antidote she needed to forget Atlanta for a few weeks.

The next few days would be interesting. Her heart took up a little Snoopy dance in anticipation as she crossed the enormous marble lobby, put on her sunglasses, and exited into the brilliant African sun.

Two

February on the plains of Western Africa was the season of "short rains." So while the dirt roads crisscrossing the vast savanna kicked up a plume of red dust behind Kess's Range Rover, the short grasses on either side were lush and green. Beyond the horizon on her left was the narrow, low-lying coastal area, to her right, and several hundred miles away, the start of the Huren rain forest.

The African prairie was dangerously beautiful. Teeming with wildlife, gently rolling hills made a bumpy green carpet as far as the eye could see. In the distance a herd of several hundred wildebeest ran parallel as the vehicle got closer. Kess almost stopped to dig out her camera when she passed a lone elephant. Its large ears flapped lazily at flies as it stood beneath the thorny branches of an acacia. While an elephant could run about twenty-five miles an hour, and was considered dangerous, this one-tusked old boy looked content to laze away the afternoon right where he was. Thank God.

Out-of-sight lions, cheetahs, and other dangerous predators stayed somewhere shady until it was time to come out and hunt at dusk. By then, Kess knew, she'd be in camp. Still, her gun was conveniently placed on the passenger seat beside her. Just in case.

She'd never even held a gun before she'd arrived here a couple of months ago. She'd gladly accepted the bulky handgun the president's aide, Chizobi, had given her on arrival. She'd been practicing shooting the thing ever since, getting lessons from anyone who volunteered as she traveled from village to village with the doctors. Carrying a gun was the norm here, and being able to shoot accurately made sense. Especially when she was close to the Huren border, and the Hureni were scary, to say the least.

Kess enjoyed adding to her skill sets. But here in Africa being able to shoot accurately was a necessity, rather than just a cool new hobby. Traveling alone wasn't optimal for safety. And while she was a pretty good shot, and it was broad daylight, she wanted to get to the safety of camp long before dusk. It was probably a stupid move on her part to leave without the president's friend. Two people traveling was always safer. But she had no idea if he knew how to use a gun, and frankly she hadn't wanted to spend four hours in the close confines of a car with a man who made her hormone level, not to mention her blood pressure, rise. It was hot enough.

He'd get to the camp eventually, and by then she'd be too busy to be bothered by him.

If she opted for speed, which she did, then she had to lose comfort, since the old Range Rover couldn't support speed *and* the air conditioner. Despite the swirling dust, she had the windows open. Hot wind stung her cheeks, and the dry air made her dig one-handed into the cooler. She grabbed a cold bottle of water, drinking as she drove. God, it was beautiful here. Stark, dangerous, and thrilling. Animals she knew from the zoo or *National Geographic* roamed freely all around her. Amazing.

How long had Simon waited for her outside the city building? Not long, she bet. He didn't look like the kind of guy to wait for anyone. On any level. Fine with her. He'd have his say in—she glanced at the inexpensive, utilitarian Timex on her wrist, trying to figure out from what time she'd left to his estimated time of arrival. "At dinnertime. Good thing the docs have antacid tablets," she said out loud, amused. "One of us is probably going to need them."

After meeting with the president she'd returned to the small residential hotel where she was living for the year she was contracted to spend here. She'd showered at warp speed. A change of clothes had made her feel female again. After repacking her duffel with fresh clothing and toiletries, she'd grabbed a twelve-pack of water from the small fridge on the rickety table crammed into a corner. She was ready and out the door in record time.

Simon-what's-his-face could hitch a ride to camp

with the relief team. Really, Kess thought, pressing her foot on the accelerator a little harder, a four-hour drive with that man would be unendurable. It would be hard to maintain a cool, professional façade when all she wanted to do was jump his—

"Never mind!"

He might be mildly irritated that he had to hang around for another few hours, but so what? She bit her lip. "Telling him I was leaving earlier would have been common courtesy, I suppose. Well, sure. But it's not as if I left the man at the alta— Oh, shit. What's that?" The vehicle was gasping like an asthmatic.

"No. No. No." Kess patted the dash. "Come on, baby. You can do it. Don't strand me out here in the middle of nowhere. Look. We'll go slower, all right? See? Foot off the accelerator." The car slowed to a painful, jerky crawl.

"Damn. Damn. Damn."

The supply trucks hadn't even left the capital yet. She was going to be stuck here, in the middle of nothing but sky and grass, for at *least* three more hours.

"No bad deed goes unpunished," she said wryly, babying the car along at barely a creep, her knuckles white on the plastic steering wheel as she willed the Rover to keep moving forward.

Her heart skipped a few nervous beats. She was out here in the worst heat of the day, and while most of the truly dangerous animals were smart enough to be somewhere relatively cool, that didn't mean her presence wouldn't annoy any of the ones lurking about.

"Good car. Good, *good* car. I knew you could go a little farther." She stroked the dash again. "No need to panic," she told herself firmly. "I'm in a car. Animals can't chew through steel. I have a cooler. Water. Snacks. Three hours isn't a lifetime." Putting both hands back on the wheel, she concentrated on willing the car to keep moving.

There was only this one road leading north. The supply trucks would have to pass her. Eventually.

There was a dark blob on the road in the heat haze in the distance. An elephant? A wildebeest? Kess didn't want to risk going off into the grass to go around it.

"Move, little beastie." It was quite a way in front of her crawling, coughing vehicle. The Rover was making so much racket that any intelligent animal would be long gone before she was anywhere near it. She hoped.

Even traveling this slowly, a collision with an elephant was going to be extremely unpleasant. For both the animal and herself. Loath as she was to do it, Kess let her foot hover over the brake.

But as she crept closer she saw it wasn't an animal, but another bulky Range Rover. She breathed a huge sigh of relief. Fortunately, going at the speed of an amoeba there was no dust, just the blistering hot air on her sweaty face. Squinting against the bright sunlight reflecting off the grille, she realized there was a man leaning insouciantly against the back of the vehicle, ankles crossed, fingertips stuck in the front pocket of his jeans.

"Impossible," Kess muttered under her breath. "No way! No freaking way." The lone man was Simon What'shisname. He did not look happy as his dark hair ruffled in the breeze and the sun beat down on his unprotected head. Kess could almost see steam coming out of his ears. The thought cheered her no end. At least then there'd be some humidity in the parched air. She pressed down on the brake and the car sputtered to a stop three feet from his knees.

She was a rebel without a pause.

"Hey," she said cheerfully, getting out of the car, but keeping the door between them. "Fancy meeting you here."

The sun struck his eyes, making the pupils an eerie translucent green. He smiled at her. Kess noticed his smile didn't reach his eyes. "Forget we had a date, Katherine?"

She blew out an aggravated breath. "My name," she told him coolly, "is *Kess,* and it wasn't a date per se. I knew the supply guys would give you a lift." Said supply guys being nowhere in sight.

"Clearly that isn't the case." He took his elegant hand out of his pocket. "I imagine they're several hours thataway." He indicated the way she'd come.

"And how does one get 'Kess' from Katherine? I thought it was a pet name Abi had for you."

"Katie Scarlett. Middle school. Bloodied noses until I was called K.S. Eventually K.S. morphed into Kess." She shrugged. "How'd you get here so fast?" He hadn't passed her, and for the last hundred miles this dirt was the only road north. She scanned the side of his car. The right side was dinged, and recently. The grassy dirt embedded in the crushed metal looked fresh.

His look burned her with jade fire as his gaze slid slowly over her, as if calculating the texture of her hair, the taste of her skin, and measuring her breasts for the way they'd fit his hands. *Whoa!* A flush that had nothing to do with embarrassment rode her cheeks as his lashes dropped and he ran his eyes like a physical touch up her legs. Wondering what they'd feel like wrapped around his hips in the throes of pleasure?

Or: Simon was staring at her hair and thinking it a too-bright mess, or admiring her cool new Asolo Stynger GTX bright orange hiking boots.

Amused at her own unlikely tangent, Kess jerked her chin toward his vehicle. "What happened? Run into an angry female buffalo?"

"A wily redheaded fox."

"No, really. Were you in an accident? What happened?"

"It fell." His expression gave nothing away. He'd make a good poker player.

Kess, who knew she'd make a shitty poker player because everything she thought was right there on her face like a freaking movie screen, frowned. "Fell?" As far as the eye could see were gently rolling hills. "Off what?"

"Never mind. Ready to go?"

"Go where exactly?"

"The village? Wasn't that your destination?"

"Does your car run?" Wouldn't that just be the straw on Kess's back having both of them break down in *exactly* the same freaking spot in the middle of freaking nowhere?

"*My* Rover is in perfect shape. Except for the dent." He paused long enough for his eyes to leisurely traverse each one of her less than stellar curves. *Again.* And it was not her imagination that his eyes flared. "Need help with your bags?" he asked conversationally.

Kess lowered her head, making a production out of adjusting her cap to block the sun's rays. She felt flushed and was fairly certain she was blushing for the first time since Trevor Mulligan had tried tongue kissing her in front of the whole third-grade class. "I'll get it, thanks."

"Fine, I'll get the air cranked up. You look hot."

Not hot like "So hot I'd like to strip you nekked and have my wicked way with you right here in this cool-looking green grass." No. The "You're so sweaty—keep away from me!" kind of hot. She opened her mouth to make a pithy comment, then snapped it shut.

Three days tops, Kess told herself, hauling out her backpack and the cooler. She stuffed the gun into the pack and zipped it closed. "Should I lock the car?" she shouted. His laugh made something inside her twinkle. "Oh, shut up," she told herself firmly, trudging to his car. Putting down the cooler, she jerked open the back door and tossed in her pack, picked up the cooler, and shoved that onto the floor after it.

"Why are you laughing?" she asked, getting into the car and slamming the door. The cold air felt so good on her hot skin she almost purred.

"We're close enough to the border for the Hureni to walk down the road and steal everything off that car until not even a spark plug is left. Think locking it will slow them down any?" He accelerated and they pulled away from her vehicle, leaving it there on the side of the road. He was right. The second the Hureni discovered the car it would be stripped down to an oil slick. But how did he know that? Hadn't he just arrived here?

Sharply aware of him, Kess turned the vent so icy air hit her face. "Probably not." She shivered. God, it felt great to be cool for a change. Being in such close proximity to the president's friend made her almost unbearably aware of him, which in turn made her hot. Not cold.

Squinting, she moved the sun visor to the side to

block the sun from her face and give her hands
something better to do than lean over and grab
him. Lord, he smelled good. Clean sweat and a hint
of something oceany. She changed her depth per-
ception to make him hazy and the background
clear. That worked. Sort of. "How long have you
known Mr. Bongani?"

"College. Off and on since."

She found herself staring at his hands on the
steering wheel. He had very elegant hands. Big.
Strong. His long, tanned fingers crisscrossed by
dozens of small, white scars. She imagined those
large hands cupping her breasts, and her nipples
ached. Redirecting the blast of cold air to mask the
obvious peak of her nipples, Kess said casually,
"Just here for a visit?"

Simon slanted his gaze over at her. "Why? Do
you have to vet all Abi's friends?"

"No. But he's an important man, and the elections are in a few days. I don't want anything to
upset him right now."

"And you think I'll 'upset' him?"

You upset *me*. Fighting for composure, Kess said
briskly, "Of course not. I was just curious as to
why you're here." This was ridiculous, she told
herself firmly, trying to ignore her very female reaction to his maleness. He drove with a relaxed ease,
one-handed, even though they were going almost
ninety.

"I'm a friend. Someone the president knows and

trusts. He *invited* me. Is that enough intel for you?"

Intel? Alarm bells went off in Kess's head. Oh, shit! "Are you in the army? Oh, my God. Is he going to declare war on Huren? Is *that* why you're here? Are you one of those guys the US sends in to plan attack strategies?" *Shitshitshit.* Why now, so close to the election?

"Jesus, woman. Do you even need an audience or can you conduct this wild-hair monologue without stopping for a breath so I can comment?"

Well, yeah. Her mind did have a tendency to race forward, running possible scenarios before she had all the facts. It was a good and bad trait in a publicist. Expect the best but plan for the worst. But still . . . "Just answer me honestly. Because if that *is* why you're here I have to go back and talk to the president about how we're going to handle the press." She hauled her backpack from the floor in back onto her lap, unzipped it, pushed aside the Browning, and started rummaging through the cavernous depths for a notepad and pen.

"Write this down, it's important."

Kess chewed the corner of her lip, and placed the tip of the pen on the first line, then cast him a quick glance. "Ready."

"Simon Blackthorne—That's BLACKTHORNE with an e—is in Mallaruza visiting his friend Abioyne Bongani, President of Mallaruza, for a little R and R, beach time, reading time, and a little sightseeing thrown in to keep the mix interesting. You're not writing."

"Funny." She stuffed the pad and pen back into the bag, then tossed it with a *thunk* onto the floor behind his seat. "Fine. You're on vacation. Here. Where there could be a bloodbath with Mr. Bongani's detractors any minute, where some weird but virulent virus slash disease that scares the crap out of *me* is killing thousands of people a day. Where the temperature is a hundred in the shade, and the beach is littered with jellyfish. Yeah. I see why a man like you would pick Mallaruza as a prime vacation spot."

"You talk a lot, don't you?"

"Well, you have to admit—"

He shoved a CD into the player and Maroon Five belted out "Highway to Hell." *Rude, but appropriate,* Kess thought, sliding her spine down into the comfortable leather seat and readjusting the cold air vent. She closed her eyes.

"Don't go to sleep. I need directions."

She snorted. What's the bet he'd Mapquested the route, got a GPS satellite reading, and called freaking OnStar before he'd set out. "Straight on until morning."

"I'm no Peter Pan, believe me."

"Hmm." The sun was baking her cheek. Without opening her eyes, Kess reached up to adjust the visor. Her hand encountered Simon's on the same mission.

Simon told himself not to touch her a nanosecond too late. Their fingers brushed, then seemed to fuse and remain still. Her skin was smooth, warm, and vibrantly female.

"I'll get it," he said at the same time as she said, "I'll do it."

He dropped his hand, suspecting that if he didn't cave she'd arm wrestle him for domination of the sun visor.

He accelerated. He had more serious concerns than an unwanted sexual awareness to deal with. He hoped to hell he wouldn't require his wizard powers for a few hours. Jesus. The simple teleportation of a 3.5-ton vehicle was nothing. He'd done it hundreds of times. Half an hour after she was supposed to pick him up outside Abi's office, Simon had been hot on her trail. He'd floored the Range Rover just because he enjoyed driving. And driving fast, on a dirt road, kicking up a rooster tail of red dust. The Rover wasn't a fighter jet, but the speed was still a rush.

As fast as he'd been going, his elusive guide was faster. Even with her head start, she was nowhere to be seen. And since Simon knew there was only one road, this one, due north, she was clocking in at speeds higher than what was remotely safe, even out here where the land was nothing but gently rolling hills with no traffic. Hitting a large animal at ninety miles per hour would, at best, leave a mark and, at worst, kill the animal, her, or both.

Fifty miles in, he'd decided to teleport himself and his vehicle to intercept her. Teleportation was one of the easiest powers. Something he'd never given a thought to.

Invisible, he'd teleported, unnoticed right overhead, and had picked a spot under a shade tree some three miles ahead of her limping vehicle. Unfortunately, his power had sizzled like an electrical outage a hundred feet off the ground and a mile short of his target. He, and the vehicle, had suddenly materialized, dropping like a rock.

His fucking power had short-circuited. Again. Good thing he'd managed a last-minute landing alteration and come down on the grassy verge.

Shouldn't have happened.

But it had.

In the last few weeks he'd had a fifty-fifty failure rate. The power outages were coming a hell of a lot more frequently. Scared the crap outta him. He supposed he could talk to his friends, but damn it, he was embarrassed. A kind of wizard performance anxiety, he thought. Unamused.

Worse, the malfunction of his powers endangered not only himself but fellow T-FLAC operatives and innocents alike. Hence the vacation.

This was bullshit on a grand scale.

He'd been lucky so far.

A wizard without powers was . . . Not a wizard, for Christ's sake! Since it wasn't just what he did, it was who he was, the thought chilled Simon to the bone.

If it happened again he'd put in a call to Mason Knight, the man who'd taken him under his wing. Mason was a combo father-figure, mentor, and friend. Surely to God he'd know how to repair Simon's powers.

He rubbed a hand around the back of his neck, casting a quick glance at his passenger. Head supported by her bent arm against the window, she gave a good imitation of being asleep. She wasn't, of course. He could practically hear her agile brain doing calisthenics, but for now he'd pretend along with her. He needed the silence, and the hypnotic visual of the long, straight dirt road ahead, to concentrate.

"I pity the poor guy you're planning to dismember." Her voice was low and husky. Simon had been aware of her observing him for the past several minutes.

"Maybe it's a woman."

She straightened up and tucked a leg under her. Her ball cap had fallen between the seat and door, and she pulled it out of the space, but didn't put it back on. Her hair, especially in the direct sunlight streaming through her window, was fiery, and seemed to have a life of its own. Now clean and shining like liquid fire, Kess's hair was stunningly beautiful. Simon's fingers flexed on the hard steering wheel as he resisted reaching over to touch it.

"I don't think so," she said with utmost certainty, her luminous gray eyes fixed on his face. She had very long, thick dark lashes that made her eyes appear as open and guileless as a child's. But she was no child. Her firm, round breasts pushed out the front of a clean white T-shirt very nicely.

"I imagine," she mused, pursing her lips. Jesus. Was she deliberately trying to make him salivate? "That if you're engaged by a woman, you treat her very well."

Simon bit back a smile. She really was a piece of work. "What if I'm not 'engaged' by her. What if she's a pain in my ass?" She was a pain all right. Right in the nuts.

"I still don't think you'd ever physically harm a woman," she said, looping her arms around her bent knee and cocking her head to look at him. Her hair slithered down the front of her shirt like magma. "Break her heart maybe," she offered. "Now if a *guy* got on your wrong side I imagine you could handle yourself pretty well."

Behind her head, and in the distance, Simon saw a herd of delicate gazelles leaping like butterflies through the grass. He was tempted to point them out to Kess, anything to break this inane turn in the conversation. Instead, he let his attention flicker to the road ahead, then glanced back at her. "Ya think?"

She lifted her shapely ass off the seat to fish a rubber band from her back pocket. "So, Simon

Blackthorne with an e, what do you do for a living when you're not vacationing in deepest, darkest Africa?" She put the band between her teeth and did that wholly female thing of sweeping her hair back and into a ponytail. The movement lifted her breasts and arched her back.

Simon had a clear and vivid image of Kess sitting on a bed. Just like this, arms raised, breasts bared. Waiting. "Any water in that cooler back there?"

She twisted the band into her hair, then leaned over between the seats to open the cooler on the floor in the back. Her shirt rode up, baring the un-believably sexy small of her back. She smelled of something floral. Something tropical. Something that reminded him of sultry nights under billowing white drapes, with the scents of the ocean and woman thick in the balmy air.

At this rate he could steer the fucking car with his cock.

She righted herself and handed him one of two icy glass bottles. "Cheers." She clinked bottles with him, then removed the cap of one, extended her hand, and switched with him.

She chugged down half the bottle in one go. "Profession? Job? Vocation?" she prodded.

Simon drank deeply before answering. "Private contractor."

"Cool." She ran her dewy bottle across her fore-head, so sparkling droplets of water ran down her temple. He wanted to stop the car, and—Fuck.

This was ludicrous. The woman wasn't giving off even the faintest of signs that she was remotely attracted to him. *She's not my type, for God's sake.*

"I've always admired people who can work with their hands," she said cheerfully, running the wet bottle down the side of her neck. First one side, then the other. "I have two left thumbs. I made a birdhouse in woodshop in third grade. I ended up with both left thumbs black and blue, *and* supergluing my fingers together." She grinned, her teeth white, one eyetooth slightly, and damn it, *endearingly,* crooked. "It was fun though. Homes or offices?"

He'd intentionally misdirected her, but he could say with absolute truth, "Home."

"And you can stay away from work like this for weeks at a time? Won't you lose business by not being there?"

Fish away, honey. I'm a professional liar. "The only house I'm working on right now is my own." That was true. Which surprised him, because he didn't share a lot about himself. Particularly to strangers. "There's a fork up ahead. Left or right?"

"Right. We'll be there in less than an hour. What kind of house is it?"

Permanent. Beautiful. Mine, Simon thought with a sense of pride and accomplishment. He was putting sweat equity into it, but the roof was on now. One day . . . "Ranch style on a hundred acres." He pictured the cedar exterior, nestled as it was right now in a blanket of pristine snow, just waiting for a fire to be lit in the mammoth great room fireplace. The rocks he'd placed there, one by one, excavated from his own property.

"Are you going to run catt— Watch out!"

A massive white rhino stood four-square in the middle of the road. "I see him." Hard to miss. Its head swiveled as the car approached, but the animal didn't move out of the way. Its inch-thick light-colored hide was stained with red dust, making the ugly son of a bitch pink. Ridiculously small ears swiveled as Simon braked and slowed to a stop a good fifty feet away.

"We could go around him," Kess whispered as the large beast snorted irritably at the car.

"His wife is on the left, the kids on the right. Look."

The female wasn't looking any too happy having the metal monster between her and the three fat little calves munching grass on the opposite side of the road.

"Now what?"

Simon could think of a dozen things they could do to pass the time. Most of them involved removing their clothes. "Now we wait until the family moves on. This is their backyard, they have right of way."

She settled her back against the door, curving her leg up on the seat, then rested her water bottle on her booted ankle. "Are you married?"

Christ, her gaze was direct. "What makes you ask?"

"You're building a house." She shrugged. "Single guys don't usually build a house unless they're married or planning to be married soon. Are you?"

Simon shook his head, amused by her persistence. "I'll eventually marry." In about three years he'd start some serious searching. For the moment he was quite content to wait for that particular "want" on his list. Right now he was enjoying the planning. The anticipation.

"Anyone in mind?"

"Yeah, I have an image in my head." So crystal clear, so specific that his future wife and mother of his future children was almost real to him. "Haven't met her yet." But he'd know her the second he saw her.

"You have an image of the woman you'll marry one day?" She drank the last of her water, and he watched her throat move as she swallowed. Simon imagined what Kess would taste like if he ran his tongue down the sweet curve of her neck, then had to adjust himself by shifting in his seat.

"Really?" she arched a red brow. "That's fascinating. Tell me about her."

Simon leaned his shoulder against the window. The rhino family wasn't going anywhere. He looked at Kess, at the way the brilliant sunshine backlit her hair like a fiery halo, at the way her sharp little nipples pressed against her T-shirt, at the way the khaki pants pulled tight across her mound. "You want to know about the as-yet-unidentified woman I'm going to make my wife?" He swigged the cold water to flood his dry mouth with moisture.

"Got anything better to do?" She reached into the cooler and removed a pack of cookies. She held up the bag. When he shook his head she reached in and took out three. Sharp white teeth crunched into a cookie. Crumbs fell onto her chest. He almost groaned out loud. How could someone this oblivious be this fucking sexy? The wild mane of ginger hair, her lightly tanned, freckled skin, the sassy mouth all added up to any man's wildest fantasies.

Making herself comfortable, she reached for another cookie. "Tell me about her."

He'd played this game, mentally, for years. But Simon hadn't even told his best friends about the house, let alone the wife and children he intended to people it with. "Tall. I don't want to get a crick in my neck bending down to kiss her."

Mist-colored eyes brightened as Kess smiled and an insidious heat seeped into Simon's blood. "She could always stand on a step stool," she offered, eyes dancing.

"Hardly handy," he told her dryly. "Dark hair. Black or a dark brown will work. Brown eyes. Pale skin. Not too fat, and not too thin—"

"Have you tried Stepford?" Kess asked, her

words brimming with amusement. She polished off the first cookie and bit into the second, leaving a fleck of chocolate on the corner of her mouth. He was getting a hard-on watching the woman eating, for God's sake.

It took everything in him not to lean over and lick that sweet smear off her mouth. He gritted his teeth at his own idiocy. Here he was describing the woman of his dreams, and he was literally panting like a horn dog over another woman. He actually felt guilty. As though he were cheating on his future wife. Kess Goodall was making him insane.

He dragged his gaze away from her lush mouth. "Great sense of humor—"

Her lips twitched. "I'm guessing big boobs are on the list?"

"I don't care about the size of her breasts."

"Well, you'll have to consider size before you put in your order. Good God, Simon. You can't order up a wife like—like a *burger.* Don't you want to just meet a random someone and fall madly in love?"

"I'll love my wife until the day I die."

"But don't you—" Kess changed her mind. He was so intense and serious that he was fun to tease. But she wasn't going to press her luck. "Look. The rhino family is packing up and going home. Oh, my God, how cute are the babies?"

She'd peppered him with enough questions, and wanted to digest everything he'd said. She'd never heard a man speak with such obvious sincerity about a subject that should be entered into blindly and with great gusto. What an interesting guy. He made her . . .

She tried to analyze her physical reaction to him and bit back a smile. He made her feel intensely, gloriously . . . *female.* And aware of her own body in a way she'd never felt before. She glanced out the side window, enjoying the way her heart beat so quickly, the way her skin felt sensitized as if waiting for his touch. She brushed a finger over her lips and felt a surge of pleasure at just being alive. With him beside her and the brilliant African sunshine streaming into the car.

Life—at least now in this exact moment—was good.

Simply . . . good.

As soon as the last of the rhinos crossed, Simon started the car and they resumed their trip. Kess could feel that her face had gotten sunburned through the window, despite the sunblock she wore religiously. No pale skin on her. One side was red, the other a nice golden brown from spending months in the sun.

Of course she wasn't brunette, tall, or Stepford either. "The base camp is in the middle of those trees. Eucalyptus," she told him. "Imported, and part of a failed attempt at a cash timber industry. I'm sure the animals enjoy the bonus shade. Honk lightly three times so they know it's us—*They* the *camp,* not they the animals." She smiled. "The Hureni skulk around every now and then."

Kess didn't mention that the sound of approaching vehicles immediately signaled danger and possible attack. Most villages were along roads, so they were easy targets for bandits, rebels, and the government army who came to pursue their various agendas: stealing food and other goods, kidnapping children, attacking villagers.

The presidential guard, when not kept in check, were frequently brutal and, despite Mr. Bongani's instructions, had burned hundreds of temporary camps of refugees fleeing just such treatment in their own countries.

Villagers had told Kess that sometimes the army parked their vehicles a few kilometers outside the villages so that they could launch a surprise attack on foot. People would leave their belongings and run off from the main dirt road or their villages into nearby fields. Many were so scared that they lived in the bush for months.

Kess bit her lip. The president's job seemed insurmountable to her. But God, he was doing his best, and she admired the hell out of him for the inroads he was making.

Simon gave the horn a triple tap as they approached.

"That's weird." Kess put both feet back on the floor and leaned forward, her hand braced on the console as she tried to see the camp up ahead through the trees and shrubs. "Usually Jackson, Dr. Viljoen's dog, comes bolting out to meet visitors. They must be upriver collecting samples . . ."

A dark shape in her peripheral vision caught her attention, and she lifted her eyes to the sky.

The air above the trees was filled with a swarm of circling vultures.

Three

Simon grabbed her upper arm as Kess flung open the door and started to jump out of the car. "Stay here," he instructed, his expression grim. In his left hand he held a small, deadly-looking black gun. Half the size of hers, but it looked twice as dangerous. Despite the intense, baking heat, she felt a frisson of icy dread watching Simon striding toward the trees. Oh, God. She hadn't told him the seriousness of the Hureni raids this close to the border. For all she knew the camp might be full of Hureni warriors. And Simon was alone.

Without further thought, she kneeled up on the seat, hauling her pack up and over onto the armrest between the passenger's and driver's seats. Yanking down the zipper, she found her gun right on top of her clothes. Her fingers barely shook as she picked it up, methodically clicking off the safety.

She grabbed her camera as well, tucking it in her front pocket, then got out of the car, leaving the door ajar just in case she needed to jump back in.

She couldn't hear herself think over the noise of the determined birds wheeling above. With their bald pink heads and dark gray bodies they looked exactly like the scavengers they were. Kess shuddered with the creepy-crawlies.

It was oddly silent once she'd filtered out the sound of the birds screeching. No talking. No Jackson barks. No Enzi singing as he started the dinner fires. No Koffi scolding the dog for getting into her clean wash.

This can't be good. Kess ran lightly in the direction Simon had gone, slipping into the trees several yards behind him. Without turning around, Simon lifted a hand in a stopping motion. Weird. As if he had eyes in the back of his head.

Since he seemed to know what he was doing, Kess stopped. And as impulsive as her action was, leaving the car, she wasn't stupid. He might need help, and while she wasn't by any means a crack shot, she usually got what she was aiming at.

This was no city park. The dangers were too numerous to count. People. Animals. Insects. All were potential threats. The camp intentionally wasn't anywhere near an animal drinking area, but it *was* close to the river. A mile to the south was the latest village to succumb to the virulent disease sweeping the country.

Soon animals would come to drink, predators would be out in search of their prey. And the ever-present Hureni would go stalking as well, though their prey was the food and medicine in the aid camps set up by President Bongani.

When Simon moved, she moved. A dozen scenarios flashed through Kess's mind as she stealthily followed in his footsteps, clutching the heavy gun in both hands, her arms outstretched.

She calmed herself by imagining less dangerous options. Like the possibility that the nomadic Fulani had come to trade goods, and the entire camp had gone off to see . . . *Oh hell,* Kess thought, fear making her mouth dry and her heart pump way too fast. The entire camp was *never* gone. Not everyone at the same time. And then there were the vultures to consider.

The weight of the gun in her outstretched arms made her muscles ache. She adjusted it slightly, her arms trembling, both from the physical weight and the ethical weight of responsibility. She hoped to hell she didn't have to shoot anyone, but if push came to shove, she thought she could do it.

Simon kept moving, his passage between the trees almost ghostlike. Kess stayed about twenty feet behind him. There was a small clearing up ahead, and while she couldn't yet see it, base camp was straight through the trees. The coarse cry of the birds swooping and dive-bombing overhead made the hair on the back of her neck stand up and a series of chills race down her spine.

Her heartbeat was thundering in her ears. She wrinkled her nose at the sickly-sweet smell thickening the hot air. God. *What the hell was that gross smell?* She tried to separate it from the pungency of the eucalyptus trees, and the green, scummy smell of the nearby river, but couldn't quite identify what it was.

A lion roared, sounding terrifyingly close to a woman who happened to be walking through the carnivore's backyard. There were many things Kess was willing to do for her job, but being torn limb from limb by a hungry lion wasn't one of them. She was equidistant from the car and the camp, but she knew, despite the overwhelming urge to do so, that running would not be a good thing. The air was still, no breeze moved the hot air between the trees. The lion could be twenty feet away, or two miles. She didn't want to be fast food should one of them decide to run her down.

Two miles would be good. Two miles would be most excellent. Stay right where you are, kitty.

Simon glanced over his shoulder and shook his head, pointed at the ground, and made a stay motion with his free hand. She stopped dead in her tracks. It made sense for her to stay put. But he'd be really sorry if he came back to find she'd been partially consumed by a pride of ravenous lions. She'd be pretty freaking sorry too, she thought wryly as she scanned the area around her for any movement.

He motioned that he'd be going ahead, and Kess took a few steps to her right. Doing a quick scan to be sure there wasn't any animal life on the bark, she leaned back against a giant tree. Using it to help support her aching muscles, she lifted the muzzle of the gun. For several long, agonizing minutes she stood there, barely breathing as Simon disappeared between the trees. In his absence and despite the gun in her hands, Kess was keenly aware of her vulnerability. Lions and Hureni weren't the only dangers. Not by a long shot. Sweat trickled down her neck.

The locals had warned her never to wander far from camp. Not all threats stood on four legs. Cobras, puff adders, and bush vipers were all common in this area as were the venomous funnel-web tarantula spider, which had venom three times stronger than a black widow. *And* its fangs could pierce through clothing and sometimes even shoes.

Or she'd just give herself a terror-induced coronary on the spot as she listed everything that could kill her while she waited.

A hundred years, and a thousand rapid heartbeats later, Simon reappeared in the clearing. "Go back to the car, Kess. Now." His grim voice carried easily. He wasn't whispering. He still had his gun in his hand, but she could tell by the line of his shoulders that he wasn't as tense as he'd been a few seconds ago. Having cleared the trees, he was highlighted by the sun as he stood just out of the tree line, and in the camp itself. The vultures were swooping through the clearing up ahead, not in the least bit deterred by his presence.

She heard him, but she was so freaked out by the

rank smell, and the roar of the nearby lion, his words didn't compute.

Putting her tired arms down, but keeping the safety off the gun now at her side, Kess walked up beside him. "Where is everyo—" She took a reactive step backward as bile rose in the back of her throat.

There'd been a bloodbath. A massacre.

Bloodied bodies were strewn from one side of camp to the other. Not all the bodies were intact. Limbs and entrails littered the ground. Blood had seeped into the ground, turning it an unnatural shade of brownish red, or pooled in the dried, wrinkled foliage blanketing the grassy ground.

The vultures barely looked up from ripping the carcasses with their sharp beaks. Half a dozen hyenas gorged on the remains, shifting aside only when a vulture laid claim to the body.

Kess's eyes saw the wholesale murder of her friends like a Technicolor nightmare spread out in front of her, but her brain could hardly comprehend what she was seeing. "What—How—God, oh, God . . ." Automatically, she lifted the camera and clicked off a fast series of graphic pictures.

Even through the viewfinder, none of the dead were remotely recognizable.

Gagging, she grabbed onto Simon's strong forearm as her knees threatened to buckle.

"Don't. The vermin will be over here quicker than you can spell puke." He spoke so quietly she wasn't sure if she was actually hearing him or reading his lips.

Swallowing convulsively, Kess buried her face against his arm. The sight, coupled with what she now realized was the stench of blood and sun-roasted flesh, made her stomach writhe and her legs weak.

"Breathe through your mouth. Slowly."

Nose or mouth, Kess didn't want to breathe in death. She shook her head, eyes squeezed shut, lips pressed hard against the tensile strength of Simon's biceps. She thought she felt his hand on her hair, but if that were the case it was cold comfort.

He was moving, and Kess went with him, still numbly glued to his side.

She heard the creak of the car door, and realized they were back at the car. "Get in," he said, gently extricating her clenched fingers from his arm. "Lock the doors, and stay put. I'm going to look around."

"Don't—" *Leave me.* "—do anything stupid," she said instead.

His lips twitched. "Ditto."

"Simon—"

He turned back. "Yeah?"

"Will you—will you check to see if anyone m-made it?"

"Sorry, honey. No one made it."

"How can you be sure?"

"The scavengers got there second. The machetes came first."

Bile rose in her throat once again at the vivid mental image of the medical team being hacked to death by dull, rusty blades. She could almost hear their screams, feel the stinging pain of slow but deadly slices ripping through skin to bone. She'd seen television footage of the massacre in Rwanda, and the thought of people she'd been with just hours earlier being murdered so methodically squeezed her chest tight.

"Keep that gun handy."

"What if the—"

"Lock the doors." And he was gone.

The protection spell, coupled with a few tons of metal, would protect her. Against human and/or wizard foes. It would keep Kess safe, but Simon knew it wouldn't keep the unpredictable woman where he'd told her to stay. He considered putting a binding spell on her, but resisted. His powers were iffy at best, and God only knew, he might need all the juice he could muster.

Loping through the striations of dusty sunlight shafting between the trees, he sent out a mental probe. The danger was still present. Not wizard. Didn't mean that a wizard couldn't slip through his probe, especially given the recent unpredictability of his powers. The massacre in the camp didn't have any of the hallmarks of the work of a wizard.

Simon shimmered, invisible, into camp. The birds

and hyenas startled, sensing his presence, shifted uneasily for a few moments, then went back to work. A quick recon showed no one had been spared. The slayings had all the signs of overkill. Unnecessarily brutal, most likely Hureni.

Suddenly the hyenas lifted their heads, ears alert, and the vultures took wing in a loud flurry of squawks and flapping wings.

Simon heard stealthy footsteps behind him seconds before the animals scattered. Five or six pairs of bare feet rustling the dry leaves. He couldn't use his three-sixty vision because it wasn't damn well working.

He glanced down. Ah, crap! They could see him clear as day. He'd materialized without being aware of it.

Hell, he really needed to get ahold of Knight and get some fine-tuning on his powers. Pivoting, he blocked the knife a warrior aimed at his ribs. Missed his ribs, but took a slice out of his arm. Stung like fire. Simon's fist connected with the guy's jaw. The blow landed on its target, then his fist slid off the tribal paint on the warrior's face, and connected with his ear. Bringing up his knee, Simon hit the guy with a debilitating blow to the groin.

The warrior doubled over, falling to the ground with a high-pitched shriek of agony. Two more came up behind him, assegais raised. Working in Simon's favor, the assegai, a long wooden spear with a metal point bound to the end, was too unwieldy for close combat. But these guys knew what they were doing, and they let fly from ten feet away. The sharp blades bit into the dry dirt at Simon's feet. Close, but no cigar.

He shimmered, teleporting behind them. It worked, scaring the bejesus out of his opponents. Spinning in bare feet, they raised their stabbing spears and started babbling, looking around for the Ghost-man, holding up their *ishlangu,* hunting shields, to protect themselves.

Two Hureni warriors, braver than the others, circled him, their frightened eyes white-rimmed in their brightly painted faces. Their dark skin gleamed with sweat and animal fat. They might be confused and afraid about what he was, but these two, protected by their animal skin–covered shields, weren't backing off.

It would be good magic for them to capture and kill him, Simon knew. Wasn't gonna happen. His punch to the rock-hard shield caught the guy on the left flat-footed and stunned him. He bowled over, his shield flying. The one on the right came at him fast and furious. Seeing that the shield his friend had held protectively against him hadn't worked worth shit, he tossed his aside and came at Simon with blood in his eye and a short-bladed hunting knife in his hand.

Simon smiled. The guy faltered.

"Come on, asshole," Simon taunted, beckoning him in with a hand gesture. "Just you and me."

They circled, their feet sending up small clouds of smoky red dust. Simon kicked the knife out of the man's hand in about two seconds. "Tsk. Tsk." He had the Taurus, but it wasn't going to do him much good against five men. More important, he didn't want to draw more attention to the current problem if he didn't have to. Hand-to-hand was fine and dandy with him. Fact was, he enjoyed a good workout, and right now he had adrenaline to burn.

The guy, war paint, loincloth, and primitive weapons aside, was professionally trained. South African trained if Simon knew his moves. And he did. Interesting. Why were these local Hurenis South African military trained? To what purpose out here in the middle of nowhere?

A warrior did a spinning heel kick with a gnarled and filthy foot, aiming for Simon's jaw. What Simon knew, and his opponent didn't, was that one never kicked the other guy above the waist if one could help it. It was the best way to get your nuts ripped off and stuffed into your mouth. Clearly, the warrior didn't know this rule.

Simon did a front snap kick at the same time, lifting the guy, his balls on the toe of Simon's boot, five inches off the ground. Having made the same incorrect tactical fighting move once himself, Simon knew the level of pain he'd just inflicted. The warrior screamed bloody murder and dropped, coiling into the fetal position on the ground six feet away, his chances of fathering little warriors now severely limited.

"Telling you just wouldn't have had the same effect," Simon said, spinning to intercept another guy. "You'll know better next time, lamebrain." He spoke in English since there were over four hundred different dialects spoken in the country, and while French was the official language of Mallaruza, Simon figured them for the dialect types and kept his fluency in French to himself.

The next warrior wasn't making the same kicking mistake as his pal. He crouched low, jabbing a short *iklwa* at the air between them. In his other hand he twirled an *iwisa,* a knobby war club, with commendable dexterity. The guy knew what he was doing.

He and Simon did the combat dance, while Simon kept a weather eye on the other three men rapidly closing in.

Fuck this slow dance. Pulling the Taurus from the small of his back, he shot the closest guy before he could put up his shield. Which wouldn't have mattered anyway since it was unlikely the skin-covered wood was Kevlar.

If more warriors came because of the sound of a weapon firing, he'd deal with them, too.

The guy circling him tripped over the remains of one of the slaughtered medical team and with a too little, too late war cry fell on his ass, legs straddling the corpse. His eyes went wild as he struggled to right himself and get away from the gore posthaste. He definitely wasn't happy. Simon aimed the Taurus and took him out, dropping him right there in a pool of dried blood and glistening entrails.

He spun on his heel. "Next?"

All he saw was a bare ass in retreat.

His adrenaline was still pumping, crystallizing his vision and making his hearing almost preternaturally sharp. "Hell." The problem, he thought, as he checked the dead guys, was that he wasn't done fighting. He still had bucket-loads of testosterone coursing through his body. He needed to expend that energy. On something.

He could give chase to the warrior. See where he was headed. Interrogate him. Get some answers. But that would leave Kess alone and vulnerable. Until he could stash her somewhere safe, he was stuck playing babysitter.

And thinking about Kess . . . The rush of sexual heat crashed with the force of a tidal wave into his already overheated blood. If a guy couldn't fight he could always fu—

"No," Simon said out loud. His voice sounded thick and alien to his own ears as he picked his way through the bodies and headed back to the vehicle and the woman in it. "Not just no. But *hell* no."

No magic this time. He'd run, and get rid of some useless, unexpended energy. His legs and arms pumped as he darted between the trees, the weeds and shrubs slashing at his legs as he hauled ass.

It was stifling in the car. Kess had decided not to waste gas by keeping the car and AC running, nor did she want the sound of the engine heard by anyone. Who knew who else was out there? Fishing another ice cube out of the cooler, she ran it over her cheeks and throat. She was so hot she was fantasizing about a deep, ice-cold swimming pool. She made do with a rapidly melting ice cube.

"Where are you, Simon?" God only knew what was going on. He'd been gone for the better part of thirty-seven minutes. Only something bad could keep him this long in a camp filled with dead bodies. "Did something happen to you?"

Holding the frigid cube to the jumping pulse at the base of her throat, she fixed her gaze on the trees ahead. Was he dead too? Had the murderers come back?

She shuddered despite the enervating heat.

Maybe he needed help. Kess's heart lodged in her throat and she had to wipe the nervous perspiration off her palms onto her pant legs. The longer she sat there waiting, the more vivid the possibilities played in her brain.

She had to get out of the car to go and check. As far as rescue went, she was the only game in town. However, the image of the animal-gored human remains, and that never-to-be-forgotten smell, kept her in the hot car.

"Get out and go and help him." Her voice sounded as terrified as she felt. "If I go to the camp and he's there and needs me, that'll be a good thing, right?" And what if he's dead? What if the bad guys finished him off like the others? "Then good will go to bad, very, *very* bad in a heartbeat."

She'd either die sitting here in the car or die out there. Six of one and half a dozen of the other. She fumbled one-handed for her bag in back, grabbed it, and took out a new SIM card for her camera. Popping out the full card, she stuck it in the front pocket of her jeans and replaced it.

As much as she hated to do it, someone had to document what had happened here. She was the woman with a camera. "Let it be noted," she said out loud, "that I am totally, and without an ounce of shame, scared out of my freaking mind."

Opening the door to let in marginally cooler air, Kess put her booted feet outside and slid off the seat, the heavy gun in her hand.

The trees seemed a long, long way away. She'd never again be able to smell eucalyptus without an instant snapshot of the massacre in the camp flashing in her head. She pressed a hand to her roiling stomach and swallowed the fear-induced saliva with an audible gulp.

It was dusk now. She had been staring so hard at the spot where Simon had disappeared, she'd barely noticed. The watering hole was about a quarter of a mile downstream from the camp. To the denizens of the plains, a quarter of a mile was a short trek for a human snack. Pretty much like leaving the family room to dash into the kitchen for that yummy last slice of chocolate cake.

"I taste like shit," she told anything with an empty belly, raising her voice barely above a whisper. Her stomach jolted with every step she took.

Talk about walking that green mile or whatever it was death row inmates walked. She put a bit of energy into her step, even though she imagined glowing, hungry, yellow eyes fixed on a bull's-eye on the back of her shirt.

"I told you to stay the hell in the car," Simon said from behind her.

Kess let out a very startled, very girly shriek and slapped a hand over her heart as she spun around to face him.

He shot out a hand, gripping her elbow to keep her from careening into him. "Where the hell do you think you're going?"

A cut on his arm bled sluggishly, and he was dusty and disheveled. But to Kess, whose heart had literally stopped when he'd suddenly materialized behind her, he looked like a million bucks. She wanted to fling herself at him and wrap her arms and legs around his body. She wanted to bury her nose in the damp place on his neck where she could see his strong steady pulse beating.

"Your arm looks like it needs stitches. The medical team should be here—"

"Fuck!" Simon said, looking over her shoulder.

One minute Kess was standing, the next she was flat on the dusty ground with Simon's large body covering hers. Just as she was about to tell him that this might work better if they were *facing* each other, a loud, reverberating *bang* blotted out her world.

Four

SMAW. Shoulder-launched Multipurpose Assault Weapon. The rocket launcher took out the Range Rover in one fiery blast. Since its aimed trajectory was five hundred meters, the sons of bitches were relatively close. Close enough to make toast out of an armored Range Rover and singe Simon's eyebrows.

While he was digesting this piece of unexpected intel, he was made shockingly aware that he had a warm female pressed between his body and the unyielding dirt when said female bucked and tried to get him off her.

When she lifted her head, the back of it connected to Simon's chin with a teeth-jarring *thunk*. She slewed around to look up at him. Her face dead white under the light tan and freckles, her eyes were unfocused and hazy. "What in God's name was that—"

No time for answers. Simon simply threaded his fingers through the silky hair at her nape and squeezed gently. Kess's eyes rolled, and she slumped back, unconscious.

"Sorry, honey. But we need to get the hell out of

Dodge before they aim one of those bitches at *us*.
And I'm praying that my powers hold long enough
not to drop-kick us right into the enemies' laps."
Crouching to present a smaller target, he lifted
Kess's limp body into his arms. "Here we go."

He shimmered, teleporting into the hills a good
thirty miles away. Finding a small cave in the rocky
hillside, Simon carried Kess inside, then cast a protective spell across the mouth of the cave. The
protective spell he'd put on the Range Rover hadn't
worked worth shit. He hoped this one fared better.

"Good thing you don't listen worth a damn," he
muttered, laying her limp body on the down sleeping bag he materialized beneath her. If she'd stayed
put she'd have been collateral damage. Shit. This
vacation was definitely turning into work. He
needed to call this in, then go see exactly who these
assholes were.

Her hair felt like hot silk as it twisted and curled
around his fingers, binding him to her. Simon
found himself reluctant to let her go. He did, of
course. Touching this woman was a mistake. A *big*
mistake. Her pheromones called to his in the most
primitive, compulsive siren song Simon had ever
encountered. She was hard to resist. He stared
down at her face in repose. She was prettier when
she was awake and animated. Now she looked
vulnerable and quite sweet with her eyes—and
mouth—closed.

He rocked back on his haunches. "Kess, wake

up." She didn't so much as flicker an eyelash. He touched her cheek. The side that was slightly sunburned. "Come on, sweetheart." He stroked the warm silky skin with his thumb. An almost involuntary movement that set off a faint, but unmistakable, warning contraction of his heart. "Time to rise and shine."

She turned her face into his hand. "Hmm. One more hour." Her soft mouth brushed his palm, sending a zing of electricity up his arm, through his chest, and down directly to his groin. "Kess." He tapped her cheek. "Wake up. Now."

Her lashes fluttered on his skin, and she opened sleepy eyes, focusing with apparent difficulty on his face. Her brow pleated. "What happened?"

"The bad guys blew up the Rover."

"Which bad guys?" She pulled the band out of her hair as she sat up, then raked her fingers through her hair. Even in the dim light inside the cave her hair was on fire. And of course, a mess of curls and twigs and God only knew what else. Simon wanted to smooth and neaten . . . No he didn't. What he wanted to do was comb his fingers through the strands, pull her face up to his, and— Lose his mind.

"Not sure," he said shortly, checking her pupils because he was close enough to do so. She was okay. He, however, felt a disproportionate rush of heat just looking at her.

Her big gray eyes mirrored her confusion as she glanced around the unfamiliar surroundings. After a few moments she looked back at him. "Where are we, and how did we get here?" Direct and straight to the point. She wasn't afraid that they'd switched location, just puzzled. Nothing seemed to squash her zest for life. Energy radiated off her in waves.

"Cave in the hills, and I carried you." Close enough. He plucked a six-inch-long twig out of her hair. Strands of silk twined around his fingers, snagging on the calluses as if holding him there, tied to her in a way that made him want to unwrap her like a long-awaited present.

He wanted to see her slender body naked, spread before him like a feast. He wanted to touch her mouth with his and kiss her senseless. Kiss her until she sobbed with need. He imagined himself inside her, giving her exquisite pleasure, her legs wrapped around his hips, her head thrown back as she came apart in his arms.

He *had* lost his mind.

Not particularly pleased by her continued effect on him, Simon made his expression blank as he studied her for any ill effects after the teleportation.

She appeared fine. Just fine.

"There aren't any hills anywhere near—" Her eyes widened and he noticed that the soft gray was surrounded by a charcoal rim. Her lashes were long and thick . . . He was close enough to count her individual eyelashes, for God's sake. Simon shifted back, out of range.

"The hills and any caves are *miles* away. You carried me *miles*?"

He shrugged, digging in his pocket. Before pulling out his hand he materialized a blue ruffly thing similar to the one he'd seen her wearing. "Here." He handed it to her. "You don't weigh that much."

Taking the tie, she grimaced comically. "Gee, thanks." She sat up fully, crossing her legs as she finger-combed her hair.

She looked at the fabric donut he'd handed her, then back at him.

"Where did this come from? Did I drop it in the president's office?"

"Somewhere," he answered noncommittally.

"Thanks. I lose these things all the time." Glancing around as she secured her hair, she asked, "Where did all this stuff come from if the car was blown up?" She indicated not only the sleeping bag, but the stack of supplies Simon had materialized along with the bedding.

"Just stuff some camper left behind." He rose, dusting off the knees of his jeans. "I'm going out to look around."

"Okay," she said absently. "Why do you think

someone would lug all this stuff up here, only to leave it behind? Where are they? *Who* are they?"

"No idea." He looked out across the gently rolling hills in the distance. The light was going fast, casting long shadows as the sun melted into the horizon. He wanted to get back to the camp and see if he could pick up any clues as to who these guys were, and why they'd targeted—hell, massacred—the doctors.

"They'll probably come back, don't you think?" Kess asked, getting to her feet and walking toward him. She meant the nonexistent campers.

Simon kept his back to her. A useless endeavor since he had three-sixty vision. When it worked. Which it did now. She chewed her lip as she looked down into the valley several hundred feet below them. "That's a hell of a climb."

He needed her to look somewhere else while he switched out with Nomis. Leaving his other self here was more expedient than sending Nomis to track the warrior. Nomis could do pretty much everything Simon could do, but he didn't quite have Simon's physical strength. Kess was safe here with him. And if a problem arose, Simon would know it the second Nomis did, and he'd be back in a flash.

He mentally checked in through Nomis's eyes to see how Abi was doing. The president was at a gala party surrounded by hundreds of people and in full view of his bodyguards. Nomis was, at this moment, redundant. Simon called him in. They couldn't appear in the same place at the same time, but his alter ego waited to materialize at Simon's word. While they had separate bodies, their minds were one. What Simon knew, Nomis knew, and vice versa.

Something he'd enjoyed as a kid. His invisible playmate was all too real.

"I'm going to take a walk. Look around for a few minutes," he told Kess. "I put a gun next to the sleeping bag. Take the safety off, and keep it with you at all times." He paused. "Do not leave the cave until I get back. Got it?"

Kess saluted. "Be careful."

He cocked a brow. "I'll be back in five. Stay out of trouble."

Cute. Like she could get into trouble way the hell and gone out here. Kess watched Simon navigate the rocky slope with the ease of a mountain goat. She grinned at his retreating back—nice ass—then went back into the cave to see what their unsuspecting hosts had planned for dinner. She was starving. Hell, she was always starving.

The first useful item she pulled out was a small camp lantern, which she lit right away. The light dispelled the black-and-whiteness of dusk quite nicely and illuminated the rough wall of the shallow cave with flickering golden light. Unpacking a cardboard box of supplies, she found two ice-cold steaks in a cooler, two enormous potatoes, butter, cream, and, for God's sake . . . chives! Strawberries and a bottle of wine. She had no clue about quality—to her, wine was wine was wine, good, bad, or indifferent. It either tasted acidy, fruity, or sweet, in which case she'd have a glass. Or not. She'd rather go for a soda loaded with sugar and caffeine. No way—there were a couple of cans of *those* as well.

Kess tried the eyebrow-lift thing that Simon did so eloquently. She couldn't quite manage it. "Who are you guys and what kind of evening were you planning?" This was no kind of camp food she'd ever seen. But hey, she wasn't one to look a gourmet gift in the mouth.

The box also held a small propane three-burner cookstove and a frying pan. These guys had thought of everything. "It wouldn't surprise me," Kess muttered, "to find a white linen tablecloth and napkins in here." She dug through the box. Glasses. Not plastic. Real glass. Silverware. Ditto. "Ah, man. No *tablecloth*? Who do you think we are? Savages?"

"Do you always talk to yourself?" Simon asked behind her. She didn't shriek at his unexpected arrival, but her heart did a few aerial calisthenics.

"Frequently," she told him, standing up and tossing him a companionable smile. The dancing light from the tiny lantern on the floor flickered around his features, making him look a little demonic. And, oh, Lord. So sexy, her blood pressure went up, and she felt as though her body was bathed in the heat of the sun. Her brain was having a total eclipse as she tried not to lean into him. His chest was so nice and broad and solid-looking, and there was a shadowy place on his throat that she bet tasted salty and delicious.

Get a freaking grip, for God's sake! "I find myself vastly entertaining," she told him cheerfully. "Especially when I'm alone. Did you discover anything interesting out there?" While she would've liked him to take a bit longer checking their perimeter, considering they'd been the target of some kind of missile, she didn't blame him for coming back to be surrounded by three solid walls of rock.

"You could've looked around a bit longer." She gently probed the hot side of her face.

"I saw what I needed to see." He glanced at the box and cooler near her feet, and the flickering light on the walls.

"I'm going to start dinner. It won't be ready for half an hour or so. Think it's okay to have the light? What about cooking? Will the smell of food give us away?" Kess asked suddenly. Somebody had just attempted to blow them to smithereens. It wasn't smart to draw attention to themselves. "Sorry, I wasn't thinking. We'll just waste all this scrumptious food—it's probably the bad guys' anyway—and hang out in the dark."

"No. It's fine. Leave it. Find what you need for a meal?"

She pulled a face. "Only if you can stomach a thick, juicy steak, baked potatoes, and green salad, followed by strawberries marinated in something fabulous. Camp food, you understand. We'll have to tough it out and eat it to keep up our strength."

His lips twitched.

Kess cocked her head and narrowed her eyes. "You look different. What did you do?" Well, he'd almost smiled. Which was certainly different. But that wasn't it. "Ah! You combed your hair the other way."

The twitch turned into a small smile. Good Lord, his eyes were an almost eerie green in this flickering light. "You think I went outside to groom myself?" he asked easily.

Kess thought he'd probably gone out to pee. She shrugged. "No clue." He did look slightly different, though. She couldn't put her finger on it, but it bothered her that she couldn't figure out *what* about him was different.

"I need to ah . . . use the facilities; can you get that stove going?"

"I prefer you don't go outside."

"Well, it's good to want things, but I have to go." He hesitated and Kess could practically hear him trying to figure out how to make her crouch in the far corner of the cave. Was not going to happen. She managed the whole eyebrow-cock thing quite well, and waited him out.

"Here." He bent to pick up the gun on the sleeping bag. "Take this." He handed it to her. "And be quick about it. Another ten minutes or so and it'll be pitch-dark out there."

Again she gave him a smart salute, almost putting her eye out with the barrel of the gun. "Yes, sir."

"Here, take the lantern, too."

It was going to be pretty damn hard to do what she needed to do with her hands full. "Aye, Captain."

"*Go,*" he said, and Kess swore he was grinning behind her back.

Simon walked through the aid camp, looking at the scene with fresh eyes. Even though he sensed no immediate danger, he maintained invisibility. So far so good. The moon was high and a brilliant white, spotlighting the area so that shadows were deep, and objects appeared as crisp and clean as a black-and-white still life. He didn't need the mag light he carried, and clipped it back into the holder next to the Ka-Bar knife strapped to his left thigh.

Christ. Poor bastards. Even he, who was used to the worst of inhumanity from man, found the breadth of the massacre to be nauseatingly graphic and horrific. Talk about overkill.

Intel had sent him images and bios of the medical team before he left Quinisela. Flipping down the mono eyepiece from his headset to download the data, he walked through the devastation, attempting to ID everyone. It wasn't easy. With the help of the optical scanner he was able to look at a body, and the electronics scanned through the intel on each individual until a positive visual ID was made. The eyepiece was also capable of capturing digital fingerprints and doing X-rays. But the visual identification was enough for this application.

It was a quick and extremely efficient form of identifying remains. Also gave him a bitch of a headache as the data flashed in front of one eye like a movie on fast-forward, while the view from the other eye was stationary. A hot, mild breeze ruffled the tops of the eucalyptus and intensified the rank smell of the rapidly decomposing bodies. What the heat and animals hadn't finished off, the insects would. Food was never wasted in the bush.

Fresh tire tracks indicated several heavy trucks had arrived and departed. Hastily. Smart move. The supply trucks sent by Abi with the relief workers to replenish supplies weren't needed now. And while Simon suspected that the new personnel were armed, he was damn sure that anyone in their right mind, seeing what had happened to the predecessors, would blast out of there PDQ. He rolled a body with his boot. A half-masticated face stared up at him from bony sockets. All he could tell was that she was female. The woman had shoulder-length hair; in the moonlight it looked like a washed-out orange. A knot formed in Simon's gut as he imagined it to be a vibrant red—the hairstyle was similar to Kess's.

Jesus. What the hell did the relief doctors think had happened to *Kess*? Had they even bothered to pause and check the IDs of the corpses as he was doing? Given the relative similarities between the corpse and Kess—height, weight, hair color and length—had anyone even considered that Kess may have been a target on her return?

He used his sat phone to contact Abi's aide to have the bodies removed. Next he called in to his Control to report in.

Vacation over.

The body count revealed two people missing. One was Dr. Konrad Straus, the other Dr. Judith Viljoen. There was no mistaking either of them by their physical descriptions. Had they managed to flee before the Hureni soldiers arrived? Had they managed to get away safely, or had they been killed a distance from camp and their bodies not yet discovered? Hell, it was possible animals had dragged them off. Simon wanted to track down the Hureni who'd done this, but more pressing was ID'ing these people before every trace of them was gone, which would certainly be long before the T-FLAC forensics team could get here. He was it, and every moment counted.

Using a special tetrabyte image capture feature

on the headset, Simon transmitted all the data directly to HQ in Montana for analysis. While he worked the scene, he tuned in to Nomis and Kess.

Nomis was shimmering—invisible, he was following Kess outside, roughly thirty feet away from the mouth of the cave. While the lantern lit Kess's way, Nomis shielded it from anyone else's view. Turning his back on her, Simon's alter image looked up to enjoy the stars in a navy blue sky to give Kess some privacy.

The protective shield around her was in place. Nomis was there, and would get her back inside the cave where that protective shield would bind with hers. Simon knew Kess was safe. *He,* however, was in deep shit.

Wizards at three o'clock.

Invisible. Powerful. And sixteen or twenty to his one.

So-so odds if these were powerless bad guys. But this kind of power required equal power. He didn't fucking *have* it. Right now he was sustaining Nomis and his own invisibility. A no-brainer. Usually. The protective shield around both Kess and the cave wouldn't usually have required more than a thought, but now he felt the pull and fizz of his power as it pulsed in and out of sync.

They were several clicks away, but if he knew they were there, they knew he was here. He materialized. Conserving juice.

He needed every vestige of his power, and he needed it *now*.

His mind raced. He was damned if he'd pull the protection spell from Kess. Without it—without him—she didn't stand a chance in hell. But if he pulled away most of Nomis's functions he'd have a tad more capability. Not a hell of a lot, but maybe enough to stay alive longer than he would without it.

Something slithery rustled in the grass near Kess's booted foot. She'd put the lantern on the rocky ground, turning the lantern down as low as she could without snuffing out the flame. The barely adequate illumination showed the blades of grass moving as something retreated. Something small. She *hoped*, doing everything she could not to remind herself that small insects and animals could be just as deadly as their larger brothers and cousins.

The heavy gun wavered in her left hand. Of course, as soon as she'd left the cave, found a hidden spot with a bit of grass, set the lantern on the ground, undone her belt, yanked down her zipper, and pulled down her pants—all while trying not to shoot herself as she juggled the freaking gun— she'd found that she no longer *wanted* to pee.

With a silent sigh, she reversed the order of things and picked up the lantern. She couldn't hunker down out here forever. Simon was going to come looking for her any minute.

Her stomach rumbled as the smell of sizzling steak drifted on the slight breeze. Yum. Mouth watering, she trudged up the rocky incline to the cave.

One minute she was watching her footing, the next Simon was directly in front of her. Lord, the man moved like a freaking ghost. "Don't *do* that," she whispered, heart pounding. Maybe she did need the shrub after all. Maybe she should think about tying a bell around his neck or something. Anything to warn her of his presence. Not that she needed a lot of warning. She was already danger-ously aware of every beautiful inch of him. The way his lips quirked when he was amused, the way his shoulders dipped ever so slightly as he walked. The outline of strong, sculpted muscle beneath his shirt. Yeah. A bell would be good.

He put a finger to his lips. Yeah. She got it. Shut up. She nodded. The meager light made him ap-pear to flicker, which, when added to the sound of creepy-crawlies slithering in the grass, a screeching bird, and the deep, gruff roar of a far—she hoped—distant lion, gave her some wicked goose bumps.

He forged ahead and she hurried after him, her boots sliding on the sandy, rocky terrain. Tufts of grass and a few shrubs would have been helpful, but she had no intention of putting her hands any-where there might be tenants.

The thought of reaching for a bush to pull herself along and grabbing a giant spider instead kept her hands firmly on her gun and lantern. Simon didn't offer to carry either.

The enticing smell of the cooking steak turned to the stinky smell of burning meat. Kess put some muscle into the easy climb. She was starving, and while she wasn't a picky eater, she hated to waste a perfectly good steak.

Her foot came down on a rock. It went one way, she the other. Because her hands were full, Kess fell flat on her face, then slid backward a few feet, still holding the lantern and gun.

Hauling herself upright, she glanced up to see if Simon was on his way back to help her up. He wasn't. From her lower vantage point, she thought he looked blurred, as though he were behind a curtain of slowly moving water. A veil of transparency that made him appear even more ghostlike than a few minutes ago.

Starvation-induced hallucination. She could see a thin line of smoke coming out of the cave up ahead. Damn it, he was burning their dinner.

Other than a scraped chin, she was fine. Not that Simon bothered to even turn around to check as he walked into the cave.

Fine. She was a big girl. A lacerated chin wouldn't kill her.

The second she stepped into the cave the small wick of the lantern gave out, plunging the cave into semidarkness. The moon was out, and a blue flame leapt beneath the steak burning in the fry pan. In a minute her eyes would adjust and she'd be able to see just fine. Kess walked toward her burning dinner.

"I'm fine, thanks," she said a little more acerbically than the injury warranted. The sarcasm lost its impact because she was barely whispering.

Silence.

"Do you want me to pull the pan off the burner, or do you prefer your steak turned to a charcoal briquette? I mean I'm okay with well done, but burnt *crispy* isn't my favorite way to—"

Silence.

Had he gone outside again? She glanced over her shoulder. Nope. He was hunkered down on his haunches at the mouth of the cave, his back against the rough wall, his gun held loosely in his right hand, which dangled between his knees. He wasn't paying her a bit of attention.

"Alrighty then. I'll just go ahead and turn off the burner, okay?"

Silence.

Over his head the sky suddenly lit up like the Fourth of July. The brilliance of the distant lightning strike made her squeeze her eyes shut as it sheeted across the black sky. "Wow, I didn't even hear the thunder, did you?" Kess blinked open her eyes. Simon was gone.

"Well, hell, Blackthorne with an *e*, the least you

could do is say good-b—" She was looking right at the cave wall when he suddenly materialized in front of it again. One minute he was gone, the next he was back in exactly the same position as he'd been before. With the hallucinations coming so fast, she definitely needed to eat before she totally lost her last grip on reality.

Five

Seven men materialized out of the darkness, stepping from the tree line into the moon-drenched clearing. Not seven wizards. One wizard accompanied by half a dozen henchmen. The lone wizard had the power of multiplication, a rare but effective ability to clone his "presence" footprint. Much like a porcupine fluffing its deadly quills at the enemy.

Simon stood motionless, feet spread slightly, hands held loosely at his sides as the group approached. If this was the wizard Abi had sent him to find, Abi was in far more trouble than he knew. Hell, Simon acknowledged, right now *he* was the one in trouble.

The wizard took the lead. Tall—easily seven feet, with morgue-pale skin and reddish-blond hair hanging straight to his shoulders, where it broke to flow halfway down his chest and back. In spite of the heat, the guy wore a duster of dull black leather, and dark pants tucked into knee-high black boots. He looked like a well-drawn manga character.

Six Hureni men flanked him. Three a side. This

time they'd eschewed war paint and loincloths for camo and efficient German hardware. Not as colorful, but considerably more practical and efficient than *ishlangu* and hunting shields.

The presence of the Hureni didn't bother Simon at all. The wizard, however, did.

Power pulsed off him in unrelenting waves. Even on his best day Simon would've had a hard time battling this guy. The stranger's power was damn strong. But since this wasn't one of Simon's best days, powerwise he'd better think fast before he turned into something unpleasant.

Like a dung beetle. Or worse—dead.

Mustering as much juice as he could, he took a step forward, drawing his power in tightly.

The wizard sent a spear of brilliant, sparking electricity in a straight line aimed at his heart. Simon had zapped his enemy in just the same way, dozens of times. But never with this amount of power. Christ. He instantly teleported a foot to his left and the strike narrowly missed him. Missed, but he felt the incredible power behind the surge. The fine hairs on his body crackled erect and his heart surged. Behind him, one of the prefab tent houses burst into flame with a *whoosh* and a shower of sparks.

He quickly absorbed the swirling magic so that he could boomerang it back. "I see we've dispensed with the niceties," he said dryly, instantaneously opening a large, deep pit beneath the feet of the seven men. Six disappeared from sight as they fell twelve feet down into the hole in a flurry of limbs and Hureni curses.

The wizard floated above the hole, his long pale hair drifting gently around his upper body as he hovered. "Amateur theatrics."

Not done yet, dick.

Simon ID'd the man's coarse accent as Afrikaans. A South African wizard? Fuck. He suspected he knew who this asshole was.

Without shifting his gaze, he conjured a thick tree branch, calling it to his opponent at warp speed. The branch struck the other wizard a resounding blow on the back of the head with the sound of a watermelon hitting concrete. The basic, yet effective, move pitched the wizard headfirst into the hole with his pals.

Simon immediately cast a magical restraining net over the opening of the pit, then strolled over and looked down. Despite his casual demeanor, it was taking everything in him to maintain the power. The second they saw him standing over him, the Hureni started firing. The barrage of bullets ineffectually hit the invisible shield, bouncing around inside the hole. Two men fell, mortally hit. A third and fourth screamed in pain as they were struck by their own bullets.

Ping. Ping. Pingpingping. Bullets ricocheted off the shield, hitting another guy who started wailing as the last man frantically tried crawling over him to get out.

"Fuck you, too," he told the other wizard. He spoke to the slow-to-learn Hureni: "Yo, assholes. Unless you want to kill yourselves sooner than later, fingers off the triggers."

He made eye contact with the furious wizard below. "Who are you?" Simon tried probing the wizard's mind, but it was sealed, as were the minds of the Hureni. "You responsible for this massacre? No answer? Why them?" He indicated the dead medics scattered about. Personally, he couldn't come up with a decent reason for such slaughter.

The wizard's eyes caught the moonlight and gleamed in the darkness of his dirt prison. "American." His voice was coldly malevolent, sending an unwelcome, and uncharacteristic, chill up Simon's spine. "Remember my name. *Noek Joubert.*"

Jesus, he'd been right. Noek Joubert. Head of the South African–based Phoenix tango group. Abi had cause to be fucking concerned. Joubert was one of the baddest tango badasses around.

Simon would recognize this guy's signature from a hundred miles away if he ever encountered him again. If he was alive to encounter the guy again. He'd heard of Joubert, but intel hadn't mentioned Joubert's level of power. And he had *intense* power. Simon felt it pressing around his body like an oppressive blanket of electricity.

The dark power held its own energy, as if it were

alive. Worse, it was ten times stronger than Simon's powers. And his own were considered, when they were fucking operating at full throttle, formidable.

"Remember it," Joubert said, his tone silky and filled with promise. "It will be the last name you utter before you die."

"Well, hell. That's depressing." Simon plucked a dead leaf off his sleeve. "I always thought I'd have some sexy woman's name on my lips as I breathe my last. Noek Joubert, huh? Never heard of you. What did a bunch of do-gooder relief workers do to piss *you* off?"

"*I* ask the questions here," Joubert snarled, looking up at Simon with venom glinting like quicksilver in his dark eyes. "You aren't one of the Doctors Without Borders. Who are you?"

"I'm the one in the position to be asking the questions." Simon's body shook a little at the amount of strength required to hold the restraining net in place. Perspiration sheened his skin, and his heart beat like a trip-hammer in his chest. He gritted his teeth, pushing back harder.

"Let's try this politely. Who the fuck are you, asshole, and what's your interest in the medics?"

"Your shield can't hold forever." Anger made the man's voice hard and vicious. "I'd suggest you return to wherever you hail from, and stay the fuck out of my business."

Joubert's power pounded against Simon's shields. Hard. Persistent. Simon stood his ground with difficulty, and for the first time as an adult felt real fear.

Even the small bit of juice he was using to maintain Nomis would help. But he was damned if he'd leave Kess unprotected. Especially now. No. Nomis had to stay with her. If something happened to him, Nomis would get Kess to safety without Joubert knowing about it.

Kess had to be removed to a safe location. Now. Delaying her departure wasn't an option. He communicated with Nomis in a mental form of shorthand. Just in case . . . It was a bit like talking to himself. But not. "And that business is?"

"I have neither the intention nor the inclination to explain myself to a mere Half wizard."

He wasn't a Half wizard, but clearly his powers were weak enough to translate as one. Fuck. The netting was losing tension. He cut off communication with Nomis. It was only with substantial concentration that he was able to keep the more powerful wizard contained.

Simon cocked a mocking brow. "Interesting observation since you're the one down in that hole. Not to mention half your posse's dead or injured from self-inflicted gunshot wounds."

The other wizard's power shot up through the netting, delivering an invisible sucker punch that knocked Simon back on his ass a good thirty feet or more.

Irritation turned to seriously pissed as he shot to

his feet, rubbing his chest. Felt worse than a bullet striking through Kevlar. Much worse. Eyes narrowed, and all his attention pinpointed and focused on the binding spell, Simon once again made the net impenetrable. Power against power. The very air around him vibrated as he forced one foot in front of the other to get back to the edge of the pit. It was like walking into a hurricane-force gale. Without the sound. The clearing was eerily silent.

The guy's silver-black eyes gleamed up at him as Simon stood over him. Simon gave him the evil eye back. "Anyone ever mention you don't work or play well with others?"

"Most people appreciate the consequences of crossing me."

Who *were* Noek Joubert's enemies? Simon wanted to give them a call, maybe buy them a beer. Whatever it took to get this asshole under control. "Crossing you—sounds dangerous. Did these doctors cross a line? Is that why you did the whole slash and splatter thing?"

The dark wizard flicked his fingers, sending a stream of sapphire-colored energy into the netting. Sparks outlined the invisible strands in a grid of electricity. Under normal circumstances Simon's protective tools were effective. But now—whether it was due to the dark wizard's stalwart powers or Simon's unpredictable outages, one flick of his fingers was all it took. The shield pulsated and started to splinter.

"I doubt your spell will be effective much longer," the wizard taunted, baring his teeth like a feral animal. "Heed my advice, American. As they say in your country, 'cut and run.'"

Simon felt his powers straining against the force emanating from the stronger wizard. He needed to buy some time. If not, the whole cut-and-run thing might just be one of two options.

"Tell me why you killed a bunch of relief workers, and I'll consider sparing your life." Simon picked up shards of electricity and power like bits of lint on a black coat. It was all he had.

The South African laughed. "Your threat is an empty one. You are neither up to the physical task nor do I make a habit of explaining myself or my actions to anyone."

"Make tonight an exception," Simon suggested, spreading his feet. "Explain yourself, or I'll hold you until hell freezes over." Never make an ultimatum you aren't one hundred percent positive you can keep. Unless it's the only fucking card you're holding.

With a spark and a flash, the netting flew off the opening to the pit and his nemesis was free.

"I was hoping you'd do that," Simon muttered, blasting the wizard with everything he had. This time, thank God, he blasted him with the full force of his resurgent powers. Joubert went flying, striking a tree twenty feet away with a bone-jarring thud and emitting a fog of green phosphorescent, foul-smelling smoke. A few seconds later he boomeranged right back, knocking Simon to the ground and enveloping him in the rank smog.

Simon saw the glint of steel through a haze, and barely felt the bite of the gleaming sword Joubert held to his throat. His skin felt anesthetized, his breathing shallow, his vision dim—Christ.

Photoluminescence. Joubert's body had the ability to absorb radiation without reemitting it until he needed to use it as a weapon. Apparently harmless to him, but not so fucking harmless to Simon.

The slower timescale of the reemission was associated with "forbidden" energy state transmission in quantum mechanics. These transitions occur less often in certain materials, like Joubert's body; the absorbed radiation could, it would seem, be reemitted at a lower intensity. For how long? Minutes? Hours?

Until, Simon's senses swam as nausea climbed his throat, *until I'm dead, or wished I was?*

No fucking way.

Using his last ounce of power, taking Nomis's strength and drawing on something even deeper, Simon conjured a sword. Using the crossguard, and a well-placed knee, he managed to lever the taller, heavier man away from his throat. Springing to his feet, Simon locked his knees until he felt steady enough to move. Jesus.

Fucking hell.

He felt annoyingly weak, drugged, and sapped,

but he managed to two-fist the heavy sword and swing. His hands were numb, and he had to trust his fingers to maintain a tight grip. He had gained a small measure of surprise fighting with his left hand dominant. But a split second was all the advantage he had as Joubert executed a point-down deflection, grabbing his wrist.

Simon stepped in hard, and executed a pummel strike to the other man's face. Joubert fell back with a curse and a bloody nose. No bullet, or bullets, would work against Joubert's wizard shield. Simon had to fight fire with fire. He poured white light down the forged steel of his blade until it burned with an icy glow, then swung it in an arc that connected the razor-sharp edge to Joubert's upper arm. Leather, fabric, and flesh split.

Joubert retaliated with a draw-cut, slicing open Simon's cheek. He laughed as Simon staggered into the swing, sidestepping the sweep of his blade. "You can't win, *Dom doos*."

"Can," Simon assured him. "And will." One lesson he'd learned, and clearly his opponent hadn't, was that physical mastery, of both the blade and your body, led to a devastating level of physical power. Never bring anger into the fight. None of Simon's blows fell by accident. Each was as precise and methodical as he was. Each move was calculated. Even under normal circumstances his fighting style was spare and to the point. Now, he dared not waste a second of precious power by grandstanding.

Joubert was stronger. Simon fought smarter.

His right hand controlled the degree Simon wanted his sword to rotate around the fulcrum of his left hand. Grounding made it easy for him to withstand Joubert pushing at his sword with his entire weight behind it. He shoved back, and the other wizard stumbled, barely catching his footing.

Joubert's sword flashed in a power cut, shooting sparks of blood-red as they came together in a thundering clash that lit up the camp as bright as day. Joubert was all over the place. *Undisciplined*, Simon thought, *no control*. No. Pissed and unable to control it.

Joubert clearly hadn't expected the strength of Simon's powers, crappy as they were at the moment. Never underestimate your enemy. His opponent's misjudgment wouldn't last long. But for now it worked to Simon's benefit, and he took advantage of it. His might be the lesser power, but he was a better swordsman because of his discipline and control. He brought the tip of the heavy sword up in the "boar's thrust," a move designed to enter an opponent's body just above the groin and slice upward.

Joubert brought his own sword down and blocked the move an inch from his dick. Then, without warning, he disappeared, leaving behind the faint stink of his phosphorescent smog. He took all of his men with him.

His voice came in surround sound. "We'll meet again, American."

"Count on it." Shaken at just how fucking close he'd come to croaking, Simon waited until Joubert's presence was off his wizard radar before he sank to his knees. "Jesus." Had to talk to Knight about this power weakness. He couldn't perform his job if he couldn't depend on his powers.

The thought scared the shit out of him.

Okay, he thought, getting to his feet and feeling ridiculous for overdramatizing the whole power outage situation. He was a fully trained T-FLAC operative first and foremost. He hadn't bested Joubert with his wizard powers. He'd bested him with skill.

Fuck. Staring up at the stark white moon beaming down, Simon ran his fingers through his hair. He'd been lucky. Damn lucky. It was a hard pill to swallow, but if Joubert had chosen powers instead of swords he wouldn't be standing here right now. And *that* was fact.

Simon needed to get in to see Knight for a fast tune-up. In the meantime, he wanted to get to Kess as quickly as possible and take her out of range. Then he needed to go to work to figure out the connection between such a powerful wizard and the massacre.

Simon teleported the hell out of there.

He found himself sitting in a cornfield in Kansas. Needless to say, he'd missed his mark. Badly.

"Fuck."

Kess. Not *Kansas.*

Standing, he brushed hay and other debris from his jeans. The only thing more irritating than his flickering powers was knowing that a few more minutes of battling Joubert and he'd have had no option but to shimmer out of range. Would've been a first. Simon didn't like running from confrontation any more than he liked losing a fight.

The last time that had happened he was seventeen and Alex Stone had knocked him on his ass. Alex had just discovered his ability to temporal accelerate, and taken it for a test drive. Unfortunately, Simon had been the guinea pig and ended up needing ten stitches to close the gaping wound on the back of his head.

With his confidence a little shaken, Simon concentrated hard on Kess, pinpointing her exact location in his mind, then shimmered, hoping he'd end up at the mouth of the cave and not the mouth of the Nile.

Despite the previous day's horrific images, despite the night's interesting observations, and despite lying on the hard and rocky ground, Kess had slept like the proverbial baby. The previous evening had grown a little chilly, and keeping her eye on the man with the gun, she'd crawled into the sleeping bag and snuggled beneath the lightweight down right after choking down the burnt steak and a bite of barely cooked potato. Four minutes after she closed her eyes she was asleep.

She woke the next morning none the worse for wear and, yawning, sat up and stretched her arms over her head. She was alone. By the slant of light trickling in through the cave it was still early, barely past dawn. But she felt refreshed. Refreshed and brimming with questions. Like, where was Simon?

She'd never forget the relief crew; their images were forever burned into her mind. Getting back to Quinisela to do her job was imperative—the families had to be notified, she'd need to write up a press release. The president would be devastated at the loss of life in a country he was trying to unite.

Tossing back the sleeping bag, Kess shot a penetrating look at the man backlit by weak early morning sunlight as he strolled inside. She got to her feet, holding the sleeping bag in front of her, almost like a shield. But the rapid beat of her heart at seeing him wasn't fear. It was the familiar tingle of excitement he ignited inside her. That zing of awareness that elevated her heartbeat and made her breasts feel fuller. Sexual awareness to the max. Just because she felt it didn't mean she had to act on it, but her heightened awareness and her level of anticipation just *looking* at Simon felt as good, if not better, than a manic ride on a roller coaster.

"Simon?"

He cocked a brow. "Expecting someone else?"

Ah. Kess carefully folded the sleeping bag, then held it over her arm as she drew in a deep breath trying to figure out where to start. No matter her own belief in her observations, saying it out loud was going to sound ridiculous.

The air still smelled faintly of the burnt meat she'd consumed last night. Her silent companion hadn't eaten anything. "Now that you mention it . . ."

"Mention what?"

She scanned his face, then frowned as she noticed the dried blood around a two-inch slash on his lean cheek. "You're *hurt*."

"It's nothing. Mention what?"

How had he cut himself? Just by going outside to pee? Had he slipped and fallen down the rocky hillside? He didn't look clumsy. In fact he looked . . . *determined*. And extremely focused. On her. The way he was looking at her this morning made all her girl parts sit up and take notice. Her brain tripped and tumbled over the erotic images that suddenly filled her head. She squeezed the sleeping bag, pressing it against her suddenly-erect nipples. God, he was potent.

"Kess?"

She blinked. "Er . . . yes. I'd like to ask you a few questions, and I'd appreciate honest answers." Of course as a publicist she knew that people *always* had an agenda. Truth was irrelevant and open to interpretation. Hence the birth of her specialty, media spin. But media spin wasn't where her mind was at the moment.

Her skin felt hot and too small as she noticed him looking at her mouth. Her mouth was dry, but she didn't want to lick her lips, or chew her lip, or do anything else to draw attention to her own acute awareness of him looking at her looking at him. The cave wasn't that big, or wide, and was fairly shallow. He walked toward her with slow, deliberate steps. Reason shouted for her to run like hell. A deer running from the powerful lion. Her heart started thumping hard against her ribs as he got closer, and closer . . .

"Do you have a twin?" It was the only logical explanation. She pressed the sleeping bag harder against her chest. Could he see how hard her heart was thumping? Could he tell that she was having a hard time concentrating on what the hell she was saying?

"I did." His eyes gleamed hot as he looked at her. "A sister. Theresa died with our parents when we were seven. Why?"

"Not a sister." Kess licked dry lips. A quick swipe. Simon's eyes flared dark green flames. "A—a brother."

"No brother. Twin or otherwise."

"Damn."

"Damn?"

"Someone was here—Was it a hologram? No. I touched him. It. Damn it. I have no idea—Who or what are you?"

He paused mid-step. "What are you talking about?"

She was so discombobulated by the way he was looking at her that Kess could hardly think straight, let alone talk. But she couldn't let this . . . this *thing* interfere with her job. Simon was the president's friend. But something weird had happened here last night. Something weird and confusing, and hell yes, a little bit scary.

"Last night," she said quickly, because she wanted to have her arms around Simon instead of the sleeping bag. She'd like to have Simon's arms around her *on* the sleeping bag, *under* the sleeping bag—*Get a grip!*

"And before you attempt to bullshit me." Kess backed up a couple of steps as he advanced. "Let me recap what I *know.* Simon Blackthorne with an e, that would be you, finger-combs his hair to the right, is left-handed, wears his watch on his right wrist, and rarely smiles. With me so far? My babysitter last night, while looking a lot like you, *wasn't* you."

She trusted herself on this, because while she'd found him deliciously sexy, and very, very appealing, she'd not had this level of lust factor with the man she'd been with last night. Taking another step back, she came up against the wall. The rough rock scraped her back through her T-shirt. "Everything was reversed, and his hair and skin were a few shades paler than yours. His eyes weren't quite as green either."

Kess dragged in a shaking breath, because he was still walking toward her like a lion stalking his prey. His eyes, filled with pure sexual speculation, narrowed, skimming her body like a physical caress.

In Kess's mind he was already tasting her, touching her. And her body responded accordingly. Still, she stood her ground while her entire body pulsed and vibrated with longing. "I don't have a freaking clue how you did whatever you did. But whoever or *whatever* was here with me last night wasn't you. He was your mirror image. Your twin—But . . . Oh, and there was that little disappearing, can-see-right-through-you thing that was *extremely* disconcerting." Downplaying that little fact had allowed her to sleep last night.

"You're very observant." He was right in front of her, only a few feet away.

"Aren't I though? Well?"

He cupped her cheek. Oh, God, she was going to melt into an embarrassing puddle at his feet. The light was behind him, casting his face into shadow. She smelled his skin. Something clean under the smell of the natural soil around here. A little clean male sweat that made her heart pound even harder.

The cut, high on his cheek, was deep. He probably needed stitches . . .

With his free hand he plucked the sleeping bag from her nerveless fingers, tossing it aside. He reached out to cradle her jaw, then tilted up her face. His thumb brushed gently across the laceration under her chin. "This hurt?"

She shook her head. His fingers slid up the side of her throat, his eyes so close she could see herself reflected there.

"It's complicated," he murmured huskily.

"Most interesting things—" he was combing his fingers through her hair over her ear. The sensation of his touch was almost like getting a mild electric shock. It zipped through Kess, making her lose her train of thought. She couldn't seem to breathe properly. "Ah—are."

His expression was purely carnal as he murmured softly, his mouth inches from hers. "We need to get back to Quinisela."

"Well, yeah." *Are you ever going to kiss me,* she thought, heart pounding as his shirt brushed her chest. Her nipples ached to be touched and she leaned into him a little. "But unless you can perform more magic and produce some sort of vehicle it's a heck of a long walk."

"I can perform more magic." He cupped the back of her head and leaned down another frustrating inch—"And we have a chopper waiting."

His breath fanned her lips. "Seriously?"

"Seriously." His eyes blazed the hot green of the inside of a flame as he curved his hand around the base of her throat where her pulse leapt manically. "Ready?"

Ready to rip your clothes off and push you down on that sleeping bag, or ready to leave? Thank God there'd been a brush and toothpaste in the pack. Incapable of dancing this dance one more second, Kess grabbed the front of his shirt in her fist. "Are you going to kiss me or not?"

Six

Hell, yes, he was going to kiss her.

She slid her arms around his waist, pulling Simon the last few inches to close the gap between them. As if he needed help. Hunger flared higher. He braced his hand on the rough stone, protecting the back of her head as he leaned in, tilting her face so her lips were on target.

Kess didn't yield to the kiss, she met it head-on as he pressed flush against her so that they touched from breast to groin. Dipping his head, he met her soft mouth in a hungry kiss.

Hungry? Starving. Hell, call it what it was. *Voracious*.

Clawing, insatiable need roared through his body as she parted her lips and welcomed him inside with a sweep of her tongue and the erotic scrape of her teeth.

Kissing Kess was like dying of thirst in the desert, then falling into a deep cool well. She tasted of minty toothpaste.

Her body molded to his as their tongues teased and explored, straining against each other to get that quarter inch closer. He felt it as their hearts picked up the same out-of-control rhythm, and he tightened his arms around her slender body, drawing her impossibly closer.

Out of breath, they separated for a second that felt like an eternity. Then he kissed her again.

They came apart for a second, both breathing hard.

Cheeks flushed a deep coral, Kess splayed her hand on his chest. "I can feel your heart," she whispered, her voice thick and sexy, her gray eyes silvered with passion. "It's pounding as fast as mine. Feel." She took his hand and placed it on her soft breast and Simon automatically adjusted his hold to cradle the soft orb in his palm. He swept his thumb across the hard peak of her nipple and felt her shudder.

His heart pounded like a jungle drum. Unable to resist her, he caught her mouth, kissing her again, without holding anything of himself back.

Adrenaline, desire, hell—the knowledge he was *alive,* filled him to the brim. Logically he knew that the desire to fuck wasn't uncommon after combat. But desire this strong? She was oil to his fire.

He wanted to take her. Right here on the stony ground. Instead, Simon pressed her tender body between himself and the unyielding rock at her back as he ran his tongue along her teeth, raking the slight imperfection of a crooked eyetooth like a touchstone. He wanted her to cry his name as she came apart in his arms.

He spread his fingers at the base of her throat. Not to hold her in place, but to feel the wild beating of her pulse beneath his palm. He stroked the smooth skin on the underside of her jaw with his thumb as he ravished the slick, sweet interior of her mouth. Kess wrapped her leg around his hips, urging him against her body. God, she was responsive. Wild in his arms.

His dick was rock-hard. Kess moved against him, but it wasn't enough. For either of them. Simon pressed his straining erection to the juncture of her thighs as he kissed her deeply over and over, until they had to break apart to suck in air. Then they went back at it.

She whimpered, running her hands the breadth of his shoulders as she tried to crawl inside his skin. Digging her nails into his scalp, she rocked against him.

Tearing her mouth from under his, Kess whispered, "Wait . . ."

Simon brought his mouth to her neck as he felt the shudders ripping through her. Nibbling her velvety earlobe he whispered, "Let go," then sank his teeth lightly into the damp curve of her throat as he rocked against her.

Fingers still buried in his hair, she shuddered, then with a soft, wild cry came apart in his arms. Her forehead dropped to his chest, as he wrapped both arms around her, holding her tightly against his own unsatisfied need. Christ. That was fucking incredible. She was incredible.

"Sleeping bag . . ." she muttered thickly. "More."

If only. He should put her down, but the slight heft of her ass beneath his arm was heaven. "Have to get back to town."

"I know." Her warm breath seeped through his shirt and she rubbed her cheek against his chest. "I'm limp." Her arms tightened around his neck. "Just a few more minutes?"

"Can't."

She sighed, but didn't let go. "Can you carry me again?"

Simon smiled against her silky hair. "No, this time you're on your own."

"Damn." She lifted her head, cheeks flushed, eyes bright. He watched as she took a moment to switch gears; lowering her leg from around his hips was a wrench for both of them. "Okay. What do we take, and what do we leave?"

"Leave everything."

"Right." Glancing around, she moved out of his loose hold. "This has been one of the oddest experiences of my life."

"Never been kissed before?" he asked mildly, leading the way outside. He was surprised at how hard his heart was still thundering—how could she not hear it? All that from a kiss, and heavy petting that had brought her eyes to slits of desire. He swallowed, his mouth ridiculously dry. And he was about to walk away as if he weren't choking on his own need.

"A few times." She paused behind him and he glanced over his shoulder to catch her stretching her arms over her head, her slender body arched. Her peaked nipples pressed against the front of her T-shirt, proof that she was still as aroused as he was, yet she had made no demands, nor had she had any complaints.

His body ached with heavy need. Five minutes, just five minutes, and they'd both be satisfied.

No. He jerked his heated gaze away. Kess was some *other* man's fantasy woman. Some guy out there in the sane world was building a house for a fiery redhead—*this* fiery redhead. Probably dreaming right now of Kess, swollen with his child. Imagining lying with her in long, cool grass as they made love.

Fuck.

The reality check was enough to piss him off. "We gotta move it. Be careful, but get a move on. I want to speak to Abi before he goes into the office."

"I'm going as fast as I can without breaking my neck," she said without rancor as stones skipped ahead of her feet shod in bright *orange* fucking boots. "Why are you so cranky all of a sudden?"

"I don't get cranky." Horny. Frustrated. But never cranky.

"We could have taken a few minutes—"

Simon's jaw ached from grinding his teeth. Let *her* try walking with an enormous cockstand. "Drop it."

"Isn't the sky spectacular?" she offered innocently, but Simon heard the smile in her voice.

"Are you always this cheerful at dawn?"

"Only after an unexpected, but spectacular, orgasm. Yes. Pretty much. Thank you for asking."

Crap.

Kess walked a few steps behind and to his right, humming something tuneless under her breath. She was sure-footed and athletic, but the going was rough due to the loose stones littering the ground. The small ridge housing the cave ran for several hundred clicks down the center of the hilly valley, like the brown spiny backbone of some giant green beast. The sandy soil hosted rocks, shrubs, and a few hardy trees and grasses, since rain eroded the hard surface, making plant life struggle to thrive. Several deer grazing nearby lifted their heads to watch them, and a rabbit hopped across their path, then disappeared behind the shrubs.

The sun crested the horizon, already baking the hard-packed ground and turning the sky into a shimmering pale blue streaked with magenta and orange. Kess came up beside him, still humming to herself.

What was she humming? It didn't matter. Simon averted his gaze from her sweat-dampened skin. The pale glow of her bare nape was sexy as hell. Damn it, now he knew what she tasted like. Joy. Damn it. She tasted . . . Happy. He wanted to bury himself hilt-deep in her wet heat and keep doing it until he got over this absurd desire.

"Oh!" She suddenly skidded down a few feet, arms flailing for balance. He stopped thinking about getting any, and shot out his hand to clasp her upper arm and steady her. The three deer grazing several yards away spooked at the noise and took off in graceful leaps and bounds. Righting herself, she shot him an incredulous glance. "How on earth did you carry me all the way up here yesterday?"

Teleportation. "Here, give me your hand." Not so altruistic. He wanted to touch her again.

Kess grabbed his hand as she slid another foot, scattering more rocks, which rolled down the hillside. "Thanks. Do you want to tell me what's really happening?" She asked the question as casually as if she were asking him his favorite food. Companionably, she linked her fingers with his, palm to palm, then fell into step beside him again.

"Do you even know?"

She wasn't talking about what had just happened between them. The non-sex sex that could rock his world.

Simon was starting to have his suspicions about what was happening in this dark little corner of the world. But he wasn't ready to air them. Not yet, and not to Kess.

"Do you feel guilty?" Kess's eyes were shadowed as she glanced up at him.

"Guilty for what?"

"Cheating on your—what do you call her—I just need to know for future reference."

Simon paused to give her a baffled look. "Call who?"

"I think it's *whom*. Your future wife."

His face felt warm. Christ. "My One Day Woman."

"Ahh. Well, don't worry. She'll never know that you kissed a redhead in deepest, darkest Africa unless you tell her."

She doesn't exist, Simon wanted to shout. But he just resumed walking. Maybe a little too fast, as she slithered and slipped behind him, and he had to haul her upright every now and then. "Slow down, Sasquatch. We'll break our necks going down at this speed."

Feeling idiotic, Simon slowed down to a safer speed. Her hand felt small against his. Her skin soft. He wondered what had made him tell her about his fantasy woman. His "One Day Woman." He'd never mentioned his need for hearth and home to anyone. Damn. He didn't need a shrink to tell him that his fantasy, hell, his fixation, was due to growing up in the foster care system. Some places had been okay. Some had been bad.

He'd started fantasizing about the wife and the life he was going to have at about sixteen. The images had morphed and grown until the entire picture was as firmly fixed in his brain, in his psyche, as if it were the real deal. He was building the house for her. That perfect woman that was going to come along any day now.

Kess Goodall wasn't the woman he envisioned waiting for him at home after an op.

It wasn't just the superficial, it went deeper than that. Damn it, she didn't match any of his criteria. She wasn't in the least bit soft-spoken, she wasn't . . . *girly* enough. She wasn't sweetly accommodating, or any of the other refinements he required of a future wife.

But her mouth felt right under his. Her curves fit his angles to perfection. And God—her response was everything a man could want. And more.

"I probably know less about what's happening than you do," he said, dismissing the comparison of the real woman and the fictional woman. He'd known one considerably longer than the other. "I'll run some things by Abi when we get back to Quinisela."

She tugged on his hand to get his attention, and he paused. Sincerity shone in her large gray eyes as she held him there, joined by their clasped fingers. "You can't think the president has anything to do with the Hureni attacks?! If you paint him with that brush, you'll tarnish all the good things he's done," she said passionately. "He's doing an incredible job holding the peace. And no matter what you may think, he had nothing to do with what happened here."

"You know this, how?" he asked, playing devil's advocate. He continued walking and she fell into step again. Interesting how quickly she jumped to Abi's defense. Interesting, too, her knee-jerk reaction to him talking to Abi. Simon helped her over a shaley patch, enjoying the feel of her hand in his. When had he ever walked hand in hand with a woman? Never.

"I know because I know the man. He'd die before he let anything happen to his people. He's devastated by every reported death. The president takes each of them personally. He's doing everything in his power to find a cure for the disease and to keep the Hureni on their side of the border."

"He's not a saint," Simon pointed out, feeling mildly—it couldn't be jealous—*Hungry*. He hadn't eaten last night.

"His people think he is." Kess's eyes turned silver as she defended her boss. "And I'm not going to dissuade them."

"You'd be out of a cush job," he pointed out, walking on. If it sounded too good to be true, it probably was too good to be true. And even though he considered Abi a friend, they hadn't seen each other in more than ten years. A man could change considerably in a decade. Simon was waiting for more intel from HQ. He'd asked for everything they could dig up on his old friend.

"Tell me about this virus."

"I like my job, and I believe in the man I work for," she said with a little more heat. "The president pays me very well to do a job I enjoy doing. Cush isn't exactly the word I'd use. Look around. Does this look cushy to you? Just once would you give a straight answer to my questions?"

"Depends."

"On *what*, for heaven's sake?"

"On if I know the answer for fact and not speculation."

"Fair enough. It started three months ago in one of the most northern villages up near the Huren border. A woman walked fifty miles, with a raging fever and her baby on her back, to the closest clinic. She reported that everyone in her village was dead. Can you—" She held out her other hand for him to take and help her over a tall boulder.

Simon helped her up, then gripped her narrow waist and lifted her down on the other side.

"Thanks. The doctor there presumed it had been a Hureni attack; they've been getting worse and worse for the last six months or so. He took a few interns to the village and discovered that everyone had died of a virulent form of hemorrhagic fever. Probably dengue. Hang on a sec." She dropped his hand, then held on to his arm as she stood on one foot. "Rock in my shoe."

Simon waited as Kess paused to fish a stone out

of the top of her boot. "They had an outbreak of dengue in Singapore last year," he said. "Got it?"

At her nod he took her hand again as naturally as if they'd been friends or lovers for years. He told himself that it was to keep her safe, and they continued down the hill. "*Aedes aegypti*—yellow fever mosquitoes." Simon tried to remember what he knew about mosquito-borne illnesses. Not a whole hell of a lot. He made a mental note to get the research department on it. "This would be the place for it. Apparently dengue is the most virulent mosquito-borne disease after malaria." And that about covered the totality of his knowledge.

"We have that too, of course. But Mallaruza hasn't had a dengue fever outbreak in thirty years."

"And now it's back," he pointed out.

"No. This has all the earmarks of a hemorrhagic dengue outbreak, but it's *not* dengue. There are courses of treatment that work for that. The president has supplied all of them to physicians across the country. *Nothing* cures whatever this is. So far three million people, and counting, have died a gruesome, painful death. And no one can figure out *what's* causing it."

"And you were doing what exactly, going to a contaminated village? Writing a press release?" he asked savagely. What the fuck was Abi thinking, sending Kess into a lethal setting?

"As a matter of fact, yes. I was taking pictures." She dismissed his condemnation entirely. "They'll go with a series of articles I'm writing to show the outside world what's really happening in Mallaruza. People need to know what's happening here. *And* how Mr. Bongani is handling it. He's working tirelessly to eradicate whatever this is. He has a lab in Switzerland working on a cure 24/7. If anyone can save these people it's their presid—

"You weren't kidding, were you? Where did this come from?" she demanded, switching gears when she saw the huge black chopper waiting for them at the bottom of the hill.

She glanced around. Nothing but sky, grass, and a few scraggly acacia trees. And a military Black Hawk. "Where's the pilot?"

Simon had materialized the chopper. No pilot necessary. "He took off. I'm flying us back."

She frowned. "Took off . . . *Where*?"

"Two choppers." He yanked open the door, lifting her in before she could tell him she could get in on her own. He liked the feel of her. The slimness of her waist, and the way her hips flared beneath his hands. He liked the way the weak sunlight set her hair into a blaze as gloriously Technicolor as the African sunrise. He liked the way she kissed, giving back everything she got. Nothing in reserve.

He liked that his mini vacay was turning into an op after all. He liked that he'd take Miss Goodall back to Quinisela. He liked that he probably wouldn't have to run into her again.

She complicated things.

Disengaging his hands from her ass, Simon walked around and got in on the other side, then started the engine. The MH-60M, like the Rover, was armor-plated. But the right projectile, meticulously aimed, could take the helicopter out just as it had the vehicle.

"Strap in." Slowly the rotors started spinning. "Only one headset. We won't be able to talk until we land."

He put on the earphones, glanced over to confirm she was secure, then lifted off in a swirl of dust.

Kess settled back against the leather seat, staring out at the rolling green hills of the savanna spread beneath their swiftly moving dragonfly shadow. How convenient for him not to have to talk all the way back to Quinisela. She had so many questions, but she knew if she pushed she'd get nowhere.

Far below, a small group of elephants grazed ponderously on a clump of thorny acacia trees, and a herd of zebra, graphic black-and-white, nibbled the grass at a giraffe's feet. Amber light from the slowly rising sun elongated shadows, making it harder to spot more than the most obvious animals.

As Simon flew over the medic's campsite, the noise of the rotors disturbed a dozen or more vultures on the ground. They flew up in a frenzy of ragged gray wings and scrawny pink heads. Kess averted her gaze from the scavengers and the clear-

ing below. What she'd seen there was indelibly en-
graved on her synapses. She didn't need to see it
again. She'd never forget.

She'd made some close friends there. People who
wanted to save lives and instead had given theirs.
For what?

The helicopter turned over the trees to follow the
road south. It didn't occur to her to doubt Simon's
ability to fly a helicopter, even as he flew off at an
angle. To their left the dense tree canopy followed
the winding Congo River. Farther downstream was
the last village Kess had visited with the medical
team. They'd hastily sent her back to base camp
when they'd seen how quickly the virus was
spreading.

God. Kess rubbed the back of her neck where
tension squeezed her muscles. For five minutes up
there in the small cave she'd been able to put the
graphic images aside and just feel. He played her
body like a musical instrument. But those few minutes didn't really blot out all that had happened.
Not by a long shot. No matter how incredible it
was.

How could this horrific disease be controlled?
Millions were already dead. The medical team had
been there to help the survivors, to take water and
soil samples for testing, to help the villagers bury
their dead. And in payment they themselves had
been slaughtered like cattle.

Kess couldn't even begin to come up with an answer that made any kind of sense.

Looking down, she saw where Simon had parked outside camp the day before. The only sign of the vehicle was the aerial view of what looked like splatter. As though someone had dropped a bucket of black paint on the dirt road. The Rover had disintegrated, completely obliterated in the explosion. Kess rubbed the goose bumps on her arms. If she hadn't gotten out of the vehicle. If Simon hadn't returned just then—

He'd damn well better answer her questions the second they landed. There was definitely something off about whatever was going on way out here. *What*, Kess had no idea. But she'd bet her last bar of Dove soap that Simon knew. And if he didn't know, then he was the kind of man who'd find out.

To do her job effectively she had to know the truth. Who had killed the medical team, and why? The last thing she needed was a native uprising at this juncture of the election. Not only did the president have to keep his focus, if the murderers were Mallaruzis it would be a PR nightmare. The fact that Bongani was doing everything in his power to help his people—bringing in medical supplies and outside aid—was commendable, but if his own people were killing those sent to help them—

Kess shuddered at the idea that she would have to come up with a way to keep that out of the mainstream media. There was just no way to spin this so it looked good.

The world already knew about the Hureni. Knew that Mallaruza's borders were under attack and that the small country's neighbors were getting bolder. It was also common knowledge that Bongani's army could only do so much when half their time was spent burying the dead.

She had a feeling her mettle was about to be tested to the max as she spun this latest crisis in the media.

Was Simon really just a friend of Bongani's, or was he something more? She turned her head to look at him. Since he was frowning, she guessed he was barely aware that she was two feet away from him. Not bothering with subtlety, Kess scanned his features, trying to figure out how this man had gotten under her skin so quickly.

There was no point pretending to herself that she wasn't fascinated by him. Just *looking* at him aroused her. It wasn't necessary to glance down. Her nipples felt sensitive, as the hard peaks rubbed against her T-shirt, and the damp spot between her legs still felt tender.

That kiss had turned her inside out. Kess enjoyed sex. She was young and healthy and found making love, with the right man, incredible. While she'd believed herself in love with the three men with whom she'd had serious relationships, she'd had a couple of spectacular one-night stands as well.

Which proved she didn't have to be in love to enjoy the act. And for the other times, there were all sorts of interesting toys.

Love? She frowned, eyeing him again. Why was she thinking of the L word? She'd climaxed from a simple kiss, plain and simple. Her brow furrowed and she squeezed her thighs together to stop them from trembling.

There was nothing simple about Simon.

Seven

Kess recognized the luxury car waiting for them at the Quinisela airport as part of the president's fleet. There was no sign of a driver. Simon certainly knew how to make things happen in more ways than one.

"Where can I drop you?" he asked, holding open the passenger door for her.

What had she expected? That he'd want to come back home with her and finish what he'd started on the ridge? "Kagunda Hotel on Zende; know it?"

"Midtown?"

Looking at his mouth, Kess nodded. What was it about this guy that made her insides feel all warm and goopy when she looked at him? On some primitive level she knew it was because he was big and strong. He'd protected her yesterday. And damn it, he'd kissed her like she was all *he* could think about.

She needed to get over that kiss. No matter how incredible it'd been. While a brief fling might sound appealing, Kess had a job to do. She was a professional, and this job meant so much on so many levels. She was *not* going to screw it up by screwing around.

"You can give me directions when we get close." Simon closed her door with an expensive snick, then walked around the front to the driver's side and got in.

After slamming his door he reached out and brushed his fingers over her hair. At his touch Kess's heart started galloping, anticipating another of his toe-curling, brain-melting kisses. Instead he untangled a twig from her hair. Tossing it out the window without comment, he started the car, then pulled out of the hangar, driving across the tarmac to the exit reserved for private-plane owners.

Well, hell. That was like expecting a Barbie camper for Christmas and getting . . . socks.

So she had tree parts in her hair. So what?

Despite a night spent who knew where, he looked well groomed, his dark hair finger-combed off his face, his T-shirt and jeans clean. His boots were only slightly dusty from their tromp downhill. She, however, felt like she'd slept on the hard ground, and wished she at least had a hairbrush. She was sure her hair looked as though she'd stuck her finger in a light socket, and her clothes were as dusty and grimy as her lovely orange boots.

A shower would take care of her grooming concerns. She'd been out in the bush for twenty-four hours, for God's sake. But it did tick her off that Simon always seemed immaculate, while every time he'd seen her she looked as though grooming was a last thought. She was more comfortable in pants, preferably jeans, but when was the last time she'd even worn a dress? Her lips twitched. Probably the last time she'd had sex. Maybe there was a correlation. She should do a study on it.

"Stop fiddling with your hair. It looks fine."

Damned by faint praise, Kess thought darkly, dropping her arms. She actually liked her hair, and thought it was her best feature. It was thick and slightly wavy, and usually had a nice shine to it, when it wasn't full of shrubbery. She got a lot of compliments on the unusual shade of red.

It was normally better than "fine." So what if it wasn't dark, like Simon's Stepford wife-to-be. Kess folded her arms and glared out of the side window. He shouldn't go around kissing redheads like that if he wanted to marry a brunette. Not that she wanted to get married anytime soon. She had a career to manage. Which, up until the day before yesterday, had looked quite promising. Now, not so much. She picked at a broken fingernail, considering the odds of the shit not hitting the fan, and everything that had happened in the last twenty-four hours turning out to be a random bunch of bloodthirsty Hureni warriors, and an isolated incident.

Kess, hating to place a losing wager, switched back to thinking of Simon. She wondered where he was staying. Not the small residential hotel where she was living, she'd bet. Either he was a guest of his friend the president or he was at the one and only resort hotel on the beach. It was the best hotel in Quinisela, which wasn't saying one whole hell of a lot. The place was fifty years old and showed its age. Not a lot of tourism in Mallaruza.

Kess wanted to change that. The area had a certain charm, and she envisioned a row of beautiful, luxurious hotels curved around the bay. She and the president had spoken at length about developing a tourist industry to rival the one South Africa had enjoyed back in the day. It seemed an odd location, but he was building an enormous church— no, it was bigger than a church—a basilica, right across the street from the beach and a few blocks from the hotel. While exquisitely beautiful, covered with creamy marble and enough hand carving to look like an expensive wedding cake, the enormous building pretty much blocked the view if any hotels should be built.

But first she had to make sure that Mallaruza was in the news only for the good the leader of the country was doing. Her job was to accent the positive. Hard to freaking do when an entire team of medical personnel had just been butchered for no apparent reason. She'd put out a press release as soon as she got to her hotel, before the media discovered the horrific news.

It was ironic that Simon had to show up now, of all times, Kess thought. Talk about bad timing, and the wrong guy. She didn't have months to persuade him that brunettes weren't that special. But damn it, she couldn't get that kiss out of her mind. And she had to. There were a hundred and one reasons, not the least of which was that Simon had already told her point-blank who his dream woman was. And it wasn't her.

Kess glanced up at the darkening sky as they took the potholed streets into the city proper. Even if she and Simon were perfectly compatible, which she knew they weren't, he was only here for a short-term visit.

She was here for the long haul. She had so much to prove to all her detractors. She was working quadruple time bringing Mallaruza and its president to the notice of the world; her boss was up for reelection in less than a week; the civil war on the border was escalating. And in six weeks she had to return to Atlanta for her court appearance.

The thought of defending her actions in a court of law depressed her. But it was time to give her side of the debacle in the firm's Atlanta office last summer. She sighed.

"Okay?"

"Hmm?"

His brow furrowed. "You sure got quiet. I asked if you were okay."

Let's see, she thought. She was in lust with a secretive man whose kisses made her dream of white picket fences. She had to salvage her reputation, tenuous as it was. For that she had to return to a city that had vilified her in the small public relations community and made her name mud. Yeah, no sweat. And she had to make sure that her boss was reelected in a country that thought killing was an acceptable form of communication.

She was fine and dandy. "Sure."

Kess almost bit her tongue as the car dipped and bounced over a series of deep potholes impossible to avoid. The sun disappeared behind a bank of dark clouds, and the air felt thickly oppressive. It was going to rain. And when it rained here it was a downpour. She wanted to go home, shower, forget about Simon and Atlanta, and be in her city hall office before the deluge hit.

"Damn. I just realized. My camera equipment was in your car. Someone will have to go and take pictures before they remove the bodies. Maybe there are clues—"

"I took pictures." Simon handled the big car with ease. Kess suspected he did everything with ease. Including commandeering a helicopter and producing a waiting car. "Already sent them in for analysis, and there's a team on their way out there now to investigate and remove the bodies and return the remains to the families."

"You're very efficient. What did you do? Give the SIM card to the pilots? What was it you said you did for a living? A builder, right?"

"Contractor. Not builder. I'm a counterterrorist operative for an organization called T-FLAC."

Oh shit! That *kind of contractor. Please tell me not.* She'd known he was holding information back, and she hadn't expected such an honest answer. "What does that mean? Are you saying there are terrorists for you to counter in Mallaruza?"

"There are terrorists everywhere."

"But here in particular?"

"I'm looking into it."

She believed him. Her eyes widened as she realized the connotation of his job. "Oh, my God, this is going to be a public relations nightmare."

"What is?"

Kess waved her hands. "All of it." Okay, she thought, her brain shuffling through options, maybe not. Simon would deal with the terrorists—she had every confidence that he could do whatever was necessary. And while he did whatever he did, Abioyne Bongani would still look rosy. She'd make sure of it. "Are you here to rout out terrorists, or to help train the president's army?" Either way would look bad. Damn it to hell.

"That was a pretty giant leap. But that wasn't the plan. No."

Twisting one leg under her, Kess turned to look at him. "Is Mallaruza going to war?"

"Not that I'm aware of."

"Would you tell me if you did know? Because if that *is* the case I have to get things—"

"Right now, we have seven people dead, two people missing in what has all the hallmarks of a Hureni attack."

"True." Kess chewed her lip, then after a few beats while she computed what he'd just revealed, asked, "What do you mean two people *missing*? How can you know that? There was so much . . . carnage." She shook her head as she said the words. "That's pure speculation."

"Wrong. What I saw at the camp doesn't lend itself to multiple interpretations. Straus and Viljoen weren't there."

"Wait. Are you saying that Dr. Straus and Judy's bod— That they weren't *there*?" He hadn't said a word. Not one freaking *word* that two people were missing. Not yesterday. Not during the night. Not today. She tensed with brimming anger, and damn it, now, hope.

"Two people were missing. Those two."

"You might have mentioned this before now. Do you think—They got away! Thank God. They must've found a cave like we did, and hidden while—"

"Possible, but unlikely. The attack was fast. No one would have had any warning. So unless they were somewhere else at the time, I don't think so."

"But they could still be alive? It's possible, right?" Her pulse leapt, two people had survived that bloodbath. Thank God. She envisioned a sweet survivor story that she could write to Abi's benefit.

"Possible? Yeah, guess so. Probable? No."

The finality in his tone dashed her hopes. "Maybe animals dragged them off somewhere." Just the thought of it made Kess shudder and rub the goose bumps on her arms.

"Possible, but I walked a mile in each direction. I didn't see any drag marks or blood trails. Doesn't mean it didn't happen. My people will do a more thorough search in the surrounding area."

All the blood left her head. "*We* have to go back and look. Maybe—No. They wouldn't be alive, would they? Of course not."

"I don't believe animals took them."

"I don't know whether to be relieved or—Are you implying that the Hureni *kidnapped* them?"

"I'm not implying anything. I'm not even sure the Hureni were responsible."

Kess frowned, her intellect taking another giant step. "You think local *Mallaruzi villagers* killed them? Why? The doctors were there to help them. That doesn't make any sense at all. Maybe t—"

"How about giving that fertile imagination of yours a rest until I get some answers?"

"I'll certainly try," Kess said dryly. Yes, she should stop conjuring up worst-case scenarios. But wasn't that her job? She had to be ready to spin this to the president's advantage. Not that a war with the neighbors could in any way be construed as an advantage. Damn it. She had to find out if the killings had been an isolated incident or the tip of a bigger problem.

"Take a left at the next light even if it flashes red. It's been broken as long as I've been here, then turn right onto Zende."

"This isn't for you to figure out, Kess." Simon shot her a glance before he turned. "Let me handle it. It's what I do."

"Are you a mind reader?" she asked with a rueful smile. "You're right. I'm not equipped to deal with this. But it is my job to know and deflect any bad press."

"I'll give you a heads-up when I discover anything. Fair enough?"

"That's the hotel on the left—Yes. Fair enough." He'd have to see her again.

Simon pulled the car under the portico and a porter, seeing the president's car, came out as if jet-propelled. "Thank you for being there. I would have been totally freaked if I'd arrived alone to see that."

Simon waved the porter off. "Don't go out of town alone again, Kess. In fact, try not going anywhere alone. As civilized as Quinisela appears, it's still Africa under the veneer of civilization. If the Hureni were bold enough to kill those people four hours away they might be bold enough to come into the city."

"I'll ask the president's aide, Thabo Chizobi, to give me another gun."

"Know how to use it?"

"Of course." Not that she ever wanted to. But there was no point in having a gun if she didn't know how to use it. "Thabo gave me some lessons. I've practiced every day."

"Good. I'll find you something lighter than the Browning. What do you have planned for today?"

"I'll be in my office in about an hour. I'll be there the rest of the day, why?"

"I'll have a new weapon and ammo for you when you get there. I'll send Chizobi to pick you up and bring you into the office. An hour?"

"It's only a couple of blocks—"

He touched her cheek. Probably subtly wiping grime off her face. "Humor me, okay?" Simon's fingers felt cool against her hot skin, and his touch lingered for several very fast heartbeats before he dropped his hand.

He beckoned the porter who raced across the parking area and whipped open Kess's door, letting in a blast of ozone-smelling, muggy air.

She got out, awkwardly waiting for Simon to say something wonderful.

"See you." He leaned across the car and tugged at the passenger door.

The second it closed, he drove off.

Kess stared after the car as the wind tossed her hair around her head. "See me *when*?"

* * *

"—Noek Joubert." Simon finished telling Abi the details about yesterday's mass execution. They'd talked briefly on the sat phone late the night before, but Abi wanted to hear everything again this morning. At the retelling his friend seemed to age ten years.

"Is Joubert the wizard you were talking about?" Abi frowned. Simon wasn't sure if it was at what he'd just said, or something his friend was watching on the silent plasma TV on the wall. "*I* was talking about?" Abi asked absently, still watching the news.

"Yeah, Abi. The one you suspected was working with the Hureni. The one you wanted me to find?"

Abi's face smoothed out, but his skin had taken on an ashen cast. "I don't think so. No. I'm sure this isn't the guy."

Really? What were the odds that two powerful wizards were wandering around Mallaruza looking for trouble? "Heard of him?" Simon asked, leaning back against the leather chair in the president's opulent office. He brought a gold-rimmed china cup of fragrant coffee to his mouth. The coffee was excellent, strong and aromatic. The fragile, ornate cup was all for show, and damn hard to handle. Simon cradled it in his hand as he glanced out of the window behind Abi, waiting for an answer.

Fat drops of rain splattered apathetically against

the windowpane and the gunmetal gray sky filled the view. Kess was probably in her small office down the hall by now. While the drops were fat, it wasn't raining that hard. Yet. But he suspected it would be a bitch of a storm when it did. He drank the last of his coffee as he waited for Abi to answer.

"Joubert?" Abi's brow creased into a deep frown. "Name doesn't sound familiar. You'd think it would. A wizard that powerful."

Beep! *Wrong answer.* Shit. Simon didn't believe him, although Abi had hidden his reaction extremely well. He'd most certainly heard of Joubert. Knew him. Or knew of him. Simon wasn't sure. But the name had elicited a small tightening of the muscles around Abi's eyes. And a telltale tremor in the hand holding his saucer so that the cup rattled as he placed it casually on the desk.

Interesting. "I have feelers out." Simon crossed an ankle on his knee, perfectly at ease. Where had Abi's and Joubert's paths crossed? More important, why keep it a secret? "Should know more b—"

"Excuse me. I want to listen to this." Abi grabbed up the remote and pointed it at the TV.

". . . current government of Mallaruza has a primary responsibility to protect its civilian population, and must therefore stop the army, *including* the presidential guard, from committing human rights abuses," Jungo Kamau said grimly, looking directly into the camera.

Abi's opponent, and currently the county's financial compass, was spit-and-polished for his interview, but had the air of a man who'd had little sleep and carried a shitload of problems on his narrow shoulders. With just cause, Simon thought.

"While I applaud President Bongani's efforts, he *must* hold perpetrators accountable." Kamau's hands, clasped on the desk in front of him, went white-knuckled. "Human rights agencies have to be allowed to establish a presence here. We can't do this alone. Especially with this virulent sickness sweeping through our country."

The reporter, a white South African woman with cotton-candy yellow hair and large blue eyes, assumed the faux, overly concerned expression used by most television journalists. "The president has offered asylum to anyone who needs it. Some consider him a saint."

"Some might," Kamau said flatly. "But look around you. We can't support our own people. Inviting millions of refugees into our country, while seemingly altruistic, is just straining our already overburdened resources."

"What do you think of the president's construction of Africa's largest cathedral, Mr. Kamau?"

"I don't think—I *know*. Mr. Bongani is spending hundreds of millions we don't have to—"

"Just a faggot shooting off his mouth." Abi turned off the TV, tossing the control onto his desk. "He doesn't have any idea what the fuck he is talking about."

Since the guy was the country's comptroller, Simon suspected Abi's opponent knew to the penny what he was talking about. He'd brought up some good points. But Abi was clearly pissed off by the interview. "Abi, about Joubert—"

There was a sharp rap at the door. A second later Chizobi, Abi's assistant, came in. His closely cropped hair glittered with scattered raindrops, and he wiped his damp face on a pristine white handkerchief. "Excuse me, *ubaba*." He stuffed the cloth in his suit pant pocket.

An elemental itch on the back of his neck made Simon set his cup back in the saucer on the edge of the desk and give the older man a more thorough inspection. In his late fifties, five-ten Chizobi was as skinny as a garden snake. He was in a position affording him respect, and relative wealth, in a country that saw its people eking out an existence as best they could, and he dressed the part in a shiny navy suit and white shirt accompanied by a skinny black string tie. He reminded Simon a little of the late Sammy Davis Jr. Without the glass eye.

If Chizobi had had a hat, he'd have been twisting it in his hands as he came forward to stand before the president's enormous desk.

From Abi, Simon knew this man was a trusted employee, and had been for close to ten years. He was serious, diligent, and devoted to his boss. And this morning he was worried as hell. His face was shiny with nervous perspiration, his brow accordion-pleated.

"I am sorry to interrupt you, *ubasi*. I am sure it is nothing. But *inkosazana* Goodall, she is not at the Kagunda Hotel. The porter, he say the *inkosazana* left half hour after she was dropped off by *ubaba* Blackthorne.

"I checked, but *inkosazana* is not in her office." The aide pulled the hankie out of his pocket again to mop his brow, his nervous gaze darting between Simon and his boss, his Zulu accent thick and almost unintelligible as he tried to relay his message as quickly as possible. "I also checked to see if the *inkosazana* signed into the building today. I regret she has not."

"Don't be concerned," Abi told him, clearly distracted. By the mention of Noek Joubert perhaps? "Kess sometimes stops at the gym on Zizwe—"

"She is not there, *ubasi*." It was apparent that Chizobi was hell-bent on showing his much-revered president that he had exhausted every logical avenue before reporting in. "I checked."

Simon stood, a muscle ticing in his cheek. Where had the blasted woman disappeared to now? He wanted to be annoyed that she'd ignored his concern and not only walked to the office, but taken a detour. He might not know Kess well, but Simon was damned sure that she would have done exactly what he'd asked her to do: wait for Chizobi to pick her up and drive her to her city hall office.

If Kess hadn't been waiting at the hotel, something had happened to her. And in Mallaruza that could mean damn near anything.

"I'll find her." Simon paused at the open door. "And Abi? Remember how you know Noek Joubert. We'll talk when I get back."

Tired of being filthy, Kess locked the door to her room and headed straight for the shower. The stall was tiny, rusty, and barely adequate, but it served its purpose. Ten minutes later, clean and wrapped in a towel, she emerged from the shower. She had a lot to process. "And Simon Blackthorne counterterrorist operative shouldn't be on my To Do List."

Something drew her gaze to the neatly made bed. She frowned.

An envelope, damp and grimy, was propped against the pristine white pillows on her bed. Not a love note from Simon, she bet.

Someone was in the room. Kess looked around wildly for her gun. The gun that had gone up with the Rover. Shit. The blood had drained from her head and the hairs at the back of her neck stood up in nervous anticipation as she looked around for the intruder.

Her room was on the fifth floor. How had anyone managed to get in? Certainly they hadn't rappelled up the side of the building in broad daylight on a busy street. Besides, the window was closed and locked, she could see it from her position in the middle of the room.

Bribed by the lazy-assed, sneaky doorman, Obi, she bet. *Shitshitshit.*

Of course there was nobody there—where would they hide? The bed had drawers under it, and there was no closet, just a few hooks on the wall. Other than the bed, an easy chair, a microwave oven, and a small refrigerator, there wasn't any other furniture.

The room smelled strongly of cigarette smoke and stale sweat left behind by her uninvited visitor. Kess ran to the door and snapped the dead bolt back in place. Spinning around, she clutched the towel between her breasts and scanned the room again. She was alone. Just the thought that someone had been here while she was naked in the next room gave her the heebie-jeebies.

Whatever was in the damn envelope could wait until she had clothes on. Staring at the envelope the whole time she dressed, Kess wished that she'd asked Simon for his cell phone number. He must have a cell phone. He'd called to have a helicopter delivered, for God's sake. Why hadn't they exchanged numbers?

Grabbing up her dusty boots, she sat on the edge of the chair to put them on. Giving Simon her cell phone number wouldn't have done her any damned good. It had been blown to smithereens in his Rover the day before along with her gun and everything else in her duffel bag.

Since there wasn't a telephone in the room, she'd have to leave the hotel, find a public phone that worked, and try him via the president's office. "Please be there, Simon. I'm totally freaking out."

What would she have done if Simon wasn't around? Called the local militia? Useless. They wouldn't even bother coming to take a statement. They had much bigger fish to fry than a break-in. She didn't have anything of value for anyone to steal anyway. Her most valuable possession was her camera, and that had gone *kaboom* with her phone.

She'd get another lock, of course. She'd already added the dead bolt when she'd moved in a couple of months ago. But that hadn't kept the person out. Especially if assisted by a damn passkey. Chills raced across her still-damp skin. The second she was fully dressed, Kess snatched up the letter-sized envelope and opened the flap.

We have Dr. Straus and Dr. Viljoen.
Bring your camera to Café Ndebani
no later than 9:30 A.M. today.
Contact no one and come alone.
Any delay will result in injury to your friends.
As incentive, we have left you a little something.
Check the top dresser drawer.

"I'm going to freaking *hate* this." The sound of her own voice wasn't in the least bit comforting.

Kess didn't bother counting to three, or trying to talk herself out of looking. Without hesitation she yanked open the drawer, then sucked in a choked gasp.

It was a bloody, severed finger. The ring finger of Judy Viljoen's left hand to be precise. Kess recognized the delicate engagement ring her friend had been so excited about receiving two weeks ago.

She closed the drawer carefully, swallowing bile as she did so. She rubbed her arms as chills raced through her body.

Her friends hadn't been dragged away by either the Hureni or wild animals. Konrad and Judy had been kidnapped. A glance at the bedside clock showed her that she had twenty minutes to make the meeting. She didn't *have* her camera. It had been blown up in the explosion the day before. Oh, God. What the hell was she going to—"I put the SIM card in my pocket!"

Upending the laundry hamper she retrieved the pants she'd been wearing and shoved her hand into the front-right pocket. *Please be here. Please be here*—"Yes!" Her fingers curled around the small disk.

She dragged in a ragged breath, holding her clenched fist to her rapidly beating heart. Now to call Simon and get backup. No way was she meeting these butchers alone. No matter what the hell they told her to do.

"Simon eats people like you for breakfast," she

said fiercely, running down five flights of stairs to
the lobby. Obi was nowhere in sight. But Simon
would help her track the son of a bitch down, and
squeeze out the information of who'd broken into
her room.

The public phone, tucked under the slope of the
front stairs, was useless. Someone had cut the cord
and stolen the receiver months ago. Damn. Damn.
Damn. Her heart was racing so fast she felt sick to
her stomach. There'd be a public phone in the
bazaar. Somewhere.

Kess checked her watch, then speed-walked
through the bazaar, heading for the small coffee
shop tucked halfway down a narrow side alley. The
marketplace was crowded with housewives doing
the daily food shopping. The brightly colored cotton print dresses of the locals were mixed with
western business attire worn by young, hip Mallaruzis grabbing a snack to take to the office or enjoying a late-morning coffee with friends.

Kess had no time to admire the colors and scents
of the outdoor market. Wiping a raindrop off her
cheek, she picked up her pace. She narrowly
avoided colliding with a woman balancing a
produce-filled basket on her head, a baby strapped
to her back.

Adrenaline racing, she looked over her shoulder.
Was someone following her? Watching her every
move? Where the hell was a freaking *phone*?
Simon? Help!

Kess shot a glance at her watch as she walked: 9:23. No time to track him down before meeting the kidnapper. She hesitated. Nothing good could possibly happen if she met these people alone.

Kidnapping anywhere in the world was a serious problem, but in Mallaruza, as in Italy, kidnapping was a way of life. Extortion of any kind was basically ignored since the entire country was rife with crime.

As crazy and foolish as she knew it was, she was Konrad's and Judy's only hope. She didn't give a damn what was on the SIM card. The kidnappers could have it.

Praying that she'd spot a phone on the way, Kess started jogging. The small café was two alleys down on the left, but it was raining in earnest now, a curtain of water dropped and people covered their heads and raced to find shelter as the sky really opened up.

What could she do if the kidnappers took the SIM card, then killed Konrad and Judy anyway? How could she prevent them from doing any damn thing they wanted? Kess bit her lip as she half walked, half ran. She'd demand proof of life. She'd insist they traded the SIM card for the two doctors, or no card. That would work. Wouldn't it? Would that give her enough time to get Simon on board and have him use his counterterrorist stuff to find the two doctors? God, she hoped so.

Hoped, but suspected none of this would go as she hoped.

And even knowing that, she was caught between a rock and a hard place. Judy and Konrad were alive. She had what the kidnappers wanted. The only thing that made her not wet her pants with fear was that she was in a marketplace crowded with people. It was slim comfort and her heart pounded hard enough for the Hureni over the border to hear it.

Thanks to the rain the coffee shop was packed and smelled not only of the strong black coffee they served, but also of ripe produce and fresh-baked bread. She scanned the jostling crowd sort of lined up in front of the glass counter.

People were looking at her, but it was no more than the usual curiosity because the color of her hair was so startling. People crowded around a dozen small round tables, sometimes two people to a chair.

A scrawny dog leapt up, snatched a man's breakfast roll right out of his hand as he got his order, then slinked outside to dine in the rain.

There was much shouting and arm waving, but no one came over to her and introduced themselves. No one made eye contact. Kess stood in the middle of the crowd with no idea what to do next. She again scanned the room from side to side, then saw a sight outside that made her heart leap with joy.

"*Simon.* Thank God." Their eyes met through the grimy window.

How or why he'd decided to look for her, and actually *find* her, was immaterial. Kess started pushing her way back to the front door. A salmon swimming upstream. No one wanted to make room for her to leave. They were all trying to get *inside.*

"*Uxolo,* excuse me, *excusez-moi.*" Nobody budged. Kess considered yelling "Fire" at the top of her lungs in all three languages, but instead used her elbows and sheer determination to clear a path to the door.

She almost fell into Simon's arms as a heavyset woman carrying two chickens in a basket on her head stepped aside more quickly than Kess anticipated.

"Simon. Oh, my God, am I happy to—"

He grabbed her by the elbow and pulled her several yards down the rainwashed alley. "What the *hell* are you doing here alone?"

Kess stopped walking, and yanked her arm out of his hold. "Knock it off. No yelling, no dragging. My hearing is excellent, and I can walk on my own just fine."

"I sent Chizobi to get you, did you forget?"

"Doctors Straus and Viljoen were *kidnapped.*" This time it was Kess who did the grabbing; his arm was damp, but warm and solid beneath her hands. Oh, God, she was so glad to see him she could have kissed him. "Simon, someone broke into my room while I was in the shower. They left a note telling me—"

She looked up just as Simon pointed a gun at her head.

Eight

Simon shook her hands off his left arm, his shooting arm, firing a kill shot at the man directly behind Kess's left shoulder. She let out an earsplitting scream as the guy crumpled at her feet. Grabbing her hand, Simon practically yanked her forward. *"Run!"*

"You can't—What—Oh, my God, Simon!" Her eyes went wild as she tried to dig her heels in. "Are you *completely* out of your *mind*? What are y—"

"Move it! Now." He started running, her hand gripped tightly in his, giving her no choice but to keep up with him. In his other hand was the Taurus. He pushed his way through people who had all the time in the world to dick around.

"Balela amathe indlal!" Get out of the way in Zulu. He hoped. By their response he might as well have yelled "Loiter right in our path and get us fucking killed."

No one gave a damn that two people were running balls out down the main alley filled with stalls of fruit, vegetables, and leather goods. Those not safely tucked away inside stood out in the rain shopping, talking, visiting, and getting the hell in his way. His ubiquitous vision showed the men behind them, closing in fast. It also showed Kess, red hair flying around her head as she ran.

"Move. Move. Move."

"I have to stay there!" she yelled, dragging on his hand. "Simon? Damn it, Simon, *stop*! We have to go back. The kidnappers—"

"Sent someone to shiv you," he shouted over his shoulder. He'd shot one of them, and there were at least five more hot on their heels. Damn it to hell. What had she gotten herself into? "This way." He turned her down a narrow space between the buildings. The passage, not wide enough to be called an alley, was littered with rank, stinking refuse. Refuse meant rats. And lots of them.

The furry rodents squeaked and scurried over their booted feet as they ran single file. Simon anticipated that their followers would miss this dark narrow pathway and keep going, giving him time to get Kess out of the middle of whatever the hell this was.

Yanking her into a small doorway, he kicked aside a rat the size of a small cat and peered down into her wide, terrified eyes. Teleportation was the fastest way out of this mess and with five guys right on their asses, he couldn't think of a more expedient way.

"Kiss me," he said.

She blinked as if he'd spoken in tongues. "W-what?"

Snaking his fingers through the thick, silken mass of her hair, Simon gave a gentle tug, forcing her head back slightly. As their mouths met, he closed his eyes for a nanosecond and envisioned her hotel room. He felt a small zing as his power flickered weakly.

Shitfuckdamn. He kissed her harder and tried focusing on a closer target. The basket shop beyond the west end of the market.

Zap. Fizzle. *Fuck.*

He'd have to do this the old-fashioned way. Just as he saw people moving about at the other end, indicating an adjoining alley filled with shoppers, Simon saw his luck had run out. Two of the bad guys had discovered their hidey-hole and were gaining fast.

There was no room to shift Kess in front of him in the tight space. Keeping a tight grip on her hand, he tried teleporting her to city hall where there were people and security guards. She might be confused as hell as to how she'd gotten there, but she'd be away from the present danger.

Fucking hell. Couldn't do it. Her damp fingers clutched his hand as she ran forward, tired of waiting for him to move. Putting a protection spell on her, Simon tried teleportation again. This time only the short distance necessary so that he was between Kess and the two men.

It worked. Protecting her behind the shelter of his body, Simon turned and fired at the front guy.

Mallaruzi, by his dress and features. He went down, much to the joy of the rats who used his body as a bridge. They swarmed over him even while the next guy kept coming. He kicked the rats aside, stepped over the body of his fellow assassin, and aimed his Smith & Wesson .40, firing from thirty feet away.

Simon fired at the same time. He felt the bullet crease his shoulder, but was more interested to see his target go down. "Stay here," he ordered Kess, sprinting forward to see if the hit man could give him any answers before he died.

"Stay h—Are you *nuts*? I'm not staying anywhere." Kess followed him, standing inches away as Simon crouched down to feel the guy's pulse at the base of his throat. "Is he—?"

"Dead, damn it."

"Probably the whole point of having the guns," she said dryly, her face pale, her eyes huge as he rose to stand beside her.

Simon wrapped his arm around her shoulders because she looked a little shaky. Or maybe because he just wanted to hold her. Or most likely, because he still had the taste of her on his lips.

"What did the kidnappers want?" Because there was no doubt in his mind that whatever *it* was, *they* still wanted it. There were a handful more guys out combing the marketplace. And they had been sent by someone. Who?

"SIM card from my camera." Kess stuck her

hand into the front pocket of her jeans and pulled out the card between two fingers. "Here. *You* take it."

Simon stuck it in his pocket. "I have to take a look at this. See what you have."

"Just pictures of day-to-day stuff at camp. A few grisly shots yesterday. Nothing to warrant two doctors being kidnapped for it."

"Obviously you captured something someone didn't want you to see."

"I don't know what it would be. Before we do anything else, we need to find a doctor for that shoulder."

He was more concerned about finding a safe place to stash her. "I've had worse injuries."

"*I* need you well," she told him firmly. "We'll find a doctor. *Then* look at my pict—"

"Pssst! *Inkosazana?*" A small boy, about nine or ten, darted into the alley from the other end, bare feet scattering rodents as he ran. "You come." He tried to grab Kess's wrist, but Simon held him off, a hand on his shoulder. Since that hand held a loaded weapon the kid dropped his hand and stayed where he was. The boy shot Simon an innocent glance from beneath long, curly eyelashes before he looked up beseechingly at Kess.

"Lutao take you Doctor Straus. *Inkosazana* come quick-quick."

"Where? Where are Doctor Straus and *inkosazana* Viljoen?"

"I take. We hurry. Bad man come."

Kess met Simon's gaze. "What do you think?"

"I think he's part of the plan, but we'll go with him and see what they want. Here." He handed her the Taurus, grip first. "Keep alert, and shoot before you ask questions, got it? That goes for man, woman, or child."

Kess took the gun from him. It fit quite well in her palm and was warm from his hand. "I'd rather you had this."

Beside her, the little boy danced from foot to foot with impatience. "*Inkosazana*. Quick-quick. You come?"

"I have another gun," Simon told her, his gaze lowering to the gun in her hand and back up to meet her eyes. "Let's see what these people want."

"I don't care what they want," she said as she hurried after the boy. "Whatever is on that SIM card isn't important enough for me not to just hand it over. They can gladly have it if they release Konrad and Judy."

"Look, I don't want to burst your bubble," Simon said, hustling her across the street. "But in situations like this it's rare for the victims to still be alive. Especially here, where death is practically a way of life."

"I know. But we have to be sure."

A dusty, dark blue, antique of a car was parked across the street. "You take." The boy handed the car key to Simon. "Lutao show where you go. Yes?"

"No." Simon handed the key to Kess. "You drive. I want to sit in back."

"Don't shoot him, for God's sake!" Kess whispered, concerned because he looked so grim.

Simon's lips quirked. "I don't make a habit of shooting kids, relax."

He didn't look in the least bit relaxed, Kess noticed as she climbed into the musty-smelling old car and coaxed the tired engine to life. Simon's attention was everywhere. He was looking for the rest of the bad guys, she knew. Despite the wet heat, Kess felt something walk over her grave, and shivered.

"Okay, pal," she said to the little boy as he climbed in and scooted his shorts-clad butt back on the rotted leather of the wide bench seat. His bare feet didn't reach the floor. "Where to?"

He pointed straight ahead, and Kess aimed the enormous car the way he indicated. She could barely see over the gigantic hood, and the car felt as though it almost brushed the buildings as she drove slowly down the alley to avoid people and livestock. "How far?" The car smelled like stinky feet, only worse. She cranked open her window a bit to get some rainy air blowing through it.

"Kwame village." Swinging his feet, the little guy looked at her with big, innocent brown eyes. "You know?"

"I think so. But will you warn me before I make a wrong turn?"

He grinned, showing three gaps in his front teeth. Two missing on top, one on the bottom. He was adorable. "I think so," he mimicked like a little parrot. Kess shot him a grin.

The rain was coming down in buckets, and she fiddled with several knobs and levers. The lights cut through the wall of rain. Then her seat shifted. Finally the wipers slipped across the windshield, barely moving the sheets of water flooding the windows. At least they worked.

Thump-screech. Thump-screech. Thump-screech.

"God, this car brings back memories," Simon said quietly from the backseat. "I haven't thought about my grandfather in years. He had a 1960 Studebaker just like this. Same color. Used to drive me and my sister around on a Sunday afternoon. God—I'd forgotten how great he was."

Kess had adored her maternal grandfather. Poppy had smelled of butterscotch candy, and done incredibly bad sleight-of-hand magic tricks to the great delight of her and her sister. "Is he still alive?"

"Doubt it," Simon said shortly. "He'd be in his late nineties now."

"He might still be," Kess insisted, wanting him to have someone in his life who loved him unconditionally. Very Pollyanna of her, but damn it, everyone needed *someone*. "My Poppy died at the ripe old age of ninety-two." He'd had a good life, but she missed him still.

"It's not something I give much thought."

Conversation closed. Kess glanced at him under her lashes. There'd been no masking the nostalgia in his voice when he'd mentioned his grandfather. Simon thought about him, she suspected, a lot.

Lutao touched her arm, and when he had her attention, pointed left. Kess slowed down to allow two women in bright soaked-through cotton dresses hauling filled produce baskets on their heads to cross before she turned. The car handled like a tank. Not that she'd ever driven a tank. "Did you lose touch?"

"My parents and twin sister were killed in a gas explosion at the house. I'd just started second grade. Theresa and my father both had the flu, and stayed home that day. Never went back to the house. Never saw Pops again."

Kess's heart squeezed empathetically. How terrifying and traumatic it must've been for a little boy to have his entire family taken away from him in one accident. "God, that's terrible. Where did you go? Did you have family?"

"Foster care."

"Was it awful? Sorry. That's a stupid thing to say. Of course it was awful. You'd lost everyone you loved." *Where was Grandpa? Too old to take in a nine-year-old? My God.* Simon hadn't been much older than Lutao. A baby.

"Some of the families were pretty bad, some of them were okay."

Okay was pretty bad to Kess. No child should ever have to tolerate an okay life. "I can't imagine what I'd do if something happened to my parents or my sister." She felt an overwhelming ache of love that squeezed her chest. "Elizabeth is a doctor, did I mention that? I'm very proud of her. She's an amazing woman."

"Are you alike?"

Kess laughed. The heavy car bounced and shimmied over the potholes and debris in the road she couldn't avoid. "Not at all. Elizabeth is very serious, quiet, and introspective. And smart and gentle." Kess felt a sharp pang of homesickness. She'd see Elizabeth and her mom and dad when she went back for her court date in six weeks. At least seeing them, having their support, would make the trip back to Atlanta worthwhile.

"Pretty much opposites then," Simon said, sounding amused. "Does she have the red hair as well?"

"Lighter, more restrained. My father swears he had a full head of black hair before Elizabeth and I were born, but he's pretty much bald now. Mom's more blond than red, but we all have the redhead temperament. Me more than the other two, I'm afraid," Kess said wryly. It took awhile for her to lose it, but when she did, watch out. She blew. Hence her day in court.

They were now on the potholed main drag leading out of town. Kwame was about thirty miles northeast. She glanced at her small copilot and he nodded to let her know she was on the right road.

"We had some pretty lively arguments growing up, especially since my mother's a defense attorney." Which of course made Kess's assault charge embarrassing for her. Kess understood. She just wished her mother understood why she'd done what she'd done. Needless to say Carole Goodall would not be defending her daughter when she went to court "How's your shoulder?"

"Fine."

"Liar," she said, catching his eyes in the cracked rearview mirror. He didn't look as though he were about to pass out, but it must hurt like crazy. If Konrad and Judy *were* in the village, one of them could look at Simon's shoulder. *If* they really were there. Kess was too scared to hope.

"Remember the guy you met the other night? The one you thought was my brother?" Simon said quietly from behind her.

"Ah . . . Sure."

"He's back."

Kess's gaze shot to the rearview mirror. Simon's green eyes looked back at her. Simon, but not. Simon in reverse. Holy shit! Kess almost drove off the soupy dirt road. She wondered briefly, very briefly, if she had somehow ingested some sort of hallucinogenic—only she hadn't touched anything.

"How—" She gave a fleeting look at the little boy sitting next to her. A little boy somehow involved in a kidnapping. A little boy with intelligent eyes, and big ears.

She dragged in a deep breath. Presumably there was a logical explanation for whatever Simon was doing. Curiosity ate at her. "You *will* explain—the *similarity* as soon as possible, ri—?"

His image in the mirror flickered for a second, then disappeared. He was gone.

Well, shit.

"Lutao," Kess said a little desperately, hoping the child didn't look in the backseat. She pointed to the left, his side of the car. "Look at the lions over there."

The distraction worked. He kneeled up on the seat to look through the window at the pride—a male and three females taking shelter under an acacia at the side of the road. "Simba no happy big wet."

Kess wasn't thrilled with the big wet either. The road was a morass of red mud as it continued to pour, and the heavy car was having a hard time not bogging down. "Almost there, right?" A look in the mirror showed that Simon2 wasn't back. Back from *where*, for God's sake, Kess thought a little hysterically.

"You go—" Lutao's grubby little finger indicated the gently rolling grassland unbroken by civilization to the right of the slowly moving vehicle.

"There's no road," Kess pointed out mildly, battling the steering wheel as the tires spun in the mud before finding traction again. Driving on what felt like oatmeal wasn't going to improve when she left the road.

"Okay," he said cheerfully. "You go." And when she didn't respond as quickly as he apparently wanted her to, the boy grabbed the big steering wheel with both hands, put his weight into it, and turned the wheel for her.

The car bounced and rocked as the wheels went from mud to wet grass and slewed sideways. "Whoa! I've got it!" Kess tightened her grip on the wheel and steered into the spin to straighten out the car. This was insane. There wasn't a sign of anyone as far as the eye could see. "Let's just stay on the road, okay? It'll take a bit longer, but this shortcut isn't a good idea." It was, in fact, a bad, bad idea.

If she got stuck on the road there was a chance—okay, a very, very *small* chance—that someone would drive by and be able to help her. If she drove over hill and dale and something happened, there wasn't a hope in hell of *anyone* finding them. Maybe forever.

When Simon got back she was going to kill him for leaving her alone with an ancient car and a small child in the middle of nowhere. She couldn't begin to think where he'd gone, because nothing she could imagine made any damned sense at all.

"Take the shortcut?" Simon's voice seemed to echo inside the rain-pounded car.

Kess met his eyes in the rearview mirror, tightening her grip on the wheel. "You are a dead man, Simon Blackthorne with an e." It *was* Simon. The original Simon. Back as if he'd never left. "You've got some 'splaining to do."

Yeah, he did have some explaining to do. But Kess seemed to be taking his powers in her stride. He hadn't planned on leaving at all. All he'd wanted to do was teleport Kess's SIM card to HQ in Montana. Simple enough. But the damn thing, as small as it was, wouldn't teleport. He'd discovered a new damned wrinkle in his outages. If he wanted to teleport something, not only didn't he have enough juice to leave Nomis in his place, he had to go with it.

No harm, no foul. The SIM card was in the hands of T-FLAC's tech department, and he was back. In the meantime, Kess was struggling to keep the heavy vehicle from sliding backward down a fairly steep hill. "Want me to drive?"

"I'm handling things just fine, thank you," she said through gritted teeth.

"I see that." He put his legs up on the bench seat and leaned back, arms under his head and propped against the window. "Wake me when we get there." He closed his eyes.

The car jounced over the lumpy ground, causing all three of them to become airborne.

"Bastard," Kess muttered without heat as she dropped back into her seat.

Simon grinned.

Lutao giggled.

Minutes later, Kess said, "I think we're here."

The small group of shanties looked like any other Third World village Simon had visited in his travels. The people were dirt-poor, eking out a hand-to-mouth existence. Mostly women and children of course, since the men who weren't either too old or too young were off fighting the Hureni, and/or part of Mallaruza's militia.

Off to the right a large military tent housed what looked like a temporary hospital. A line of about thirty women, some clutching babies and small children in their arms, huddled against the side of the wind-billowing tent. Seeking whatever shelter they could find as they waited to see a doctor.

Simon knew that many of these people would walk a hundred miles to seek medical help, especially if it was their child who was sick. This small village, no more than thirty ramshackle houses, was forty miles closer to help than the big city of Quinisela.

"Where are they holding Dr. Straus?" Kess slowed the car to a crawl, and turned to the kid. "Damn it to hell!" The car jerked as she slammed her foot on the break. "He can do it, too?"

"Shit." Simon stared incredulously at the front seat where seconds before a small boy had sat kicking his feet. Lutao was gone. A wizard had lured them here. A wizard that Simon should have been able to sense. And hadn't. A small, engaging child, and a replica of his grandfather's old Studebaker, coupled with his malfunctioning powers.

"Simon? What the hell is going on? You are totally freaking me out with all this disappearing crap."

"Your friends aren't here, Kess," he said grimly. "Move over. I'll drive."

Oh, how she wanted to say no, he could see it in her set jaw, but she scooted over to the passenger seat as Simon shimmered behind the wheel. "Brace yourself," he warned, then changed the antiquated car into a military ATV Phoenix Prowler.

Kess stared at him, sodden strands of hair stuck to her skin. "Hell, if you can do this, why don't you just conjure up a damn helicopter? Or at least get us a getaway car with a roof?"

"I tried for the chopper. No go. I seem to be experiencing technical difficulties at the moment. That's a machine gun up there. If I walk you through the firing of it, think you can cover our flank?"

"Cover our flank? Which way is our flank?"

"God help us."

"You don't need the Almighty, you've got me— and I get to fire a machine gun? Hot damn." Kess laughed. "Talk me through it. I've never fired a machine gun before."

"I hope you won't have to fire one now." Ubiquitous vision showed no one following them. Yet.

"Oh, boy. I hope I *do*. This is amazingly cool. Whatever *it* is."

The light tactical mobility platform of the Prowler was perfect for this uneven terrain. At the touch of his foot on the accelerator the powerful four-stroke liquid-cooled engine took off like a rocket, spewing clods of mud and vegetation at a ground-eating speed as Simon headed away from the rain-drenched village.

This wasn't Pops's car. Not by a long shot. This baby was stripped down to its sealed steel-frame, chrome-alloy ROPS, with a machine gun attached to the cargo rack. It wasn't pretty, but it performed like a champ. The low center of gravity, tight turning radius, and high ground clearance made it seem as if they were flying. "I'm going to slow down over the next hill, then I want you to stand and strap yourself in."

"Cool."

What an incredible woman, Simon thought as Kess tilted her face up to the rain. Not only was she drenched to the skin and not complaining, she wasn't asking a million questions. She would, of course. But for now she was in this—whatever *this* was—with him. One hundred percent present.

The concept staggered him.

"Where are we going?" she shouted over the

wind and pounding rain as she held on to the dash with both hands.

The cave was too far, they'd be boxed in there. Her hotel, his hotel, and Abi's place were all out of the question. And T-FLAC didn't have a safe house in Mallaruza. "Cape Town."

She grinned at him, her beautiful gray eyes filled with excitement, her cheeks flushed peach and dewy with moisture. "Beautiful place."

"You're nuts, know that?" Simon shouted into the wind. He thought she was the bravest, most exciting woman he'd ever met. And just looking at her, hair wet and wild, T-shirt transparent and sticking to her skin, heavy orange boots braced against the floor, and grinning at him like a fool, he felt a strange double clutch in his chest.

Kess Goodall was all kinds of trouble.

Nine

They didn't make it to Cape Town. Instead Simon found a room in a motel on the edge of town. To say it was a dump was giving the motel an enormous compliment. A row of nine rooms faced a deep valley, currently the local landfill, surrounded by chain-link fencing, scraggly trees, and a swarm of birds eager to scavenge a free meal. While the place didn't stink, it looked as though it should. It was still pouring buckets and she and Simon weren't just a little wet—they were drenched from top to toe. Other than being uncomfortable, being wet didn't bother Kess much. Cold and wet would have made it worse, but it was warm and wet, so she was mildly out of joint instead of freaking miserable.

She pulled a face as Simon unlocked the door to room five. "The last time a guy took me to a hotel this bad I made him sorry." Standing in front of her, Simon chuckled as he reached in a hand and turned on the light, blocking her view. "Hell—close your eyes a minute, don't open until I tell you to. How old were you?"

"Seventeen." Kess closed her eyes—almost.

Peering through her lashes, she peeked around Simon's arm. Ew! Unlike the outside rain-washed air, the room smelled of stale cigarette smoke, pot, and filth. It looked worse. The single bed had a crater-sized dip in the middle and gray-tinged sheets that hadn't seen a washing machine since they were combed in wherever cotton was combed. She almost preferred the rat-infested alley. She swallowed back a complaint.

It *would* be nice to get out of the rain. Perhaps have a hot shower. She closed her eyes as instructed. She felt Simon's heat all the way down her front, although they weren't touching. Little tingles of electrical current arched between their bodies. Pheromones. Animal attraction. Whatever it was sparking between them made Kess want to melt against his body and nuzzle her face into his neck.

"Did the guy get lucky?" There was a smell about him. Not soapy or shampoo-ish. She couldn't even describe it, and she could usually describe *anything*. It was her job. "Are you kidding me?" Fresh. Clean. Male. If she could bottle this scent, she'd make a fortune and wouldn't have to worry about her reputation.

Thinking back, she remembered the Central Motel and Peter Silverman's bike. She'd really been that innocent. "No. I just wanted to ride his Harley. He thought a quickie at his uncle's motel out in College Park would be an equitable payment." Even at seventeen she'd understood the ex-

NIGHT FALL   161

change rate the moment Peter had presented it. If it had just been an expectation, she'd have walked off in a huff, not broken the guy's jaw. But he hadn't asked, or hinted. He'd tried to rape her.

She'd walked all the way to Hartsfield International before finding a cab to get her back home. Then filed charges when her temper had cooled enough to call the police. It was a lesson well learned.

The air suddenly smelled like . . . the ocean? Kess blinked open her eyes.

Gone was the cramped two-bit motel; in its place was a spacious cabana on a beach. Sheer drapes billowed gently in the balmy breeze wafting through the large open windows that overlooked a turquoise sea and a long expanse of sugary sand. Palm trees added their subtle music of rustling fronds to the sound of the gently lapping surf. Gulls swooped and cried as they wheeled in a cloudless robin's egg blue sky. Enchanted, Kess turned in a circle.

Simon was magic.

The room was all white, no color other than the sea and sky viewed through the window and a colorful mound of fruit in a clear glass bowl on a whitewashed table. The center of the room was dominated by the biggest bed she'd ever seen. Her heart skipped.

"Did you kill him?" Simon asked behind her. He didn't sound as though he cared if she had.

Kess trailed her fingers over the round table holding the fruit bowl. "What?" she asked absently. The painted wood felt cool and smooth under her fingertips. It was real. Solid. She turned to face him. Who was this man? *What* was this man? A frisson of excitement made her blood race effervescently through her body as her eyes locked with the deep green of his. Magician or hypnotist. Whatever, whoever he was, he made her skin tingle and her blood pound through her veins. She stepped into the square of buttery sunlight separating them on the bleached wood floor.

"No," she said, her voice thick and husky as she took another step. Her entire body was aware that he was watching her mouth as she spoke. "Of course not. But I did hit him hard enough with his own motorcycle helmet to knock him out *and* break his jaw."

They met in the middle of sunlight. Simon cupped her cheek with a cool, strong hand. A hand with calluses and small white scars across his fingers. "What put you off?" His breath fanned her face. "The crappy motel, or the guy?" His fingers slid over her skin to comb through her hair, making goose bumps of desire roughen her skin.

Kess lifted her face, sliding her arms around his waist. She held onto his shirt at the small of his back as their wet clothing caused a delicious friction on her nipples. "The crappy *guy*."

Simon brushed his mouth over hers. "I have a Harley."

"A real one?" Kess's lips wanted to cling, and she fisted the back of his shirt to bring him closer. His erection brushed the juncture of her thighs.

He brought his other hand up and brushed the corner of her mouth with a gentle thumb. "Yeah. I'll let you ride it anytime."

She opened her mouth slightly, licking the edge of his thumb. Simon's pupils dilated, dragging in the light until they were the color of a black forest. Could he hear how fast her heart was beating? It sounded deafening to her own ears.

"What color is it?"

A muscle jerked in his cheek. "Any damn color you want."

Kess's laugh sounded breathless. She *felt* breathless, and giddy, and spellbound. "Why did I know you'd say that?"

His fingers curled in her hair as if he had to hold on to her to remain in control of his own strong urges. "Even if you say no." Simon trailed his lips across her cheek, then brushed them across each eye. "The sheets—" he kissed her lid, "are clean—" he brushed her other lid, "and the room stays."

Kess spread her hand up his back. His skin beneath the wet shirt was on fire, hot and smooth under her palms. "I'm not saying no." She reached up and nipped him on the hard edge of his jaw with her teeth and he gave a muffled groan as he pulled her hard against him.

Kess felt as though she were melting inside. Fast-moving lava flowed through her veins, her entire body one giant pulse, throbbing and beating like a tribal drum. "Do I have time for a quick shower first?"

He lifted her in his arms. "You have time for a quick shower *in between.*"

Simon carried her easily, placing her in the center of the big bed as if she were made of spun glass. "I'm not going to break, you know." She grabbed the front of his shirt and pulled him down next to her, and he laughed, a full-out roar of laughter that made her laugh with him.

He rolled over, then braced a hand on either side of her head. "No slow seduction?" he asked, amusement and something else in those deep fathomless green eyes.

Kess's smile faded because her heart ached in a good way when she looked at him. Her blood sang through her veins at the heated, feral gleam in his eyes as he looked at *her.* "Yes," she murmured, touching her fingertips to the lingering smile on his mouth. "How about fifty-fifty?"

He pushed strands of hair off her face, his touch light, but weighted with intention. "Is there any other way?"

"Probably." She threaded her fingers through his

hair, pulling his face down. His response—hungry and greedy—mirrored her own desire. Kess slid her tongue along his, tasting his urgency. She kissed him with everything in her, wanting to know this man as she had no other.

She had a million questions. Wasn't sure she'd like any of the answers. But right now, here in his magical white room on the beach, the only answers she needed were in the brush of his hands and the curve of his smile. She didn't think he smiled that much, and knowing that he did so for her tangled her up with the dozen other emotions tripping over her heart.

"I love the taste of you," he whispered thickly against her mouth just before he kissed her again with a fierceness that made her fingers tighten in his hair. The very rawness of his kiss brought out something wildly female in her. Kess rolled on top of him as they kissed. He was warm and solid beneath her, his erection blatantly obvious in the prison of his jeans, but she felt no urgency to take him inside her body. Not yet.

She wanted to taste him all over, she wanted him to taste her. "How long do we have?"

There were flickering lights in the room, she noticed vaguely. Tiny pinpoints of clear white illuminated dust dancing in the air around them. How odd.

She closed her eyes and trailed her lips along the

hard bone of his jaw. His skin felt hot and bristly under her mouth. The smell of him, male, musk, magic, made her body burn.

He stroked his hand around the back of her neck, his touch electric. As she kissed a trail up his throat to his ear his fingers tightened in response. "As long as we need."

She couldn't even dredge up a smile because her entire body was ratcheting up just in anticipation. "This could take a while." She pressed her thigh gently against the bulge between his legs, and his body jerked in response.

The skin tightened over his cheekbones and his eyes absorbed the light as he looked up at her. "Oh, yeah." He fisted his hand in her hair and brought her mouth back down to his. Then kissed her again until every pore in her body wanted him. *Mine. Mine. Mine,* this man belonged to *her,* not some imaginary Stepford wife. She was real, as was her passion. Surely Simon would feel and sense the difference between his ideal woman and the reality of the primal need they shared for each other.

She flattened her body on top of his, stretching out over him like a blanket. With a low murmur against her cheek he wrapped his arm around her, letting her direct the kiss. One large masculine hand cupped the back of her head, the other slid down to caress her bottom.

God, she loved kissing him. Hot and slow. Just the way she liked it. Kissing Simon was a full-body contact sport. Kess felt insanely euphoric as they made love with their mouths. Her breasts pressed against the hard plane of his chest, her nipples, hard and sensitive, ached for his touch. She needed his hands on her.

Both his hands moved to meet on the hem of her T-shirt. The air felt cool on her overheated skin as he drew the fabric up her body. Kess reluctantly dragged her mouth away from his as he tugged the shirt up and over her head. Simon closed his eyes as if in pain, then Kess felt his fingers unerringly on the clasp of her bra.

"I've never seen anything this beautiful in my life," Simon said, filling his hands with her breasts as she arched her back to give him full access. Of course in doing so she ground her pelvis against the hard ridge under her, making them both suck in a sharp breath.

Her nipples, grateful for his touch, were so hard that contact with his slightly callused fingers made Kess moan low in her throat. She skimmed her hand between their bodies, trying to touch him, but they might as well have been glued at the groin because a bit of paper wouldn't have fit between their bodies. She desperately needed to feel his skin against hers. "Could we pause half a second to get nake—"

Simon slid her body up his in one smooth move that placed her breasts directly over his avid mouth. Kess bracketed his hips with her knees as his lips closed around one nipple, hot and wet. He sucked until her body arched. "Oh, God—*yes*. Just like—ah . . . that." When her brain could function well enough to let her move, she slid her hands under his T-shirt. His stomach was rock-hard and ridged with muscle. His skin felt like hot satin under her hands. She trailed her fingers lightly up the line of crisp dark hair bisecting his abs, following it as it widened to cover his chest.

Her hands shook as she dragged his T-shirt over his head. Kess hated breaking the contact his mouth had on her breast, but the urgency driving her needed them both naked. *Now.*

His chest was broad and tanned, his nipples small dark buds amid the dark hair. She groaned his name, bending her head to taste him. Salty male. His taste and the smell of his skin were an aphrodisiac that easily fogged her brain. "Clothes. *Off,*" she begged, tearing at the button front of his jeans with fingers made clumsy by lust. The tiny lights spun and glittered around them like fireflies on speed.

"Off. Off. Off," Kess chanted, as Simon pushed her useless fingers aside and did the job himself. His penis sprang free, long and hard, and her body literally contracted at the sight of him. "Oh, God—hurry, please, Simon—"

For a dizzying moment she thought she was hallucinating as all of a sudden they were skin to skin. Their clothes nowhere in sight.

She laughed, half relief, half disbelief. "Explain . . . that . . ." Throwing a leg over his hip, Kess impaled herself. "Later," the last word came out as a sigh as she slid down on him, her palms braced on his shoulders.

His hands settled on her hips as she started to move. "Have your wicked way with me. I'm putty in your hands."

"There's—not—a—damn—thing—soft about you, Blackthorne with an . . ."

The climax came at her so fast she barely had time to suck in a shuddering breath.

Dazed, her breath sawing in and out as if she'd just climbed Everest, Kess collapsed on Simon's chest. Still joined, their damp skin stuck together as they gasped for air.

She suddenly noticed that it had gone from day to night without warning. Soft moonlight made a coverlet over their naked bodies as they lay facing each other, arms and legs entwined. Simon brushed Kess's fiery hair over her shoulder, then stroked a lazy hand down her arm. Her skin felt warm and silky smooth, and although they'd made love, and he'd touched her all over, he couldn't prevent himself from caressing her now.

He had the weirdest sensation in his chest. A feeling of fullness. Of—God. He couldn't begin to describe it. He gave up and stopped trying. Kess rested her hand over his heart, lazily playing with the hair on his chest. "This might be a good time to explain how you do what you do."

He loved the way her eyes lost focus when she looked at him. Loved the way the soft gray darkened to charcoal as if she could read what he was thinking. Not hard to do since he'd had the quickest sexual recovery he could remember since he was a fifteen-year-old with an unquenchable libido. Ten minutes after a mind-blowing climax, and he was hard again.

"Why don't I show you?" he murmured, cupping the satiny weight of her breast, before trailing his fingers over her hip. Stroking his hand down her thigh, he repositioned her leg over his hip to gain access to her damp heat.

"This wasn't exactly what I meant by tell me," she muttered with a small unconvincing frown.

"Complaining?" He slipped inside her.

"Not at all—Could you—Yes."

He brought his fingers between their bodies. "Here?"

"Hmm."

"How about here—Jesus, sweetheart. I'll go off like a rocket if you t—" She moved against him with purpose, her expression adorably intent. "You like to live dangerously, don't you?"

Her lashes flickered up when she looked at him. "Living dangerously is my middle name."

"I thought it was Scarlett," he said through gritted teeth as the orgasm raced from his toes to the base of his brain like a comet.

"You have a good memory."

His brain went blank as they climaxed together with muscle-clenching intensity.

Maybe they slept. Maybe they were unconscious. God only knew. Simon felt as though every bone in his body had been somehow transformed into overcooked pasta. Pasta had never felt so good. Jesus. Any more of this and they'd kill each other.

"How're you doing?" he asked, shifting her limp body over his so he could touch her all over without moving. Even his lips were relaxed.

"Fantastic," she said cheerfully, sounding wide-awake and ready to talk.

He almost groaned. A couple of hours' sleep right now sounded like sheer, fucking heaven. She had ridden him hard and put him away wet. Making love with Kess was a combination of teeth-gritting pleasure and acrobatics. His lips twitched. If she was interested, and she most assuredly was, Kess touched, tasted, bit, or licked. Clearly she enjoyed sex, and nothing was out of bounds.

She waved a languid hand in the general direction of the room. Since her face was buried in his neck at the time, he figured she was multitasking. He felt the light flutter of her eyelashes against his jaw. "Is this real or an illusion?"

He knew she wasn't talking about the phenomenal sex. "It's real."

"Where are we?" she asked, shifting to lean on her elbow. Seeing her plump breasts swinging free, nipples tight peaks just waiting for his touch, he stroked a finger down the gentle slope and touched the nipple with the edge of his nail. She sucked in a sharp breath and batted his hand away.

"Still at the crappy motel." He brought his hand back to her breast, trailing his fingers along her soft skin. "I just brought paradise to us." She was as close to paradise as Simon would ever get. God, she was responsive.

She walked two fingers down his chest. "Could someone else see it if they walked in?"

"I have a protection shield around the place, so no," he said, disappointed when she didn't continue heading south. He didn't think he had another erection in him, but a few more minutes of her touching him, and he thought he might very well surprise himself. What the hell had she just asked—Oh, yeah. "But if that shield collapsed, then yeah."

Kess sat up cross-legged on the bed, pulling a pillow onto her lap, resting her elbows on it and covering his favorite bits. "Tell me how you do it," she demanded. "Is it some clever spy stuff connected with the work you do for T-FLAC?"

"The organization has a paranormal division,"

he said carefully, watching her face for any sign of horror, or worse, fear. There was neither. She was intrigued and totally engrossed in what he was saying.

"Paranormal? Like ghosts." She touched his forearm. "You're pretty solid for a ghost. Are you an alien?" Even the idea that he might be an extraterrestrial, which amused the hell out of him, didn't faze her.

Simon smiled. "No. I'm a wizard."

"Really?" Her eyebrows went up. "Like Merlin? Were you born that way or did someone cast a spell on you?"

He should've known nothing like a little magic would derail her interest. He reached out to brush her knee, unable to keep his hands off her. "As a matter of fact, yes. I was born this way."

"That is amazingly cool. Are there other wizards about?"

"Millions of us."

Her eyes, one of her best features, after her hair, her breasts, her—lit up. How could ordinary gray be so warm? So filled with light and energy and a sheer love of life? Kess's entire attention was focused on him. Interest in what he was telling her made her face glow. "Really? Do they all work for T-FLAC?"

"Want something to drink?"

She shook her head, then changed her mind.

"Sure. Fresh squeezed lemona—" A glass filled with crushed ice and citrus-scented liquid materialized in her hand. "Okay. That was show-offy, but *damn* cool." She brought the glass to her lips. "A bit more sugar?" she requested with a smile that showcased her crooked eyetooth and made her eyes sparkle. She tried the drink again. "Perfect. So *do* they all work for T-FLAC?"

"No. Just a few hundred of us." He took the glass and sipped. Not bad. He handed it back to her. "And not all of us are good guys. Make no mistake, there are evil wizards out there by the thousands. Good, bad, and everything in between. Just like any other group of people." *Noek Joubert for one.*

"It would seem to me that being a wizard and being evil would lend itself to a lot of bad wizards being really bad people. Robbers, murderers, terrorists."

"Absolutely. They use their magical powers to gain wealth, or fame, or political power. It's a hell of a problem worldwide."

She frowned. "And your powers aren't working right?"

Yeah. *That* inconvenient little glitch. "It's like having power surges. One minute something works, the next it doesn't."

"Are *you* sick—Physically? Maybe it's something you need to check out with a—a wizard doctor? Like immediately?"

"I had a complete physical two months ago. So no. I don't believe it's physical."

"So it's your *powers* that are sick?"

He smiled. "You think it might be contagious? A virus of some sort? I've never heard of such a thing, but it's not out of the realm of possibility. I'll have to ask."

"Are any of your wizard buddies at T-FLAC having these power outages?"

"Not that I know of. I haven't asked. It's not like we sit around a campfire at night eating those marshmallow chocolate things, baring our souls."

"S'mores," she said absently, still frowning. He didn't like seeing her frown and placed a finger between her brows to smooth the little line there. She batted his hand away, scowling even harder. "Is that what happened to the Rover you were driving? You had a short circuit in your power while you were teleporting?"

"I was trying to get ahead of you. The car dropped out of the air unexpectedly."

"God, Simon. You could've been killed."

"I wasn't. Probably because the vehicle was armored. But yeah, it was close."

"How long have you been having these problems?"

"Couple of weeks."

"Is there someone you trust? Someone you can confide in that knows about your wizardness and can fix whatever's wrong?"

"I don't know if he can fix whatever this is, but there *is* a man I trust implicitly. Mason Knight has been an incredible influence on my life, and a mentor when I badly needed one. He's a wizard, and a powerful one, and a good friend. I've already left a message for him to contact me when he has time."

"When he has time?" Her voice rose a little. "He better find time *now*. This is urgen— This doesn't seem to worry you, does it? Or, you're making light of it because you don't *want* to know?"

"I'm not sure if it's fixable, or if for some reason I'm actually losing my powers."

"Would you hate not having them?"

"I wouldn't be a wizard."

"And? You wouldn't be less than who you are now. You wouldn't lose your job, would you? You wouldn't lose your friends, or your T-FLACy skills, or your good looks."

"Being a wizard is who I am. And yes, I believe that not having my powers would intrinsically change that."

"I don't agree with you, but I absolutely understand what you're saying. Are all your powers on the blink like this? Or are some of them still operational? And while we're on this incredibly fascinating subject: What else can you do?"

"My powers?"

She nodded. "Let's start with the guy who looks like you and isn't your brother."

"Nomis. He's a duplicate. He has—usually—all my powers. Basically I can be in two places at once."

"Handy. But might I suggest that in the future you have him comb his hair the same way you do, and switch wrists for his watch? He's exactly like you—as a mirror image. Someone else might notice the difference just as I did. Keep going. What else can you do when you can do it?"

"I have ubiquitous vision." At her frown he said, "I can see three hundred and sixty degrees."

"Do you have eyes in the back of your head? I didn't feel them."

He smiled. "No eyes in the back of my head. Just another power." He wondered if she might be onto something important, and decided to ask, discreetly, if anybody else was having problems. "I use teleportation more than all of my other powers combined. I become invisible and can move between point A and point B almost instantaneously, all without being seen."

"That is really cool . . ."

"When it's fully operational, yeah. When it's not, I could appear midair without warning. Usually I can teleport an object wherever I need it to go. You, for instance, up to that cave. Earlier today I tried teleporting your camera's SIM card to our lab in Montana. Couldn't do it without me going with it. And by doing that I didn't have enough juice to leave Nomis with you."

"No teleporting until we figure out what's wrong with you."

Apparently, Simon thought with a combination of amusement and alarm, Kess had just made *his* problem *her* problem.

Ten

Simon had brought Kess back to the city a couple of hours before. He'd taken her to pick up a
few basics at a local mall because he didn't want
her returning to her room at her hotel. They'd been
led away from the city. To what purpose Simon had
no idea. But he wasn't letting Kess out of his sight
until he knew.

Now they were in the president's office as Abi
got ready for a press conference.

Hair gleaming like a new penny, and skin glowing from their manic bout of lovemaking earlier,
Kess stood beside the president searching through
a flat box of neatly laid out silk ties on his desk.
Simon sat in the chair opposite, admiring her focus
despite the turmoil around them.

"I don't *need* you here, Kess. I want both of you
to go with the supplies," Abi told them. "I'm sending fifty of my militia with you—just as a precau-
tionary measure, of course. I don't expect any
trouble."

Fifty militia didn't sound like not expecting trouble. Fifty militia sounded like Abi expected some

action. That single sentence told Simon just how much his friend had changed in the time since their college days. As he absently rubbed the pad of his finger along his chin, Simon read Abi's body language and facial expressions as well as listened to the subtext of his conversation.

Maybe it was the evolution from carefree collegian to political power broker. Whatever the reason, *this* Abi was drastically different from the man he'd known. Simon felt a warning tickle at the back of his neck. Normally, he would have acted on his intuition but this was an old friend, so he tamped down the disquiet and turned his attention to Kess. Not exactly a difficult task since she was one hell of a distraction. Pleasantly so.

There was to be a press conference in fifteen minutes, and Abi had sent the camera crew to wait outside his office until he was ready. They'd set up the lights, leaving them directed at the president, so that he and Kess were spotlit while Simon, sitting farther back, was in shadow.

For a moment Simon simply watched Kess talking to Abi. He knew he had to get a grip on how often he looked at her. But that was easier said than done. He constantly found his gaze lingering on the sweet curve of her smiling mouth, or the way her gray eyes lit up with amusement. Maybe it was her lightness to his darkness that he found so damned fascinating. Perhaps it was because he found her unbearably sexy in a non-overt way. Her animation and zest for life, her interest, and her passion for her job, intrigued him.

Everything about this woman captivated him. It shouldn't have. She was about as far from his ideal woman as possible. He'd always envisioned sharing his life with someone who'd be content to live in an isolated house in Montana. Not a June Cleaver, apron-wearing housewife, but definitely someone who would accept the demands of his job and be there waiting for him when he returned home.

He almost smiled. He had no doubt Kess would support her husband's job, only he was fairly sure she'd insist on standing at his side rather than staying at home.

Just looking at her fully clothed and unaware of his scrutiny filled his mind with images of the two of them, naked limbs entangled, making love in the sunlight, or candlelight, or fucking moonlight. Didn't matter. It was only a couple of hours since they'd left the motel, but he wanted her again. He'd tasted her skin and felt her come apart in his arms. Now he needed to feed the addiction again.

Her lashes and brows were much darker than her hair, but in the bright lights he noticed the tips of her long eyelashes were dipped a pale ginger. He had the insane urge to run his tongue lightly over her lashes to feel their softness.

"Hey?!" Abi said a little too loudly, drawing Simon's attention back to him. The president frowned. Simon suspected he wasn't annoyed because he wasn't paying attention. What was going on in his friend's head? Hard to tell. The lie about Joubert still had to be addressed. He suspected Abi was giving him busywork, which intrigued him even more. Why did Abi, who'd contacted him for help in the first place, suddenly want to send him out into the bush?

"You want me to go with the supplies," Simon repeated, leaning back in his chair. Whatever was going on in the other man's head, he was keeping it damn close to the chest. "A complete waste of time, but I hear and obey."

"Kess and you." Abi's lips quirked a little. "You always played by the rules, didn't you, Blackthorne? No coloring outside the lines. No shades of gray."

Simon's entire life was shades of gray. Always had been. And now that was the nature of the business he was in. His job was to seek the dark and eradicate it. Activities that went from dingy white to pitch black were all just degrees of gray as far as he was concerned. Some of those shades needed to be caged, the rest needed to be dead. Simple as that. "Rules and order are what keep us civilized, and make sense."

Abi rose and walked around his desk to clamp

him on the shoulder. "You need to live a little. Haven't I always told you that?"

"Yes, indeed." Simon smiled. Abi had been a chick magnet at college. Simon had been the quiet one. "And both times I listened to you we almost got our asses expelled. And oh yeah. There was that time your 'live on the wild side, Blackthorne,' almost landed us in jail. You go right ahead and color outside the lines, Mr. President. I'll stick to following the rules."

"Hell, Simon. You need to live a *lot*. What do you say after the election we go to Bahrain or Paris and kick up our heels for a week or two?"

"With all due respect, Mr. President. No kicking of heels, and no Bahrain," Kess told him firmly. "You're going to win this election by a landslide by being everything good your people believe you to be. And *after* the election you're going to continue doing just that. No vacations for a while."

"The woman's a slave driver. I'll be as discreet as I've always been, Kess. But I'm not a monk, and I refuse to behave like one."

She held a tie up to his shirt, then bent to select another. "It wouldn't hurt for you to have a wife." Kess winked discreetly. "Sorry to be so blunt, sir. But we all know a wife and family represent stability and commitment. Good qualities in a leader."

"I'll look for a lovely wife next year. Will that make you happy?"

Yet another tie in hand, she smiled. "Find one who makes *you* happy. Your people will be ecstatic to have a first lady."

Kess might as well give up trying to play matchmaker. Abi was a confirmed bachelor who Simon doubted would ever settle for just one woman. Hell, he only had a few years left to sow his own wild oats before he found his luscious brunette and started filling his Montana house with children.

He'd be home. Kess would be . . . Simon cut the mental musing mid-thought.

"Okay, you two," Simon interrupted them. "What's the situation at this village, and what do you want me to do when I get there, Abi?"

Abi sobered and went back to sit in his mammoth chair behind his desk. "Over seven hundred villagers are already dead," he informed Simon tightly. "More than half of the village. I want to be there myself to see what is happening to my people. It's about a three-hour trip. You two go on ahead, I'll follow directly after the press conference. We should arrive close to the same time." He met Simon's eyes. Abi wanted no magic. He needed Simon to arrive in a normal length of time.

Abi would teleport and join them there, appearing to have traveled with them. Simon nodded. "Kess can stay here and help you with the press. I'll go check it out for you, and report back."

"No. I want Kess to go with you. Everyone knows she's my publicist. They'll talk to her. Show her things they won't show you. Kess will be my eyes. You'll be my muscle."

"You're sending fifty men, plus me, as muscle," Simon said dryly. "If you don't expect trouble, Abi, why such a show of force?" Simon rubbed a hand across the back of his neck where a chill of foreboding made the short hairs stand on end. He wished to hell one of his powers was mind reading. He was damn good at reading facial expressions, and right now Abi's was closed, resisting the topic.

"There won't be trouble if you and Kess accompany the relief team to the village. I'd like your opinion on this virus. You don't need to stay long. Take a vehicle and come back in a couple of days."

Jesus. Did the man not know what was happening out there? Did he just glance at reports and dismiss the gruesome truth? The idea that Abi wanted to cavalierly send Kess into the dangerous unknown pissed Simon off royally. "You've sent Kess into God knows how many villages filled with the dead or dying already. This is bullshit, Ab, since you don't know what the fuck this is, or how to cure it. You're the president, but with all due respect your actions are irresponsible." His accusation came out more harshly than he'd intended and both Kess and Abi started at the vehemence in his tone. Fuck. He was too personally involved here, something that had never happened before. He was starting to become dangerously consumed with her. He had to stop.

Easier thought than done.

"It's not just this unknown killer." Standing, Simon was suddenly, surprisingly, *furious* that Abi, and Kess, damn it, were being so fucking careless with her health. "How about her encountering one of your other top four? Bacterial diarrhea, hepatitis A, typhoid fever, or how about fucking malaria?" He paced the room, uncomfortably aware that Kess's eyes had darkened with an unnamed emotion.

Kess, a tie clasped in each hand, stepped around the desk. "I'm not stupid, Simon. I've had every shot there is, plus I'm on every antibacterial, antimalaria, and antiviral known to mankind."

"Which is great for a run-of-the-mill ear infection, but not guaranteed against whatever is killing the villagers. It's irresponsible of Abi to think you'll be protected against *everything*. Especially now that millions of his people have dropped like fucking flies."

Kess gasped and she shot him a horrified look. "Simon!"

The five-carat diamond on Abi's pinkie shot multicolored sparks on the wall as he raised his hand to halt her protest. "It is all right, Kess. Simon is right. I should not have sent you into danger—"

"You didn't send me." She spiked a narrow-eyed glance at Simon. He gave her a noncommittal look back. "I *offered* because I needed an accurate account and photographs. And yes, I'll go to this village with the relief team to record the situation.

"The last thing we need this close to the election is a hint that you're in any way trying to sweep this epidemic under the rug. The people need to know that you're one hundred and ten percent committed to getting to the bottom of this outbreak. Simon can come or go as he likes.

"Here." She handed the president a conservative yellow tie with some small print on it. Abi took it from her, then lifted the collar of his white shirt and wrapped the thing around his neck, his dark eyes fixed on Simon's face.

"All right. We'll both go." *And I'll wrap Kess in so many layers of protection it'll take a nuclear bomb to get at her.* "I'd like a look at this firsthand." *Thank God I never have to wear a tie,* Simon thought sourly, watching Kess fuss over her boss's navy pinstriped suit with a lint brush. She started instructing Abi on the talking points she'd written and printed out for him, studiously keeping her back to Simon.

As they talked, and ignored him, Simon strolled to the window, his temper banked. Abi's city hall office overlooked the crescent-shaped bay. While the sky was once again a hard, cloudless, blue, the rain from the day before was evident in the glistening water-filled potholes in the street and the darkened stone of many of the buildings.

Simon listened to Kess's melodious voice. God, even her voice turned him on. Yeah. He *definitely* had to nip this itch in the bed. Damn it. *Bud.*

Squinting against the brightness, he stared out at the view, tuning out his ubiquitous vision as Kess leaned her bright head close to Abi's, resting her hip on his chair as she pointed to something on the papers in his hand. She could talk to her boss just as easily from across the desk, Simon thought, mildly annoyed that he'd even noticed how close they were.

The sun was out. Hot and beating down unmercifully on the people filling the streets and sidewalks below. A guy in ragged shorts, and not much else, herded seven cows and a calf down the middle of the street, the speed of the stick he wielded in no way translating to the speed of the cattle. Traffic going both ways had to wait him out.

The women's colorful cotton dressing vied for attention with the men's bright clothing. Simon raised an eyebrow and lightly shook his head as a guy in a flower-print, red-and-yellow, three-piece suit tilted his red felt hat jauntily at a woman buying fruit from the stand on the corner.

A four-lane street fronted the Government Building, on the other side a wide stretch of scraggly grass, mostly comprised of dirt patches where a young girl was allowing her sheep to graze. Where they were going, and where they had come from, here in the middle of the city, was a mystery.

Beyond that was a row of shops and beyond that the deep, dark turquoise of the south Atlantic Ocean as far as the eye could see.

The small marina curved to the left. On the right the dockyard, and in the middle the small curved beach and resort hotel. The hotel was a piece of shit. Old, run-down, badly managed. The marina had brand-new berths, but currently boasted one small yacht and several beat-up fishing boats.

Right on the beach, almost blocking the view from the hotel, was an enormous structure that looked like a German castle. Abi was proud as hell of the biggest church ever constructed on the African continent. Simon pulled up some numbers in his head from the intel dump he'd received before he came to the country. Only twenty percent or less of Mallaruzis were Catholic. Islam and indigenous animist religions made up the balance.

Where did Abi think the shitload of Catholics needed to fill that cathedral would come from when it was completed next week?

But that was Abi. Bigger, brighter, more expensive. That was just the way he liked it.

Simon did a visual scan of the docks. Two container ships rode low in the water. A third cut a frothy white line diagonally across the bay on its way out to sea. Mallaruza exported mainly crude oil, agricultural products like cassava, rice, and peanuts, and some exotic woods.

He wondered idly why the other two ships didn't

take off if they were full. He'd noticed them several days ago, before his and Kess's little adventure, and the ships hadn't moved since. If they were already loaded for export, they were wasting time sitting in dock. If they had imports, they should've been off-loaded by now.

He rubbed a hand across the back of his neck. Hell, he had bigger problems than the maritime snafus caused by the inept Mallaruzi longshoremen.

"Ready to rock?" Kess asked coming up beside him and putting her hand on his bare arm. He had an instantaneous primitive physical reaction to her touch, and this time was no different, despite their difference of opinion.

"All done?"

She shrugged, not understanding where Simon's irritation came from. This was her job. And weren't the two men longtime friends? Hard to imagine today. "The trucks are already on their way," Kess told him reasonably. Maybe he was having sexual remorse. Like buyer's remorse, only worse. Maybe in the heat of passion—literally—he'd forgotten that she wasn't his future Stepford wife, and now he felt—God. Kess had no *idea* what he felt.

Was Simon a sulker? Was he jealous of her relationship with his pal? No, nothing so emotional. The logical explanation was that he had more important concerns, something deeper and totally unrelated to her. He was a professional, and so was she.

"I'd like to stay here and make sure this interview goes as planned, but he wants us to go. Please don't make a big deal out of it, okay? He's under a tremendous amount of pressure right now. He doesn't need any more aggravation."

Simon shot a frowning glance at the president, who was now talking to his aide in quiet undertones across the room. "He's a shoo-in, where's the pressure? Fulami and Kamau don't stand a chance, you told me so yourself."

"Just because he's going to win reelection by a landslide doesn't mean he isn't under pressure. Historically there have been more coups d'état than free and fair democratic elections in Mallaruza. The country's been plagued by political instability and mutinies originating from development, security, and economic crises for years. All you have to do is look around to see the political climate is tense. The only way the current president can rule his country right now is by pursuing a military solution against the Hurenis and whoever else's political agenda is to overthrow him."

Kess searched Simon's face for hints as to what he was thinking. "Do you have issue with his policy?" Simon wasn't just a closed book; Mr. Counterterrorist operative deluxe was a closed, *locked*, book. The skin over his cheekbones was pulled taut, and his green eyes glittered like emeralds under fire. She didn't like it.

"What's *wrong* with you?" she burst out, totally bewildered that he could go from hot to frigid in one short drive across town. "Care to tell me why you're so damn touchy? You and Mr. Bongani have been friends forever, so what's got you in a snit?" *You seemed to be a happy camper two hours ago when you had your tongue in my mouth.*

"You forget that it's been more than a decade since Abi and I spent a measurable period of time together. We're friends." Simon shrugged a broad shoulder. "Or at least we were. From what I've seen, government control and services outside of the capital of Quinisela range from minimal to nonexistent." He brushed a finger up her frown line. "Don't scowl at me, sweetheart. Abi's doing his best. But this is a monumental problem added to an already monumental problem."

Sweetheart? Kess blinked at the endearment. Simon didn't seem to have noticed that he'd called her anything.

"Put it this way: Lacking the authority to govern and protect its borders, Mallaruza is an easy launching pad, training ground, or rest and relaxation spot for armed groups from *neighboring* countries. Worse, your president is inviting millions of people into a country already overflowing with refugees he's been letting in for the last couple of years."

"Which shows how compassionate he is."

"Maybe." Simon glanced across the room at the president and his aide for a moment. "The northeast province is a haven for irregular armed groups from Huren. Wasn't last year's attempted coup reportedly launched from that area? Plus foreign forces have also come into the country from its porous southern border with the Democratic Republic of Congo.

"So while I admire your dedication and loyalty to Abi, and don't get me wrong, I'm not saying it isn't warranted, there's something—Hell. Call it a gut feeling. Instinct. Something is off and I can't quite put my finger on it."

"He's scared! Wouldn't you be with that kind of responsibility?"

"Yeah. I would. But there's scared and then there's scared."

Kess decided not to pry into the psyche of a male unlike any she'd ever met before. If he wanted to tell her what had his boxers in a knot, he'd tell her. If not, then . . . then not. "You're hungry." Because she certainly was. "Come on." She tucked her hand in his arm and gave a little tug. "There's a little café down the street that serves the best BLTs, and we're early enough to miss the lunch crowd. We can go and grab a bite to eat and then catch up with the trucks."

He looked like he'd argue, but then her stomach rumbled and he gave in.

They ate lunch, Simon finding enough of an appetite to eat his sandwich and fries before finishing hers. They walked back to city hall to pick up a vehicle, not holding hands, but sharing a companionable silence. Simon was quiet and introspective the entire time. Since he wasn't normally chatty as far as she knew, this wasn't exactly a large leap from normal. But it was enough for her to notice.

"Are we going to teleport?" The idea thrilled her.

"No."

The power outages, and what they might mean, scared her. "Because of the short circuits?"

"That and the fact that Abi wants us to take our time so he can join us near the end of our trip."

"How could he possibly . . . do . . . that?" She spun around, walking backward as she realized what the subtext of Simon and the president's early conversation had been. "He's *also* a wizard?"

"You're going to trip over something walking like that."

Kess turned around, but she was looking at Simon as she walked. "Is he?" He hadn't been kidding. There were wizards all around them.

"He's a Half wizard."

"Are you half or whole? What's the difference?" Fascinated, she wanted to ask a million questions. But one glance at Simon's closed expression told her he wasn't likely to answer any of them right now. "Never mind." She tucked her hand into his elbow. "We can talk on the way."

Simon made a noncommittal sound as they headed to the car pool behind city hall.

"Are you feeling okay?" Kess finally asked as they headed north out of town in a brand-new, tricked-out, black Range Rover bearing the presidential flag on the hood.

"Yeah." Simon put on a pair of dark glasses and adjusted the visor. "I'm good."

He looked damn good. Which made her heart flutter, and instead of asking about his health, she blurted, "Do you want to tell me what's going on in your head?" *Like you're sorry as hell you had sex with a non–wife candidate? Couldn't be. Men weren't that squeamish about having sex with a willing woman.* "Does your mood have anything to do with us?" Crap. There, she'd said it. Her words hung in the air for a moment.

Simon's jaw clenched, but he was all tough silence as he pulled the heavy car to the verge of the road. They were just outside the city limits, and the abandoned commercial buildings on either side of the road looked sad and depressed. He wasn't going to answer. Kess glanced around. Junk cars, newspapers, and a mangy cat sitting on the burned-out skeleton of a car. Nothing moved.

Maybe now wasn't the time or place to act like a girl. She checked the lock on the door. "Nice neighborhood." She felt eyes on them from all around. Probably rats, or men with machetes, or drug dealers. Or gang members waiting to steal the tires off the car before murdering the two people in it.

The sun shone brightly, but a shiver ran up her spine at the urban decay and the absolute isolation of the place. She'd driven by this area dozens of times, but it wasn't exactly a scenic place to park.

"Do do, te do do, te do—" she sang. "I'm just waiting for the Jets and the Sharks to come out snapping their fin—"

With a smothered laugh Simon reached over and slid his hand under her hair, then pulled her up against him and kissed her. Hard. Kess's brain melted as his tongue swept into her mouth and his fingers slid up to cup the back of her head. "I've been wanting to do that for hours. I hate to be thwarted."

She could taste his bad-boy smile. Sweet and salty and addictive. She was in such big trouble. Kess wrapped her arms around his neck and kissed him back. No confusion or second-guessing here. Simon wanted her as much as she wanted him.

He kissed her for an eternity, until Kess wouldn't have cared if the rats carried them off to their lair, car and all.

They broke apart, both breathing heavily. "You're a five-pound bass on a two-pound line, woman."

She blinked, trying to regain her sense of balance. "You're sort of smiling, so I'm guessing that's not a bad thing." Her entire body pulsed with desire. Holy Mother of God the man was potent.

Simon started the car and pulled back onto the road. There wasn't another vehicle in sight. "Not a bad thing—a puzzling thing."

A bright flash of sunlight highlighted the scars across his long, tanned fingers as he drove. Kess scooted closer to him, drinking in the smell of his skin, enjoying the heat emanating from his body. Reaching out, she touched a finger to the back of his right hand. "How'd you get these?"

"Had a hard time with spelling as a kid. One of the women paid to take care of me was a good speller. She thought the metal edge of a ruler would improve my learning curve."

Kess felt sick. "That's child abuse. How old were you?"

"Eleven."

She sucked in a breath.

Simon chuckled. "It's all right—go ahead, ask me how to spell onomatopoeia."

"It's not all right." She bet he'd mastered all sorts of skills as a kid. Her eyes prickled and her heart ached with empathy. "Were all the foster homes that awful?"

"No. Some of them were worse. Some tolerable. Learn and grow. I did both. Have you noticed anything different in Abi's behavior lately?"

God. She didn't want to talk about the president, her heart ached for Simon. She could see by the tight line around his mouth that the subject was closed. Kess grabbed his hand and draped his arm around her shoulders. He didn't resist, just brought the other hand up to steer. Kess leaned against him, tucking her body against his. They fit perfectly.

"He's been the same as long as I've been here," she answered. "Different how?"

"Tell me about his opponents."

"Ffumbe Fulami got his law degree at the University of Cape Town. He was born right here in Quinisela. He's forty-six, married to the same woman for twenty-four years. They have a twenty-two-year-old daughter, Efia, who's attending the Sorbonne in Paris."

"And he'd make a bad president of Mallaruza why?"

"Other than his series of underage girlfriends? Or his affiliation with the Russians? He's weak, susceptible to bribes, and spends a lot of time in the South African casinos."

"What about the other guy?"

"Jungo Kamau is single. Forty-two, likes to sail—that's his fancy yacht in the marina, but he's very low-key. Has a *lot* of money. Some of it family money from timber exports, but most of it was smart investing and a thriving export/import business as well as working as the minister of finance. I must admit that he's done a pretty amazing job bringing the country—if not into the black, then reasonably close. No easy task."

"Women?"

"He has a live-in lover. Male. I believe they've been together for something like twenty-five years."

"That means married, not single. Does the fact that he's homosexual impact how the voters perceive him?"

"I don't think so. If he wins the election the country will get not only a savvy businessman, but the bonus of a first husband who's a City Planner. Why?"

"I'm trying to figure out who would be the best president and why."

"The current president will *be* the best president," Kess told him firmly. Lightly she ran her fingers through the hair on the arm slung over her shoulder. She'd rather bury her face against it, but the man *was* driving and while there was nothing but grass and sky around them, they did have a destination. She wondered what he'd do if she started undoing the buttons of his jeans as he drove. Hmm.

Titillated and amused, she let the idea percolate. "Abi's young, single, well educated, and, more important, he's proven that he cares deeply for his people." Simon's legs were spread as he drove. One foot on the accelerator. His well-worn jeans stretched over the natural bulge of his penis as his foot pressed down on the accelerator.

"Ever heard that when something is too good to be true, it usually is?"

Kess placed one hand very deliberately on his hard thigh. "I've heard it, but it's not always true. Abioyne Bongani's a great man, and he'll put Mallaruza onto the world stage."

"Would you believe that if you weren't his publicist?" Simon asked dryly.

"Yes." Her cell phone rang and she hooked the handle of her new bag with her foot to grab ahold of it without letting go of Simon. She checked caller ID, then answered, "Hi, Nelson." Nelson McKay was her attorney in Atlanta. This was only the second time he'd called her since she'd been in Africa. She crossed her fingers that he had good news.

"Sorry, Kess. The lead we had on Angela Sidel hit a dead end. Have you thought of anyone else we can call as a witness?"

Kess shifted out of Simon's loose hold, sliding across the seat. The scenery whizzed past the window, and even though there wasn't a freaking cloud in the sky, everything was suddenly overcast. "We've been through this, Nelson. No. No one. Angela was the one I was— No one that I can think of. I'm sorry."

"Me, too. Look—this PI is costing you a bundle. Want me to tell him to keep looking, or have him stop?"

He only had to look for another couple of weeks. If Angie didn't show up, Kess's goose was cooked. "Keep looking. Please."

"All right. See you in court. Two weeks."

"I'll be there. Thanks, Nelson."

"Look after yourself over there," he told her. Nelson had never been out of Georgia, let alone to another country. He'd thought she was certifiable for taking this job. He thought she should have accepted being fired, and if her assault charge was dropped, sued the company for loss of wages, etcetera. Just thinking about it made Kess's head ache.

"I will." Kess disconnected and tossed the phone back into the open bag.

"What are you appearing in court for?"

She felt a sigh hovering inside her chest, but didn't let it out. "Aggravated assault."

Simon shot her a flatteringly amazed look. "You're joking, right?"

"No. Because of who the victim was, the DA upped it from misdemeanor simple assault to aggravated assault. The sentence is three to twenty years if I'm convicted. The son of a bitch was over sixty-five, which carries a stiffer penalty."

"I can't begin to imagine you performing aggravated assault on anyone. Were you set up?"

Kess's eyes welled. "Other than my family, you're the only person to ask me that question. But no. I *did* assault someone. Before I came out here, I worked for Wexler, Cross, and Dawson in Atlanta. I was with them for four years. Loved the work and my clients, but my boss, Todd Wexler, was a sleaze. Fortunately I didn't have much interaction with him, other than being able to see him through the wall of frosted glass between our offices."

Simon reached out and hauled her back against his side, then wrapped his arm around her shoulder. "Cowardly piece of crap that he was—" Kess rested her head against Simon's broad shoulder— "he'd target some poor woman in the office who needed the job and couldn't report his improprieties. Someone like a single mother, or a recently divorced woman. Then he'd sexually harass them, forcing them to have sex with him or they'd be fired."

"Jesus." Simon squeezed her upper arm, his tone savage. "Did he rape you?"

"Me?" Kess lifted her head an inch. "Hell no. I gave him a black eye when he tried to grope me on my first day there. No. He pretty much left me alone after that. But his personal assistant—"

"Angela Sidel?"

"She came to work for him last year. She was in an abusive marriage, and has a six-year-old son with Asperger's, she *needed* that job. Over time, she'd gradually opened up to the rest of us a little about her hellish marriage and abusive husband. The women in the office rallied around, and convinced her to report him, and get help. She was remarkable, and finally got a divorce."

"Why do I have the feeling *you* were the cheerleader in the Save Angela Sidel campaign?"

"There were nine of us, and we all worked toward a common goal. She got a divorce and her ex landed in jail for breaking the restraining order. That was the good news." Kess wrapped an arm around his waist and sank into his strength.

"Wexler raped her?" Simon asked, his breath ruffling her hair.

"He'd been raping her for months. She was too scared to tell anyone. But one evening I stayed at work late to finish up a report I was doing. He kept Angie late as well, and didn't realize that I was right next door and could see their shadows through the glass. I suddenly realized that she'd been hinting about the assaults for months. None of us had listened."

Simon's even breath let her finish the story.

"I raced in there, so furious I could barely see, to find he had her spread out on his desk. His pants were around his knees, and he'd definitely taken his Viagra because he didn't even pause when I rushed in.

"Angie just lay there not making a sound, her

head turned to the side, tears streaming down her face. Her eyes looked dead. All I could think of was what she'd already endured, and I went nuts. Picked up his complicated damn phone system and hit him on the head with it."

"Good for you. I hope you killed the bastard."

"Unfortunately not." Her jaw ached and Kess realized that she was clenching her teeth. As if he realized it at the same time, Simon brushed a knuckle back and forth along her jaw. "The entire time I was yelling at Angie to get up and *go*, but she just lay there, stunned. Wexler staggered back, a big gash in his forehead where I'd smacked the son of a bitch with the phone, he tripped over his pants—or his freaking penis—and he went down, crashing into his chair, which shot across the room and into the glass wall. Of course *that* shattered into a billion pieces.

"Then he came at me with one of those Boy Scout knives—I didn't realize until he cut my arm, right here." She indicated the faint white line on her forearm. "I swung the phone again, knocking it out of his hand. By this time Angie was up, and she was hysterical. Begging me not to hurt him. And I'm thinking—'Not hurt *him*?' I had blood running down my arm as she raced out of there as if the hounds of hell were after her. And I thought, 'Good. She's safe.'"

"What about you?"

"I was mad as hell and running on sheer adrenaline. He had his pants around his scrawny white knees and came at me with a big brass table lamp, trying to yank up his pants at the same time. I hit him—this time on his arm."

"Jesus, Kess."

"I know. I broke it. My hand, not the lamp. Insane. I was so angry I didn't really know *what* the hell I was doing."

"And without Sidel nobody believed you that you were protecting her from rape?"

"Right. She disappeared. I quit, or was fired, depending on who's telling the story. I was picked up and charged the next morning." She blew out the painful gust of air trapped beneath her sternum. "Honest to God, Simon, I've never lost my temper like that. It was an aberration. And now I'm going to have to pay for it."

"Unless we find Angela Sidel and her son."

"The election comes before my trial. I have a two-hundred-dollar-a-day PI looking, but so far there's no sign of her. And even if I *did* find her— would she testify on my behalf? She was scared before I exposed this new abuse. What if she's gone so far underground we'll never find her? And hell, if I were in Angie's shoes, I'd stay hidden as well. Wexler will crucify her in court."

"I'll have her found." Simon's voice was grim as he took out a tiny phone and punched a number. "And T-FLAC will sure as hell protect her. Give me any info that you remember, and I'll get a team on it immediately. Steve? I need a four-person team in Atlanta—"

Kess hoped Simon didn't think she was undoing the buttons of his fly out of gratitude.

Eleven

One-handed, Kess spread open his jeans and he sprang free. She murmured low in the back of her throat, making the hair on his body stand to attention along with his cock.

"Let me get back to you on that," Simon said into the phone, his voice strangled as he disconnected. Hard as a rock, he could barely contain his moan as her cool hand fisted around him. Instinctively he thrust into her hand. "Jesus H. Christ . . ." He tossed the sat phone onto the dash, taking his foot off the accelerator at the same time. The top of his head was about to blow off. He didn't want to hit a tree or an animal . . .

Kess bent her head, her bright hair spilling over his lap. Her warm breath fanned across his groin, making his entire body tense in anticipation. She placed a firm hand on his knee and used a little pressure to keep his foot on the gas pedal. "Uh-uh. Don't slow down."

"Don't sl—"

"Faster."

The person holding the joystick had all the control. Magically he put the car on autopilot. A hundred mph. The vehicle sprang forward in a plume of red dust. Not that Simon noticed; his glazed attention was on Kess licking her lips a breath away from his straining erection. His heartbeat ratcheted up even higher and his fingers tightened on the steering wheel even though they had no need to be on the wheel at all.

He sucked in a breath as her tongue painted a sensual line from base to tip while her short nails scored lines up the inside of his thigh through the too-thick fabric of his jeans. When she cradled his balls at the same time as her mouth closed gently around the head of his dick, Simon almost ripped the steering wheel off the driveshaft.

His T-FLAC training made it possible for him to see and compute; sunlight spilling through the windows and turning Kess's hair to liquid copper as it spilled over his lap, the speed of the car, the rich greens and umbers of the passing vegetation; he recognized each animal dotting the plain within his line of sight. And he was cognizant that the vehicle stayed on the road and was heading toward the correct coordinates.

The other ninety-eight percent of his awareness was between his legs.

Painfully hard, balls tight, he held his breath as Kess's hot, wet mouth closed around the head of his penis. His eyes glazed as her teeth scored a delicate path along the sensitive corona where shaft met head.

Every nerve and muscle strained for release. At that point Simon didn't give a damn if they hit a tree. He arched his back—

And found himself sitting on the floor in his empty, half-completed living room in Montana.

Alone.

He threw his head back and roared, "Fuck!"

Suddenly, Kess found her nose pressed to the leather seat in a car going a hundred miles an hour without a driver. For a moment she just lay there, trying to figure out what had just happened. The delicious sexual haze left her body like air from a slowly leaking balloon.

Oh, hell. Simon's defective powers had extremely bad timing.

Pushing herself upright, her brain kicked into gear and she started to laugh. Oh, God. Poor Simon. Scrambling to get her arms and legs to coordinate, she awkwardly managed to slip into the driver's seat.

"That annihilated the sex buzz in a hurry," she said with a grin, half amused, half horrified by Simon's abrupt disappearance. She bet he wasn't in any way laughing right then.

Even pumping the brake didn't slow the car, but at least she had control of the steering. The speed and the adrenaline still racing through her bloodstream surged into a different kind of excitement as red dust cut through the green blur that was the swiftly passing scenery and the heavy vehicle practically flew down the road. "I'd enjoy this a whole hell of a lot more if you'd come back," Kess told the absent Simon. She hoped he was okay. Had his disappearance been as much a surprise to him as it had been to her? Or had he planned it?

Somehow Kess didn't think a man would plan to disappear at quite such a critical moment. Nope. His powers had malfunctioned again. She sobered as she saw a herd of thirty or more zebra running across the road ahead. Beautiful. And soon to be very dead if they didn't move out of the way. She pumped the brake, but kept going. "Hurry. Hurry. Hurry." She pressed her palm on the horn hoping they'd get out of her way in time.

"You have a thing for speed," Simon said, materializing in the passenger seat without warning.

She'd never driven so fast in her life, but yes, she liked it. A lot. Kess gave him a brief glance. He had a powdering of snow in his dark hair. She bit her lip and averted her gaze to look up ahead. "Are you okay?" she asked, keeping a straight face with some difficulty. She felt his pain, she really did, but his expression was priceless. Frustration. Disgruntlement. And he was clearly still aroused.

"*Coitus interruptus* is one thing," he said flatly, wiping a trickle of water from the rapidly melting snow off his temple. "But I can't protect you if my powers aren't fully functioning. And Christ only knows, they aren't working worth shit. Turn around

and head back to Quinisela. I don't want you anywhere near this damn virus without a protective
shield around you. Especially if I can't depend on
my powers to keep you safe."

Kess could tell by his tone of voice that he was
pissed about his power outage, but beneath the an-
noyance was a thread of . . . What? Fear? She
couldn't imagine Simon afraid of anything. Yet his
powers were very much a part of him. She could
only imagine how the unreliability would impact
him. "You still have all your super-spy skills though,
right?" she asked. "That's enough for me. Besides,
despite the little spat thing you and the president
had earlier, none of the doctors or relief workers
have been infected. There's no reason to suppose
we will be either."

"Why ask for trouble when it's easy enough to
avoid it? Wait a minute. Are you telling me that in
the last half a dozen months that millions have
died, *none* of the victims were the people sent in to
help them?"

"Right."

"That doesn't make any damned sense at all—"
Simon paused to interrupt himself. "Want me to
slow the car down now, or are you still enjoying
playing Indy 500?"

"As long as I don't mow down anything," Kess
told him, happily relieved when the zebras cleared
the road ahead. "I'm loving this. No. No one else
has been infected. It's the one thing that's puzzled

all the virologists and scientists the president has working on a cure."

"Is that a fact?"

The pleasure of racing through the countryside at breakneck speed disappeared at the serious turn in the conversation. "Take your voodoo off and give me control, please." The car slowed instantly. "To be honest this has been bothering me as well. First, why is it taking these virologists so damn long to figure out what this virus *is*, and second, why aren't the medical personnel being infected?" She shifted to a more comfortable position in her seat.

"Good question. When we get to this village I'll take samples and send them to T-FLAC's labs. See what they have to say." Simon reached out and grabbed his phone from the dashboard where he'd tossed it earlier.

It barely had time to ring on the other end before he spoke. "Teleport a couple dozen hazmat test tubes to me at these coordinates," he said without a greeting or saying who he was. "Make sure there's a lab in—" he paused, "Make it Cape Town. And have a three-person team waiting for me at my hotel in Quinisela at oh-eight-hundred tomorrow." Another brief pause as he listened. "Yeah, this is a psi op. Any more intel on Noek Joubert? How the fuck is that possible?! Dig deeper."

Simon stretched out his legs in the cramped footwell, and Kess noticed immediately that the bulge in his jeans hadn't gone down at all, in spite of an unexpected disruption. "Any word on Angela Sidel? Keep looking." He closed the tiny phone and shifted in the seat, apparently getting comfortable. "The turn's up ahead."

Seeing Simon aroused was turning her on, too. Her nipples pushed against the soft cotton of her T-shirt. "Nothing on Angela?"

"Not yet." He used his thumb to dial. "But they will."

She believed him.

"Mason? Yeah, great hearing you, too. Look, I have a situation with my powers."

He sounded way too casual about it.

"Power surges, outages . . . Hell, yeah I'm concerned. About three weeks. No, exactly twenty-three days . . . No. No pain. Just malfunctioning. Where are you? Can I swing by later tonight or tomorrow and have you che— A beach, a bikini, and a babe? Yeah, it can wait a few weeks, I'm in the middle of an op in Africa—anyway. Mallaruza. Remember Abi Bongani?" Simon asked with a smile. "Nah, he's toned down his wardrobe some, he's running for president again so he's keeping it conservative.

"Heard of a powerful wizard in Africa? Name's Noek Joubert? When you get back to civilization would you see what you can find out about him? T-FLAC intel hasn't found a damn thing. No, I know, impossible. But that's what we have on him right now. Nada. Sixteenth? *El Jadida?* Sure. See you then."

He clicked the phone closed, tossing it back onto the dash. "Now. Where were we?" The vehicle suddenly picked up speed. Simon must've put it back on auto.

Kess laughed. "Oh, that ship has sailed, sailor."

He slid his hand under her hair and closed his fingers on her nape. "Ya think?" Using his free hand, he gently brushed her hair over her shoulder, then bent forward and nibbled on her ear.

"Hey!" A bolt of electricity shot directly from her ear to her groin, making Kess shudder. "You can't exchange tat for tit."

"No exchange." He licked a path around the shell of her ear, then nibbled on her lobe. "Just continuing on. Jumping ahead a little."

"What happened to my clothes?" she demanded, finding her bare behind on the leather seat and her breasts being warmed by the sun shining through the windshield. "Funny how your powers don't seem to be malfunctioning now. That is *so* not fair. I can't make your clothes disapp— Hmm."

She cast him an admiring look. He'd done a little hocus-pocus and made his own clothes disappear too. He gave her a wicked look. "Bed or backseat?"

Kess laughed against his mouth. "Oh, backseat by all means—*Oomph.*" They landed on the backseat, wider than it had been moments before, Simon on top. "Watch that elbow, sparky."

"Not my elbow. The box of vials I asked for. Here, let me get them out of the way." The small box disappeared.

"Magic is *so* handy. Can it be taught?"

"Nope." He slid down her body, kissing her all the way down her chest and belly, then kneeled in front of her, a hand on the inside of each thigh. Kess knew she should be blushing, he had her in the most intimate position, but his piercing eyes held hers as the fingers of both hands slid inexorably toward his goal, teasing and seductive, and pushed her thighs apart to accommodate his body between her legs.

She ran her fingers through his hair, pushing the silky strands out of his eyes. "You aren't going to disappear again, are you?" she asked in a thick voice. "Because if I don't have one of your parts on all of *my* parts pretty damn *soon* I'm going to internally combust."

"I'll take care of that problem for you," he assured her, maintaining eye contact. The fact that the car had no driver was immaterial as he brushed his lips on the inside of her left knee. Nothing mattered but Simon and the delicious things he was doing to her body.

"Excellent start," she told him, her heart racing faster than the car. Her breathing was erratic and she had to lick her lips to whisper hoarsely, "Carry on."

She leaned back, one hand in his hair, the other supporting her body in the hurtling vehicle. The dirt road made what they were doing more . . . interesting. A delicious shiver skated across her skin as he blew gently on her damp mound. Her fingers fisted in his hair.

"Cold?" he asked, laying his face against her thigh. His jaw was bristly, rough against her smooth skin, and his humid breath so close—so damn close—caused her own breath to hitch.

"Hot . . ."

He kissed the tender skin on her inner thigh, then licked an intricate design with the tip of his tongue—higher. Higher . . . Kess's fingers tightened in his hair as Simon licked a path along the crease at the top of her leg. His shoulders eased her legs farther apart and he covered her with his open mouth. Kess strained for deeper contact, and when she felt his tongue enter her, whimpered with the need.

Her head rolled back and forth on the seat back as he teased and tasted her. He eased up just enough for her to think she might be able to catch her breath, and then he'd start all over again, using his tongue and teeth to drive her wild.

He skimmed his hands around her hips, then cupped his strong fingers around her bottom to draw her even closer. "Ripe as a juicy peach," he whispered against the very heart of her. His breath fanned the sensitive, swollen bud and she shuddered. It was too much. It was too little.

Unerringly his tongue discovered her clit. He nuzzled gently, then a little harder, until Kess squirmed and moaned against the unbearable sweetness of the building climax. She squeezed her eyes shut as he sucked and licked, lifting her pelvis to grant him better access. "Don't stop. Don't ever stop!"

The orgasm rolled over her like a tidal wave. She arched violently, tethered to his mouth only by his fingers gripping her butt.

He held her safely in his hands as she crested, her entire body convulsing bonelessly. While her head was thrown back, and her body still quaked, Simon slid two fingers inside her. Kess bucked as her internal muscles contracted around his fingers. "I don't think I can—" The second orgasm tacked onto the first, rendering her deaf and blind as the power of the climax turned her body to liquid.

"Ready for more?" he murmured against her belly.

"Yes." The hot African sunlight spread over his head and shoulders through the windows. His skin was bronzed and satiny smooth, and looked darkly male against her own lighter skin. Kess had never felt more feminine, nor as powerful in her life. The motion of the car enhanced the experience. "God, yes. I want more. I want *everything* you have to give me." *And then I want more.* His mouth trailed up her body as he whispered what he wanted from her. What he wanted to do. With her. To her. She strained against him, trying to fit the puzzle pieces, but Simon was in no hurry.

"Cruel and unusual punishment," she told him, her voice guttural. Her breasts ached, swollen and tender.

"Oh, we haven't even gotten started on unusual," he whispered wickedly, taking a little nip on her hip, then smoothing it with a delicious swipe of his tongue.

Blood surged through her veins and her heart was doing calisthenics and triple somersaults. Her body hadn't subsided from the previous orgasms and Simon kept her hovering on the pinnacle of release, tense, expectant, craving him more and more as he nibbled and licked his way to her left breast. "Please . . ."

He closed his fingers around her right breast, kneading the resilient flesh, making her nipples ache and throb. He rolled the tip between two callused fingers, making her whimper and shift restlessly beneath him. "Suck my nipple, damn it!"

His chuckle vibrated on her skin. "Bossy woman. Patience is a virtue."

"I'm fresh out of vir—" The hot wet cavern of his open mouth closed on the hard peak of her left nipple. Kess's back arched against the leather seat as she gripped his shoulders. "Pleasepleaseplease."

Teeth and tongue gently rolled the tip until Kess whimpered, moving restlessly against him. The careful foreplay, while enough to drive Kess out of her mind, wasn't enough. "I want you inside me. Now!" she demanded as Simon took his torturously sweet time exploring every inch of her body. She was like a rubber band stretched white, a spring straightened, a sun about to go supernova. It was impossible to breathe, impossible to hear anything over the thunder of her blood racing at warp speed through her body.

This was torture. Bliss. A madness she couldn't contain. "I. Need. You."

"I'm here," he whispered against her mouth. Then he kissed her, a carnal, rapacious kiss that tasted of her and stole the last of her breath. Wrapping her legs and arm around him, Kess drew him inside her eager body. He was hard as marble, big enough to stretch her. Close to pain, but beyond ecstasy. His hand tunneled under her body, lifting her hips, and she lifted her knees over his broad shoulders.

"Stay with me, sweetheart," he said, pumping into her hard. "Stay with me." They found a rhythm immediately, and this time it wasn't tender or gentle. They wanted each other too much for that. The sound of damp skin slapping against damp skin resonated inside the close confines of the vehicle. Their breathing, rough and raw, somehow synchronized, a thread of controlled violence laced through their lovemaking. Harder. Faster. More intense. It couldn't last.

It. Could. Not. Last.

Kess bracketed his jaw, bringing his face up to hers. She kissed him deeply. It seemed as if sparks flew and fire surrounded them as they came together, then collapsed, limp and satiated in the backseat of a driverless car.

Twelve

The latest village hard hit by the virus was a hundred and fifty miles northwest upriver. The small community, dirt-poor and already struggling to subsist, consisted of mud huts with moth-eaten thatched roofs. Like most villages, it was a mile or more from the river because of the Mallaruzis' fear of the water gods drowning their children. Still, the sound of the fast-moving river carried on the hot breeze made Simon long for a cool, invigorating swim.

Making love to Kess again had been an earth-shattering experience. Odd, since he typically abhorred aggressive women. No, he thought shooting her a quick glance as they drove into the village. She *hadn't* been aggressive. She was his equal in every way and wasn't shy about telling him what she wanted.

A brisk swim in cold water and a couple of hours spent with his passenger on a wide, soft bed was the only thing he wanted right now. Another aberration, since once he was satiated, he wasn't consumed with the idea of sex for a while. Usually.

Eyes shut, Kess was slumped against the passenger door. As the car came to a slow stop, Simon stole a few seconds to look at her. He should have been thinking about villagers and viruses but his full attention was on the small smile curving Kess's kiss-swollen lips. "We're here." He brushed the back of his fingers across her warm cheek. "Rise and shine, Sleeping Beauty."

She blinked a couple of times. "I'm not asleep," she said around a big yawn, then extended her arms to the car's roof in a long, sensuous stretch.

"God, you're sexy," he said roughly as her T-shirt rode above the waist of her jeans, exposing a smile of pale skin and her incredibly sensitive belly button. He'd been extremely sorry to have to return her clothes. He liked her naked. He liked her naked a lot.

"Don't even think about it," Kess told him firmly. Knowing what she was digging in her pockets for—and sure not to find—Simon handed her a bright blue ruffly thing out of his own supply tucked in a back pocket. "Thanks." She grinned and bundled her hair into a messy ponytail halfway up the back of her head. Tendrils, both straight and curly, hung down her nape and tickled her face. Her big gray eyes looked slumberous. Anyone taking one look at her pink cheeks and mussed hair would know what she'd been up to.

"The supplies made it." She pointed to the six relief trucks parked nearby as she opened her door. "Oh, God—"

Thump. Thump.

Medical tents had been set up nearby, but it was evident that the villagers would be better served with a detail of grave diggers. The place was littered with black plastic body bags piled in parallel rows on the edge of the village, awaiting removal. Simon calculated there were more than a hundred victims of the mysterious illness. Abi was having the dead cremated in hastily dug pits downwind of the village. The supply trucks were playing double duty. Having unloaded the medicines and food, the drivers were now slinging the bags onto the trucks.

"God, that's grotesque," Kess said, swinging her feet to the ground. Simon, who'd come around to her side of the car, brushed his fingers across her disheveled hair. She got out, coming flush against his body, invading his space with an engaging, if distracted, smile.

He stepped out of her orbit. "If I suspect the protective spell is breaking down, and I tell you to hightail it out of here, you'll go like a bat out of hell. Right?"

She put on her sunglasses, then gave him a two-fingered mock salute. "Yes, sir."

"I don't like you being here at all." He glanced around camp. "It's dangerous and unnecessary."

"You mentioned that already," she said, bordering on flip. But Simon knew she wasn't. Kess was aware of the danger. She just thought she was immune. He hoped to God she was right. "Let's find Dr. Phillips, she's in charge."

They didn't have to go far. A creamy-skinned brunette wearing jeans, boots, and a light blue cotton shirt came toward them. Trim and tall, she carried herself with confidence and a distracted air. "Miss Goodall? Mr. Blackthorne?" She put out a slender hand in greeting. Kess first. Then Simon. The doctor's hand was cool and smooth.

"I'm Rachel Phillips. The president told me to expect you." Her black-rimmed glasses and clipboard made her look very serious. Hell, it was a dire situation. Anyone in their right mind would be serious.

Simon looked around. The smell of death was everywhere. There was no sign of people, but he heard the soft susurrus of voices nearby. "We don't want to take you away from your patients—There *are* survivors?"

"Only forty," Dr. Phillips said grimly, indicating a large tent behind her. "Their deaths won't be easy, and if this follows the progression pattern we've observed thus far, by this time tomorrow we'll lose three-quarters of them."

She walked fast. Simon kept up with her easily, but Kess had to practically run to catch up. "To put this new medical crisis into context," the doctor said flatly, "consider the following: Central Africans can expect to live until only forty-one years of age; life expectancy has decreased in the last decade.

The maternal mortality rate in Mallaruza is already shockingly high, as is the infant mortality rate. Between the staggering HIV/AIDS rate and this new disease, millions are dying every day. *Every day,*" she repeated bitterly.

"With these poverty indicators, and more than five percent of the population displaced, one would normally expect a significant response from international aid organizations, yet the country has never received much attention. In recent years it has become fashionable to speak of 'forgotten emergencies.' But the act of forgetting implies prior knowledge. The crisis in here is not a forgotten emergency; it is virtually unknown and unrecognized."

Kess caught up, matching their steps two to one. Dr. Phillips was angry and impatient, and clearly exhausted trying to stick a finger in a dike.

"I've sent articles and photographs of our hardships to newspapers and news agencies all over the world on Mr. Bongani's behalf," Kess told her. "Help will come."

"We needed it five months ago," Dr. Phillips snapped, walking even faster. "Come this way and we'll find something relatively cold to drink, then I'll show you around and answer any questions you have. I don't have much time, so I'd appreciate it if you kept your questions brief."

She had a trim figure and a pleasant, if distracted, smile. Simon smiled back, then noticed

Kess watching the two of them as if at a tennis match. He lifted a brow, but Kess ignored him.

"I've been with the CDC since I got out of med school and I've never seen anything like this," the doctor told them, escorting them to a tent set up as a lounge area for the doctors, out of the sun. The tent was empty. Simon presumed all the other doctors and medical staff were with patients.

"Any press you can generate on this will be appreciated," Dr. Phillips told Kess. "We feel helpless and frankly abandoned here. Not everyone comes to us for help. People live in makeshift dwellings in the forest far away from their villages." The doctor rubbed her hands as if in prayer.

"They flee abuse or attacks by bandits, rebels, and of course the damned government troops. Conditions are dire: People desperately need shelter, food, health care, clothing, blankets, soap, and potable water. The absence or limited availability of clean water and medical care aggravates diseases like malaria, typhoid, and meningitis, and now this new disease is killing even more people."

"What's your professional opinion of the source?" Simon asked, looking at the charts and pictures pinned to the side wall of the tent. Gruesome. Gut-wrenching. He was looking at graphic photographs of hell.

"We're fairly sure this isn't airborne. Educated guess at this point? Something in the water. Proximity to the river is the only common denominator we can definitely identify. But every test we've got is coming back negative."

Simon shook his head when the doctor pointed to a row of gray coolers on a folding table. Kess opened one and withdrew a dripping bottle of water. The drips immediately plopped on her chest and her nipples peaked under the thin cotton T-shirt. Simon angled his body toward the doctor.

"Can you point out the virologists on the team? I'd like to get their take on things."

Dr. Phillips's face grew mottled. "The president hasn't sent replacements."

"You do understand why," Kess offered gently. "After the massacre in the last medical camp, President Bongani has no choice but to put a minimum of doctors in the field." She gulped down half the bottle of water. "The government is doing its best to provide the population outside of Quinisela with security—"

The doctor gave a sarcastic laugh. "Which is piss-poor. Security is a joke, don't pretend it isn't. So is access to potable water, electricity, or anything more than rudimentary health care. Forget proper education." She waved a slender hand in an impatient, dismissive gesture that spoke volumes.

"We need *more* help. Médecins Sans Frontières and the Red Cross can't do it all. And frankly we haven't been getting the supplies they promised us, so we're in desperate straits here."

"The World Food Program *is* providing food.

The ships are unloading in the harbor right now as we speak," Kess assured her. "And the Office of the UN High Commissioner for Refugees recently trained local humanitarian observers and they're reporting back as well. The UN has mostly traveled with government armed escorts—"

"Which are susceptible to ambush by rebels and renders the UN incapable of accessing the most vulnerable people," Dr. Phillips pointed out harshly. "It comes with the territory," she added. "Outbreaks rarely occur in industrialized areas. We're all used to remote locations and we all know the risks inherent in our work. The president has been generous in every other way, so I find his hard stance on the matter extremely disappointing. Especially since he's been so quick to provide us with other resources. Don't think me ungrateful; I, and my colleagues, appreciate everything the president is trying to do.

"He even went so far as to pay for duplicate blind testing on the blood and tissue samples. The man personally called Dr. Grable in the UK. Apparently they crossed paths at some UN function. Grable's lab is state-of-the-art and he's considered *the* expert diagnostician."

"I remember the president mentioning the lab in England, Dr. Phillips. I spoke to him about adding more experts to the on-site team." Kess rubbed the sweating bottle across her cheek. "At this point, as you can appreciate, he's reluctant to put all the medical resources in the middle of the outbreak when we still don't know what happened to the other doctors. But you need to know that you have his full support and he's one hundred percent behind saving his people." Kess leaned against the table and twisted the cap on the water bottle. "Trust me." She took a sip of water. "The doctors back in both Switzerland and the USA are working around the clock, as is Dr. Grable."

As Simon listened to the interchange, he felt the knot between his shoulder blades relax. Simon didn't know Grable other than saying hey, but he knew *of* him. His reputation was stellar, but Simon seriously doubted Abi had met the man at a UN function. More like a Wizard Council meeting. Grable was a skilled wizard. His unique power of magnified vision allowed him to observe things even the most powerful microscope in existence couldn't see.

It made sense that Abi would call on Grable. Grable was a slight, nerdy guy who often found himself on the receiving end of hazing, wizard-style. Until Abi stepped up and appointed himself the man's friend and protector. Obviously the two had stayed in touch over the years. Knowing who was on Abi's team alleviated most of Simon's concerns. But why hadn't Abi mentioned his friend's involvement?

Kess assured him that Abi's full attention was on the crisis. Seeing the camp and hearing Abi was doing everything possible made Simon feel a little guilty for doubting his friend's commitment.

His phone vibrated in his pocket. "Excuse me. I need to take this." Leaving the two women, he moved to the other side of the tent.

He stepped away long enough to check with his control. Still nothing on the missing doctors. At this point, the general consensus at T-FLAC HQ was that they were probably dead. There wasn't any logical reason to kidnap two doctors. Neither had substantial assets, so ransom was unlikely. While they were competent, they weren't Nobel Laureates, and even if they were, it was highly unlikely that the Hureni militia would be aware of that fact. No, it was far more likely that they'd been killed along with the others and either their bodies were taken as trophies or animals had dragged them off for later consumption.

Of equal interest to him was the childish game played to lure Kess away from Quinisela the other day. Obviously, the familiar car had been a decoy specifically for Simon; an "innocent" child and the promise of finding her friends had persuaded Kess. But Simon hadn't been that taken in by it. He'd gone along simply to see how they were going to play it.

But who the fuck were "they"?

Was Noek Joubert involved with Abi? Simon ran his fingers through his hair. What the hell was Abi involved in? Who was he in bed with? And why?

Politics did strange things to people. It was entirely possible that Joubert was infusing cash and God only knew what else into Abi's reelection bid. From what he'd observed, Abi's commitment to retaining his office was genuine and if his decisions were colored by his inner politician, he'd take any and all help offered.

"Mr. Blackthorne." Dr. Phillips got his attention and then beckoned him over. "I was just about to explain to Kess in a bit more detail, and I know you wanted to be brought up-to-date. Do you mind if we do this now? I want to get back to my patients."

"Simon. Please. I appreciate you taking a few minutes to talk to us." Taking Kess's bottle of water from her, he helped himself to a swig, then handed it back before turning his attention to the notes tacked up on a board.

"What are hemorrhagic characteristics?" Kess asked, pointing to one of the notations.

"This disease or virus presents much like Ebola. Quickly worsening flulike symptoms. Upper respiratory system difficulties. Then the really nasty stuff starts."

Kess's fair skin grew paler by the second. "Nastier than being unable to breathe?"

Phillips nodded. "As the organs shut down, they literally start to explode. Blood seeps from every orifice—eyes, nose, mouth. The lungs fill with blood faster than the patient can cough it up. Then the victims literally drown in their own blood. Tough way to die."

Kess swallowed hard, the color draining from her face. "I've seen—" She closed her eyes. "God. It *is* a horrendous way to die." She turned her head and Simon saw how deeply she was affected. "We *have* to find both the cause and the cure *soon*."

"Yeah," he said grimly. "We do." One would think with the best minds in virology working on this for months, that something would have been found by now. "The president should be here soon, he was right behind us," Simon said easily. "I'm going to look around until he gets here. Kess, want to take a look, or would you rather stay here?"

"We'll be having our main meal of the day in two hours; if I can get away, I'll meet you back here. Otherwise I'm afraid you're on your own," Dr. Phillips said. Simon was pretty sure Phillips wouldn't be back. Having to stop working with her patients, even for these few minutes, clearly annoyed her.

"She's dedicated," Kess observed, watching the doctor walking swiftly out of the tent. "It must be god-awful trying to help people who are going to die no matter what one does." She shaded her eyes as soon as they were outside. It was midafternoon and broiling hot. The healthy glow of Kess's skin looked luminous beneath a sheen of perspiration. She had a dirty smudge on her cheekbone from who knew where, and strands of fiery hair were glued to her neck.

"Which way?" she asked.

She really had the most extraordinary eyes. Wide and frank and usually brimming with humor and intelligence. The convo with Phillips had taken Kess's incandescence down several notches.

"River." Simon looked toward the shrubs and trees up ahead. "I want samples of my own."

Her brow pleated as she hastened her steps to keep up with him. "Can't you just get samples from Dr. Phillips?"

"No, I want to do this under the radar."

"Do you have concerns about the testing? I can promise you, the labs the president selected are top-notch."

But everyone has a price or a motivator. The only lab Simon trusted was the one ninety feet below ground in Montana. "Yeah, well, I'm just crossing *T*s and dotting *I*s."

"Why didn't you tell Dr. Phillips you had reservations?"

"Because other than the two of us, and the T-FLAC lab, I have no intention of telling anyone anything."

"Really? Not even the president? Why not?"

"A, because it could be nothing, and B, because I find it highly suspect that three different labs have had zero success and keep coming up negative with everything they've tested. Doesn't feel right."

"It could just mean this is a new strain of something, couldn't it?"

"Possibly? Yeah. Probably? No." He glanced down at her. "Need a hat?"

"No—Oh, sure," she smiled when a pink ball cap materialized on her head. She adjusted her ponytail through the keyhole in the back. "Thanks. Can I have my sunglasses t—Excellent." Kess pushed the glasses up her nose, then cocked a thumb over her shoulder. "Shouldn't we stop at the car for those vials?"

He raised his brow. He'd have them when he needed them. It was a mile or more to the river.

She shot him a small smile. Obviously the novelty of magic went a long way toward lifting her spirits.

Unlike him, Kess wasn't used to death, so the debriefing from the doctor had hit her hard. So hard that it had taken every ounce of his willpower not to pull her against him and comfort her

"Being a wizard is *so* damn cool."

He couldn't help smiling back. "It has its moments."

"Who do *you* think has the two kidnapped doctors?" Kess asked as they walked through the thigh-high grass. She figured if there were any snakes or other creepy-crawlies Simon would deal with them. "You can take care of vermin and other critters, right?" She wasn't afraid exactly, but there were all sorts of poisonous and dangerous things lurking in the grass.

His lips twitched. "Was that all part of the same

train of thought, or was it stream of consciousness?"

"Both."

"I think someone has them. If they're still alive,
my people will track them down. Eventually."

"I'd like to say tell them to hurry, but I suspect
'your people' always do everything necessary, so
I'll shut up and hope for the best."

"Are you an only child?"

"No, I told you. I have a beautiful, brilliant,
wonderful sister, Elizabeth. She's a doctor. In fact
I'm meeting her in Cape Town the week after the
election, and after appearing in court. Unless of
course I'm in the clink with Bubette. She's going to
a medical symposium there."

"Who's going to a— Oh, your sister. Cape
Town. Got it. Older? Younger?"

"Three years older. And before you ask, no, we
aren't alike—Crap! Is that a snake over there?" She
moved closer to him and pointed.

"Stick," he said, turning it into one. "And your
parents?"

She cast the "stick" a dubious glance. "We have
a full set. The reason I'm so incredibly well adjusted
and sane." She smiled at him, enjoying the walk,
enjoying the sun on her shoulders, enjoying Simon.
She needed a time-out to regain her equilibrium.

"This is because I had a normal and pretty wonderful childhood. My mom told us we were capa-

ble of doing anything we put our minds to." Kess thought of her overachieving, literature-loving mother, and quiet, very funny father, and got a little homesick. Maybe she could persuade them to come back from Atlanta with her and they could all meet Elizabeth in Cape Town. She pushed the thought of having to appear in court out of her mind, alongside the horrors of the virus. A few hours to clear her mind and she'd be ready to go back into the fray. But for now she wanted to be in the middle of nowhere. With Simon.

"So coming to Africa wasn't an aberration?" Simon sounded amused. He indicated that they go left around a thicket of shrubs.

"Well, it was partly to keep a low profile in the hope that people would forget that I attacked my boss with a freaking lethal telephone," she said, compelled to be honest. "I saw an advertisment in the *New York Times*. The job seemed like a godsend. Hell, at that point *Timbuktu* wouldn't have been far enough away from Atlanta as far as I was concerned. The distance was a big draw but part of it was also the excitement of coming to Africa. Especially a part of Africa that the world knows little about. I thought it would be a fun, interesting job for a year. I found out after I arrived that the ad had run for three months and I was the only applicant. The president is a complex, interesting man. And he's faced with a crisis in his country right before his election."

"Why *didn't* he want you there for this press conference? Isn't that your job?"

"He doesn't like anyone in the room other than the press when he's doing his monthly addresses to his people. It's a superstition of his. I'm used to it." She shrugged. "Besides, going it alone makes him look confident, involved, and concerned. I write his speech, and then prep all the possible questions and answers with him beforehand, then let him field the press after his speech at his own pace. He's a natural, and the press loves him. He'll do fine."

It didn't take long to walk the mile. Kess told him about falling out of a tree when she was six, trying to teach her older sister how to hang upside down. "I have a scar, right here." She pushed up the bill of her cap and showed him the tiny scar on her temple. "It was amazingly cool . . . There was a *lot* of blood, which I found more fascinating than frightening. My father thought I might have brain damage—Hey, don't give me that look! I got my first ambulance ride. It was the thrill of my life at the time."

"I bet you gave your parents gray hair."

"Still do, probably. But they're smart enough not to mention it. They love us both, but Elizabeth is the golden child. She's so smart, and focused, and dedicated. God. She just loves what she does and everything that goes with it. But as far as personalities go—she and I are complete opposites. She's low-key—"

"And you're exuberant?"

"Right. Every year I try to drag that little stay-at-home workaholic with me on some European trip. She has fun when she comes, but holy crap, I have to use a crowbar to get her motivated.

"Did I mention Elizabeth's a doctor? We're very proud of her. She was the youngest in her graduating cl—"

Simon whipped her around and kissed her.

Thirteen

He couldn't resist her. Kissing Kess here, in the middle of a wide-open area, was madness, but he did it anyway. He hastily materialized a blind of shrubs to hide them, then sank into the heat of the kiss.

She wrapped her arms around his neck and leaned into him. He loved the way her lips molded to his, firm, yet soft and resilient and eager enough to make him want more. She tasted of joy. Pure, unadulterated *happiness*.

"I love that I turn you on," Kess whispered against his mouth. "And I love that I get turned on by you."

"Have to pull those samples . . ." he murmured against the curve where her neck met her shoulder. The smell of her, the texture of her skin beneath his mouth, made Simon forget sampling anything but Kess. Soft, perfect Kess.

"The river's not going to dry up while you kiss me again." She nibbled his ear and a shudder of pleasure ran up his spine.

"True."

For several minutes they just stood there, their

bodies perfectly aligned, their mouths tasting and teasing until Simon firmly took her shoulders and set her away from him.

"You're a hard woman to resist."

"Fortunately you're a man with a strong work ethic. *Your* way things will get done. *My* way one of us would have a sunburned butt, and the other grass burns. Will you come back to see her?" Kess asked, keeping up with him as they walked. Perspiration trickled down her temples and she absently wiped it away with both hands, then readjusted the bill of her cap to shade her eyes. The air was hot and still, not a breath of a breeze. Insects buzzed and droned around them, and Kess kept a sharp lookout for snakes in the long grass.

"She?"

"Dr. Phillips is a brunette, smart, and clearly passionate. Your dream woman, right?" The second the words were out of her mouth Kess wished them back. Several days ago the comment would have amused her. Today it depressed her.

He wasn't interested in buying, only renting for a while. She got it. But thinking about him with his dark-haired ideal woman hurt Kess deeply. She wished she could take the high ground and tell him she wasn't going to have any more sex with him. The thought of his lean, powerful body covering someone else made her hackles rise. Thinking about Simon whispering endearments and raw sexual demands to another woman made her—She blanked the thoughts from her mind.

She wasn't prepared to fall on her sword just yet. He wasn't married. For God's sake—he hadn't even *met* the future Mrs. Simon Blackthorne yet. For now he was hers, and Kess wasn't prepared to waste one precious moment with him anticipating regrets.

"Forget it," she said cheerfully. "None of my business. Where are you going to send your samples?"

"Directly to T-FLAC's lab in Montana," Simon told her, not responding to the Dr. Phillips question. "I'm going to have to take them myself." He pushed his damp hair off his forehead, and Kess noticed he was frowning as he looked into the middle distance. "Unless I can teleport the vials successfully without accompanying them. I'll give it a shot. If I have to go I'll have Nomis accompany you back to Quinisela."

"I can go back with the president," Kess offered.

Simon glanced at her. "He's not coming."

"But he said . . . He's not?" The sound of the river was becoming much louder; a row of trees and shrubs hid it from view. "So the president didn't plan on coming, and we're clearly in the way. Why did he send us all this way for nothing?"

"Not for nothing."

"Well, yes." She slanted him a flirty glance. "The sex was spectacular. And that kiss was delicious.

But I suspect that wasn't why he wanted to get rid of us."

"Quick, aren't you? What do you know about those ships in the harbor?"

It was Kess's turn to frown. "The ones bringing in food and medical supplies? Those ships?"

"Two of them have been there for three days."

She shrugged. What did supply ships have to do with why her boss wanted them out of the way? Kess mentally tried to connect the dots. "Sometimes it's impossible to find the manpower to unload."

"In a country with an unbelievably high percentage of unemployment?"

She'd had the same thoughts, but the president's answer had made sense. "People would rather work on the church," she admitted. "It's a problem. The money's the same, but they think their souls will be saved if they work on a church."

"That's not a church. It's a multimillion-dollar basilica. The largest cathedral on the continent. He's brought the Vatican to Africa, for God's sake."

"Hey, you're preaching to the choir. I'm not happy the president's building such an expensive, elaborate structure right before the election either. To say his timing is off is putting it mildly." She felt disloyal voicing her concern. "He believes that religion will bring all the small countries in central Africa together—"

"What do you estimate the percentage of Christians, let alone Catholics, is in Mallaruza?"

"Twenty percent, maybe a handful more."

"Has it been consecrated by the Pope? Can't be a basilica if it hasn't been."

Kess bit her lip. "I have no idea. I didn't think of that. I'll have to check."

"I suspect not. Will anyone attend Mass there, do you think?"

"God, I hope so. Simon, the building has cost him—no, not the president—cost his *people* something like forty million US dollars so far. And it isn't finished yet."

While the enormous building sat right in the middle of prime real estate, it was also situated in one of the poorest, most destitute countries in Africa. Go a few miles outside Quinisela, and most of the homes didn't have running water or adequate sanitation. There was no infrastructure. No basic system for delivering food, water, or services to the tens of thousands of people still living in medieval-era conditions.

They came to the trees and Simon magically cleared a path through the dense undergrowth. His magic was a handy skill. "You mean four hundred million." He held a branch for her. Kess stepped under it and found herself on the riverbank.

"No." She raised her voice a little to be heard over the sound of rushing water. "He told me in confidence—I gather from your expression that four hundred million would be closer to the mark?"

"Oh, yeah. I suspect four hundred and climbing. The outside looks more like a palace than a cathedral with all that hand-carved marble, and he mentioned the other day that he has Italian stonemasons and artists working on the inside as well."

"Hundreds of them," Kess told him. "He has people working 24/7 on the interior so that it will be finished by the time he's reelected. Once it's completed it'll seat seven thousand people in the nave, and have room for about a thousand people standing. He wants the ceremony performed there."

"And if he's not elected he'll hand over a legacy of debt to his successor." Simon removed several vials from the case he carried and crouched on the bank to fill them.

Kess grabbed his shoulder. "God, Simon. Don't stick your hand in there! Wear gloves or something."

"Protective shield. Where are the funds coming from?"

"I—Hell. I don't know. There's never been that much money in the country's coffers according to Jungo Kamau. And he would know."

"Yeah," Simon said, straightening, then inserting the filled vials carefully back into the case. "The comptroller would know. And why doesn't Abi, do you think?"

Kess rolled her head on her neck as tension crept up to grab her shoulders in a vise. "I have no freaking idea. All I do know is that in the two months I've been here I've seen a man working his ass off to help his people in any and every way he can."

"And you didn't ask any questions?"

"I asked hundreds of questions," she said impatiently. "But considering what he has to deal with on a daily basis, I've been giving him some slack. Maybe you should too."

Simon placed the small box in his hand in the fork of a nearby tree and came to stand in front of her. He tilted her face on his finger, his eyes chips of dark emerald. "Just so you know, I felt not an ounce of attraction for Dr. Rachel Phillips."

Kess's heart skipped several delicious beats. "No?"

"No."

A smile tugged at her mouth. "If you teleport to Montana, can I come with you?"

"It's the middle of winter and snowing."

"You'll keep me warm, won't— Holy crap that was fast!"

His eyes glittered, and his lips twitched as he steadied her with his hands on her upper arms. The expression in those catlike eyes made her toes curl inside her impractical orange boots.

"You didn't ask what would happen if this teleportation didn't work," he pointed out.

"There's a reason for that," Kess said, eyes wide

as she looked around the long, empty corridor where they stood. The walls were a soft gray and hung with stunning black-and-white photographs of buildings from around the world. "Ignorance," she said cheerfully, stepping forward to look at a photo of an old woman selling flowers in a Paris market, "in this case was bliss," she finished, clearly distracted.

She shot him a quick smile over her shoulder. "If there was the possibility that my atoms, or whatever, would be scattered all over creation, I didn't want to know about it." She paused. "I don't look like a Picasso painting, do I?"

"You look—" Adorably disheveled, a little sweaty, and wholly kissable. "Fine."

She pulled a face and removed the pink ball cap, stuffing it into her back pocket. "I don't suppose there's somewhere I can wash up before we bump into anyone, is there?"

He kept a room here, had for the past ten years. It was convenient. He'd never brought a woman to HQ before. No need. Not in all the years he'd worked for T-FLAC. While it wasn't exactly something the powers-that-be encouraged, women, Simon presumed, were allowed to spend the night. He glanced at his watch. Eight A.M.

Or an hour or two . . .

"We don't have time to linger," he said, more for himself than Kess. If he had to imagine her in his room, in the shower, he'd never finish what needed to be done here. "Dr. Phillips is expecting us back at camp for dinner in a couple of hours, remember?"

"Okay. Fine. Where exactly are we?"

"Ninth floor of T-FLAC's HQ in Montana. Come on, the lab's this way."

And his almost completed house was only fifty miles down the road. When habitable next summer, it would be close enough to drop in here after ops.

His house. His *home*. He wondered what Kess would think about it.

They dropped the vials off in the lab, and were told by a young, male receptionist to wait in the next room and not to leave in case someone had questions. Simon took the order in his stride, sitting in one of the easy chairs and picking up a science magazine.

The large room looked and felt more like someone's living room than a waiting room outside a lab. Squishy, chocolate-colored chairs, the leather as soft and comfortable as an old jacket, were grouped around coffee tables with current magazines piled haphazardly. Sepia-colored photographs of children playing lined the walls. The room smelled pleasantly of coffee.

He glanced up from the glossy magazine. "You're going to wear a rut in the floor if you keep pacing like that."

"I hate sitting around," she admitted. "Want some coffee?" Kess asked, nodding to the space-agey looking coffeemaker on a table across the room.

"Sure," he muttered, not looking up as he turned a page.

"Black, I presume?" How odd. They'd slept together, but Kess realized she had no idea how Simon liked his coffee.

"Yeah. Thanks."

Happy to have something to do, Kess poured fragrant coffee into a ceramic mug. She loved the smell, but hated the taste. "You know what I'd really love to do is have a tour of this facility." She crossed the room and handed him the steaming mug. "How big is it? How many people work here?"

Not only was she curious about T-FLAC's facility, Kess was fascinated with seeing where Simon worked. She wanted to meet the people he interacted with. See who he was in his natural habitat.

Simon's teeth flashed white as he gave her the half smile that was somehow connected to her heart. The organ fluttered in response.

"You know if I tell you I'll have to kill you, right?"

"How long do you think we'll have to wait? Perhaps we have time to—"

He scanned her from top to toe. "Cold?"

She didn't have to glance down to see that her

nipples were hard little buds beneath her T-shirt and her goose bumps had goose bumps. "It's not a hundred in the shade in here."

"True."

She suddenly found herself wearing a long-sleeved sweater in a delicious cinnamon color; it felt as soft and luxurious as cashmere. "Thanks." She wandered over to look at one of the large framed photographs of two little girls on a merry-go-round. They were about three or four, and both were laughing uncontrollably, their sweet faces scrunched up with mirth as they hung on each other. Kess smiled, then went to look at the next picture.

When she'd inspected all of the photographs she ambled over to sit on the arm of the sofa, swinging her foot as she waited. Simon caught her eye and patted the seat next to him. "Come sit here and keep me warm."

Just as Kess jumped to her feet the inner door opened. A tall woman with pixie-short black hair, wearing a pristine lab coat, came into the room. Simon immediately got to his feet and crossed to meet her.

"Blackthorne? I'm Dr. Kelsey Roberts. I've been working on your specimens, and found the results, quite frankly, intriguing."

No shaking of hands, no smile. The doctor—Kess presumed scientist not medical—was all business. She was also attractive, clearly good at what she did, and part of Simon's inner circle. Kess felt a tightness in her chest that she accurately interpreted as jealousy. Here was Simon's One Day Woman personified.

Not that he exhibited any signs of interest. He was too focused on what he was here for. An analysis of the water samples. Kess felt small, reacting the way she did. She had no claim on him. None. Something she should remember. She admired that he was a man who took his job seriously. She'd just happened to be in the right place, at the right time.

She still had ten months to remain in Mallaruza on her contract with the president, unless Mr. Bongani asked her to stay after his election. Or unless he lost. Or she was in jail.

Simon would go somewhere else in the world on some black ops T-FLAC mission. And one day he was going to be in the same place and at the same time as a tall, beautiful brunette. He was going to claim his Stepford wife and live happily ever after.

Kess wanted to kick something. Hard.

The doctor practically did a U-turn as, the niceties over, she wanted to give Simon the information he needed and apparently required them in another part of the lab. "Follow me."

Kess tailed along as the doctor led them into another room. This one was all white tiles and antiseptic-looking. Actually it looked a bit like Kess imagined the inside of a spaceship would look. Like the coffeepot in the other room, it looked very space-agey and quite cool. Kess wanted to explore. In particular she wanted to look through one of the extremely scientific microscopes and see things she'd only seen on the Discovery Channel.

Dr. Roberts dimmed the lights and went to a computer on one of two long counters filled with machines and an odd assortment of equipment Kess didn't recognize. The room was cool. Cold. She rubbed her arms through the cashmere sweater, but didn't move closer to Simon's heat, much as she longed to.

Through a large window she observed technicians in what Kess presumed were some sort of close-fitting Hazmat suits that covered them from head to toe. They looked like black-garbed space aliens. She sucked in a nervous laugh. For all she knew that could be exactly what they were. Fascinated by the possibility, she walked over to the window for a closer look.

"The preliminary cultures show it's a genetically engineered derivative form of dengue fever," the scientist told Simon, her tone grim. "As intriguing as that is from a scientific standpoint, I can't stress strongly enough that this is much worse than we originally anticipated."

Alerted to the combination of excitement and foreboding in the woman's voice, Kess turned her back on the people moving silently in the next room and looked over at where Simon and the other woman stood side by side.

"Our DNA tests matched the alleles to a particularly virulent outbreak in Chechnya last year." The woman's slender, ringless fingers flew across the computer keys and an image came up on the large monitor.

Simon narrowed his eyes to glittering slits. "Someone from Chechnya visited Mallaruza and brought dengue fever with them? Intentionally?"

A shiver, like a cold hand on her spine, made Kess move in closer to see what the doctor was about to show Simon. She knew she wouldn't have a clue about whatever example the woman was about to use. But Kess needed to be closer to him. She needed to feel his warmth. Needed his calm. Because, while Dr. Roberts was talking in a cool, scientific way, the subtext was starting to give Kess a really bad feeling. A quick glance at Simon's face showed he was sensing the same thing.

"Dengue fever has four subtypes," Dr. Roberts told him. "DEN-1 through DEN-4. Once someone has been exposed to one of the subtypes, they have lifelong immunity. Outbreaks of all the dengue subtypes have been reported in Mallaruza, making it statistically improbable that a strain of the disease could be responsible for the incredibly high mortality rate and alarmingly swift spread in the current situation."

"Fascinating." Simon leaned in to look at the monitor and the examples of . . . whatever it was the doctor was showing him. Twisting ribbons of . . . something important and scary-looking.

Simon absently stepped behind Kess, laying his open hand on the small of her back. The heat of his fingers warmed her, but more, the fact that he was touching her made her insides jump and shout. Looking at him, one wouldn't know that he was even aware that she was in the room with them. His touch meant that he was tacitly aware of her, even when focused on his job.

"So we're looking at a naturally occurring disease that was normally transmitted?" Simon asked with a frown, "and the only unique aspect is it screws with your statistical probabilities?"

Doctor Roberts ran her fingers through her short hair. "You're missing my point."

"Easy to do with all that DEN-1, DEN-2 mortality rate bullshit."

The scientist keyed up another graphic. "This." She used the pad of her forefinger to bring up a photograph of dots in varying density in long rows. "This is an electropherograph of the genetic material we extracted from the water sample you gave us."

Simon inched Kess forward so he could get a closer look. "Okay." His thumb ran a small circle in the middle of her back, even though he was looking intently at the screen, not at Kess.

Dr. Roberts tapped the screen. "Let me overlay a second electropherograph in a contrasting color scheme so you can see what I mean. This is from the Chechnian sample we had on file."

"What are those extra dots?" Kess asked, intrigued even though she didn't understand most of what the doctor was telling Simon. While it was clear that whatever the doctor had discovered was something incredibly bad, as in not good and very scary, Kess still found the entire process fascinating.

The woman shot her a Where-did-*you*-come-from look. She put more electro-whatevers up on the screen, and Kess had to concentrate hard to see the subtle differences.

"The extra *dots*," she said with patience and a touch of amusement, "are DNA alleles from leptospirosis."

Simon stiffened behind Kess, making her aware of how much tension he was already holding in his body. The fact that Simon was tense made her tense. "These two diseases don't normally coexist?" he demanded, his fingers tightening on Kess's back.

"They can," the doctor said flatly. "But in this case, they aren't coexisting, they're a singular organism."

"Gene-splicing?"

The woman nodded. "By someone who knew what they were doing. It's simple but brilliant."

"Unleashing two separate but deadly viruses at the same time?" Kess asked as her heart started racing. Someone was killing millions of people on purpose? Who? Why?

"Not separate," Dr. Roberts said. "Someone took a sample of the dengue fever outbreak and joined the dengue from Russia with a sample of leptospirosis, probably from the most recent outbreak after the flood in Nicaragua."

"Why?" Kess whispered, horrified.

"Because dengue is a mosquito-borne illness and leptospirosis is a waterborne illness," Simon told her grimly. "Splicing them together created a form of dengue that can be transmitted through drinking water."

"Correct," the doctor agreed. "Not just any dengue, but *hemorrhagic DEN-4*. It's genius. You can spray an infected area to kill the mosquitoes when you have a normal dengue outbreak. Just as you can treat water to kill off leptospirosis. But whoever came up with *this* knew that unless the genetic manipulation was discovered, none of the conventional treatments would work."

"There's no way this could be some freaky thing in nature?" Kess asked.

"Absolutely not. There's no way the DNA from your sample would match the DNA from Chechnya. There are always slight variations in the alleles in nature. The leptospirosis is caused when animal urine contaminates drinking water, and while I can't pin down the exact origin of this strain of leptospirosis, I can tell you that the gene types wouldn't fuse without the aid of human manipulation under carefully controlled conditions."

Simon's breath fanned the back of Kess's head. Not in a loverlike way—she was pretty sure he wasn't even aware that he was so close against her back that a piece of paper wouldn't fit between them. "Who has this kind of sophisticated, advanced technology?" he demanded.

"We do," the doctor admitted. "T-FLAC does this sort of cutting-edge technology right here."

Fourteen

"God, this is amazing," Kess said, wobbling as they materialized beside the river in Mallaruza. She grabbed his forearm to balance herself; he'd brought them in a little closer to the water than he liked and Simon steadied her before they both went into the river.

"Teleporting is the only way to travel." She laughed. "Who needs planes? And for someone who likes instant gratification, teleportation as a means of transportation can't be beat." Her cheeks were flushed, and her eyes sparkled. Her hair was a wild orange-red nimbus around her shoulders. Botticelli's Venus. Sensuous and strong. Irresistible.

Finding it impossible to keep his hands off her, Simon cupped her warm face between his hands, feeling her fiery hair slide over his fingers. "I've never met anyone as fearless as you."

She grinned up at him, her perfectly imperfect teeth very white in the golden glow of the late afternoon sun. "I'm not exactly fearless," she admitted, her good cheer dimming slightly. "Spiders still scare the crap out of me, and that is ratcheted down from the paralytic terror I had before I went to the Atlanta zoo at twelve, and *begged* them to allow me to handle every spider they had."

"Arachnophobia?"

"Off the charts." She shuddered dramatically. "Hated them since I was an itty-bitty little kid. But learning about them, and handling them every day, gave me a healthy respect for them."

What an amazing woman she was.

"The situation with the gene-splicing, and this virus business, scares the crap out of me." Kess's shudder this time was the real deal. "But right this second I've just made an extraordinary journey few other people will ever experience, and I'm standing here—in Africa—in the arms of a man I trust implicitly. So right now, Simon Blackthorne with an e, living in the here and now isn't scary at all."

"Christ, Kess, what the hell am I going to do with you?"

She stood on tiptoe to brush a kiss against his lips. "Feed me. I'm starving."

He glanced at his watch. "We can make it back in time for dinner."

"Sweet." She tucked her hand in his as they headed back across the open expanse of grass. "Oh! Stop a minute," she whispered, pointing to a pair of lions under the shrubs Simon had conjured earlier to conceal their kiss. "I've never seen that before. Have you?"

"Lions having sex?"

Kess tilted her head, her cheeks a little pink. "It doesn't look as if she's enjoying it very much."

The young male had the female pinned to the ground, his massive mouth and sharp teeth holding her by the scruff of her neck as he mounted her.

Surprising himself, Simon felt a rush of raw heat when both animals roared as the male started thrusting. When the male was sure his lioness wasn't going to toss him on his royal ass, the lion released her neck, then nuzzled his face against hers.

"He's kissing her! That is so sweet," Kess said softly. In seconds it was over. The lion did a graceful dismount and rolled over and yawned. Kess laughed. "Oh, my God. You guys are all the same."

"I have never bitten the back of your neck." Simon ran the flat of his hand up her soft, pale nape. She shivered. "Right . . . here." He trailed the edge of his nail across the smooth skin and delighted at her responsiveness as she bent her head with a whimper.

"They'll nap awhile, then be back at it every fifteen or thirty minutes for the next couple of days." With a strangely human-sounding moan the young lion rolled over on his back like the giant cat he was, his legs spread as he slept.

Kess's eyes twinkled. "No wonder he's king of the freaking jungle. Nonstop for a couple of *days*? Holy cow."

"We'll take the long way round so we don't disturb their postcoital glow."

"Thirty seconds hardly warrants his smug smile," Kess observed as they circled the pair.

"What he lacks in quality, he makes up in quantity."

"You lions all think the same way."

"Don't tempt me; right now the thought of grabbing you by the scruff of the neck and throwing you down in the grass has a certain piquant appeal."

Kess shot him a sassy glance. "Nobody's stopping you, Leo."

Simon's laugh disturbed a small flock of tiny brown birds with yellow throats. "I'm thinking bed, clean sheets—"

"Hmm. Shower. Wine. Can we teleport back to Quinisela after dinner?"

"You enjoy that mode of travel, do you?"

"If it gets me alone with you, I'm all for it." Her smile dimmed as if a cloud had suddenly slid behind the shine in her eyes. "Simon . . . Dr. Roberts didn't *literally* mean that the splicing was done by someone at T-FLAC, did she?"

"Jesus. I hope to hell not. But no. She meant that we have that capability."

Kess grimaced. "God, that's scary. Why?"

"Because we need to at least keep up with what the hell tangos around the world are doing. Want to lose the sweater?"

"No, actually I want to keep it, just take it off."

"I'll send it to the car. The color looks good on you. Lost your hat I see." Simon teleported the sweater, and replaced the ball cap. Mint green this time. Kess smiled happily and adjusted the brim.

His sat phone vibrated in his hip pocket and he hauled it out. "Blackthorne—"

"This is Gonzales from trace. Found your Angela Marie Sidel working in a diner in Nome, Alaska. What do you want done with her?"

"Good work." In an aside he told Kess, "My guy found Angela—First of all," he told Gonzales. "Stick to her like glue and don't let her out of your sight. Second, contact Nelson McKay. He's Kess Goodall's attorney in Atlanta. Tell him you have Sidel and set up a meet so he can get her sworn statement."

"Then . . ."

"Get back to me." Simon closed the phone and shoved it back into his pocket. "Good news."

"Yes—i-it is."

He stopped and put a finger under Kess's chin. "Are you crying?"

She wiped her wet face with both hands. "Absolutely not." And then because she was Kess, flung herself into his arms in an exuberant hug, half laughing, half crying. "Thank you, thank you, thank you."

"She'll have to give a statement and the attorney

will subpoena her to testify. He'd better be damn good."

"He is."

Yeah. Simon had checked. McKay was an excellent attorney. While Davis's team had been searching for Kess's only witness, Simon had the legal department check out McKay. Kess was in good hands and had T-FLAC's legal eagles for backup. While she did her job here, Simon was ensuring that her legal troubles disappeared.

"How come I've slept for hours and I'm still tired?" Kess asked. She yawned, then stretched, looking around to see where they were.

"Stress," Simon told her as they pulled into the parking lot behind the hotel. His hotel.

They'd eaten alone after all. The doctor was too busy to join them. They hadn't lingered; the food and the depressing atmosphere weren't exactly conducive to a romantic evening together. By mutual agreement they'd driven back to Quinisela instead of teleporting. Kess, lulled by the movement, had dozed most of the way back.

"Who do you think is doing the gene-splicing?" she asked, rubbing her eyes, trying to wake up fully. The parking lot was large, and dark, as clouds covered what had been an almost full moon earlier. The black clouds were ringed with silver as the moon tried to penetrate. It was pretty in a creepy, vampire way . . . "Please don't tell me the president."

"He's the first person that comes to mind," Simon admitted, getting out of the car. He came around to open her door, a sweetly chivalrous action that he did without fanfare. "But there's someone else I believe has a lot more to gain."

Kess let out a sigh of relief. "Good, because I like Mr. Bongani, and I'd hate to hate him if he's responsible for all these deaths."

She threaded her fingers between his. Simon's hand was reassuringly solid, his cool, strong fingers twined with hers. It was a simple pleasure to hold hands companionably as they walked, their steps matching. She loved the way he slowed to accommodate her shorter stride.

"Who do you think it is?" she asked as they crossed the pitted and weed-infested parking lot to go around to the front entrance. The air smelled strongly of the ocean, which was just across the road. It also smelled of dank, heavy expectancy, as if it was about to rain any minute.

"There's a South African wizard, head of a terrorist group called the Phoenix. I had a run-in with him the other day." Simon's tone was grim, his jaw set. "He's powerful, determined, and *here*."

A shiver danced up her spine. "Here in Quinisela?"

"No. But in Mallaruza."

"It's a fairly big country, he could be anywhere. Maybe he's gone."

"He's not gone, I can assure you. But he's not anywhere nearby. I'd know if he were within a hundred miles."

"Is he as strong as you are?"

"Stronger."

She gripped his hand a little tighter. "Oh, great. As if there wasn't *enough* weird crap going on already."

"If Abi is involved with this guy we have cause to be concerned. Joubert is incredibly powerful, and if he wants something I suspect he'll stop at nothing to get it."

"Concerned? *I'm* allowed to be *scared*." She glanced up at his grim expression and a shiver of apprehension shook her body. She stepped in a little closer. "You, however, are not."

"Oh, I'm scared, believe me. I'd be damn stupid not to be. Nothing wrong with being scared shitless. It's all in how you handle your fear."

This was arachnophobia times a hundred.

They turned the corner of the building where it was considerably lighter due to the enormous working lights on the basilica a couple of blocks down the street. The lit-up basilica looked like a storybook castle. Pale glittering marble from Italy, exquisite stained-glass windows from France, and tall spires.

"I don't think I've ever been this scared in my life,"

Kess said, startled by the admission, and ridiculously happy to be out of the dark parking lot. She'd feel even better with a solid building around them. "I don't mean scared because I was about to get a speeding ticket, or even scared that I might go to jail for the rest of my natural life if this court thing goes to hell in a handbasket—I mean really, truly, deep down *terrified*."

Simon stopped, bringing his free hand up to cup her chin. His eyes glittered. "And now you are?"

Kess bit her lip and nodded. "It started when we drove into camp the other day and I saw all those vultures, and has been insidiously building every day since. The trip to your headquarters, and everything Dr. Roberts told us, ratcheted it up a few more notches."

He wrapped his arms around her, and she rested her forehead on the hard plane of his chest. His lips brushed her hair, and she was comforted by the steady beat of his heart. "I'm not going to let anything happen to you, Kess. I promise."

She reached up and pressed two fingers over his mouth. "Don't make promises you may not be able to keep."

He kissed her fingers. "Trust me."

"I do. But I also want you to teach me, or tell me, how to protect myself from this other wizard. I don't want you to have to worry about keeping me safe if the guy goes totally off on us."

"Nobody is going off on *you*."

"From your lips." She stood on tiptoe and brushed her mouth over his. "It's late. Can we go to bed now?"

They almost didn't make it to a bed. By the time they'd kissed their way across the empty lobby and traveled up four floors in the antiquated elevator, kissing and touching all the way, it was a miracle they managed to get the door open before they were naked.

The room was bright as day as it faced the ocean and the brilliant lights from the basilica. He wanted to see her, wanted to see what he was touching, what he was tasting. Kissing her, Simon backed her over to the bed, then it was a simple nudge that had her on her back, and his body flush against hers. He wanted to watch her expression as she came, he thought as he followed her down onto the lumpy mattress.

They made love with a kind of mad desperation that left them both filmed with sweat and satiated. "Shower?" Kess asked weakly. She was sprawled on top of him like a silky blanket.

"Good idea," he mumbled against her damp neck. He didn't move.

"Tonight, do you think?"

He was right on the brink of sleep. "Hmm."

She trailed her fingers lightly across his ribs. "Are you ticklish?"

"Yes." He rolled her over onto her belly, and slid over her body, bracing most of his weight on his arms. Sweeping her hair off her neck and shoulders, he bit her gently on the tender, pale skin of her nape. A shudder traveled the entire length of her body, and Simon felt every ripple all the way down his front.

"Oh, my God." Her voice was muffled by the pillow. "That is seriously amazing. Do it again. A little harder . . ."

Simon bit a little harder, not enough to break the skin, but hard enough to know he'd leave a mark there. Mark her. Claim her. Brand her as his. He rolled her over. "Shower or here?"

Her eyes were glazed as she looked up at him. "Shower *and* here."

"Yeah. What I thought too."

They made love again. Slowly this time.

It was almost dawn by the time they dragged themselves into the shower. Still wet, they fell onto the rumpled sheets.

"Wake me up in a month," Kess mumbled, pulling his arm over her eyes. There was hardly a place on her body that Simon didn't know better than she knew herself. And vice versa. But a girl could only have so many good times before her body demanded rest.

"Election's in two days."

"There's that." A burst of love, so intense she could hardly contain it, swelled in her chest. She loved this man, and dollars to donuts he was going to break her heart when this was all over. Limp as she was, vulnerable as she felt, Kess tried to live in the moment and make the best of the time they had left together. Unfortunately, if they had sex again anytime soon, it might very well kill her. There wasn't a muscle or tendon in her body that wasn't begging for mercy while she was grinning like a Cheshire cat.

She sighed. She couldn't move. She really couldn't. "I'm not going to be able to sleep with that light shining in. Can you close the drapes?"

"Sure." After a few seconds she opened her eyes as he muttered, "Well, hell." Gloriously naked, he got off the bed and padded across the room. Clearly his power wasn't functioning or he would have closed the drapes from a prone position. She wondered what it must be like for him, losing so much of himself.

Scary. Not that she was complaining seeing him naked and full length. She admired Simon for having enough stamina to make it the three feet to the window. He didn't have a spare ounce of fat on him. Annoying man. His back was broad, his hips narrow, and his bottom was a thing of beauty. Kess came back to life just looking at it. "What are you looking at?" she said huskily. "Come back to bed, I don't think I'm done having my wicked way with you just yet after all."

He smiled at her over his shoulder. "Hold that thought." He held out his hand. "Come over here and tell me what you think that building looks like."

With a put-upon groan, Kess levered herself off the bed and walked over to stand beside him. Wrapping her arm around his bare waist, she leaned her forehead against his upper arm and yawned. "What building? The basilica?"

"What does it remind you of?"

She squinted into the lights. "Cinderella's castle?"

"Yeah. What I thought." Absently he snugged her against his side, his arm around her shoulders. "That's not any damned church. And that's why Abi hasn't had it consecrated yet. That's *not* a basilica—it's a *palace*."

"I don't think Disney would go over that well here—You're serious."

"Ever been inside?"

"No."

"Know anyone who has?"

"Why would the president build a castle right on the most valuable beachfront property in Mallaruza?"

"Because," Simon said grimly, "the son of a bitch plans to *live* in it."

Fifteen

There was a knock at the door. "Uh-oh. That sounds like Simon," she told Nomis, who sat on the couch flipping through a Swahili language magazine. "I'll get it."

Instead of replying, Nomis flickered and distorted, his image undulating like a bad projection. Kess's lips tightened. Poor Simon. No wonder he'd come back so soon.

She flung open the door. "Are your powers short-circuiti— Konrad!" Dr. Konrad Straus looked like he'd been dragged through hell and back. His shirt and pants were ripped and bloody, his hair dull and disheveled, and he sported a black eye. Lacerations and bruises covered his face and arms and pretty much any bare skin visible.

"Oh, my God." She rushed to wrap her arm around his waist, helping him into the room before he collapsed. "I'm so glad to see you! How on earth did you find me? Never mind. Come in. Let me hel—"

The door slammed behind him. He grabbed her arm hard enough to cut off the circulation. "Kess, you *have* to give them the camera. If you don't they'll kill Judy. They already—" His eyes welled. "Jesus. They cut off her *finger*. They're going to kill her if I don't return with you in an hour."

"I—Kon, this is Simon Blackthorne, a friend. Simon, this is Dr. Straus."

The two men nodded, but didn't shake hands.

"The kidnap victim?" Nomis asked, his expression, so like Simon's, not in the least bit friendly.

Kess could see why they didn't shake hands. Konrad's were badly swollen, the knuckles bloody and cut. She tightened her arm around his waist, taking a lot of his weight as she steered him toward the sofa. "There's coffee, or water if you like. I think we should get you to the hospital. It's only a few blocks away, and we have a car."

"Jesus, Kess. Shut the fuck up, will you?!" Konrad snapped, pulling away from her. "Just bring the camera and come wi—"

"Watch your mouth, Straus," Nomis said savagely, standing right next to her and glaring at the doctor. Kess imagined dogs circling, their hackles raised. "Let's take this outside." He gave Konrad a meaningful glance.

Kess stepped between them, laying her hand on Nomis's arm. He felt as solid and real as Simon. Only not. "It's okay. I understand." She turned to Konrad. "I'm sorry, but I'm not going anywhere, Konrad. You know that doesn't make sense. But I will give you the SIM card from my camera. You can use it to bargain w—"

"Stop dicking around, Kess. They want *you* and the pictures. You're coming with me."

"Here." She raced over to her new knapsack, digging through it. Give them— What the hell are you doing?"

Everything happened almost simultaneously— Nomis shimmered directly in front of Konrad, and the doctor was suddenly pointing a large black gun inches from Nomis's chest. Before Kess could compute what was happening there was a god-awful *bang* and Nomis flew across the room to land tangled in the full-length drapes.

She let out a little shriek of horror and started racing across the room.

Konrad grabbed her arm, jerking her back against his body. Kess struggled and strained to get free. "What's *wrong* with you?" Why shoot Nomis? Why? It didn't make a damn bit of sense. She'd never seen Konrad behave this way, and he scared her to death. Kess hadn't even seen him pull the gun out of wherever it had been hidden.

"Let me *go*! Damn it, let me *go*!" His fingers were a vise around her upper arm as she tried to yank it free. "What happened to your damned Hippocratic oath?" she shouted. Did Nomis feel pain? Could—oh, God—could Nomis *die*? And if Nomis died, did Simon die as well?

"Why did you shoot him? My God, Konrad, what did they *do* to you?" She was blubbering, tears streaming down her cheeks so she could barely see Nomis's still form and the bloom of blood forming on his white T-shirt. His eyes were closed and he wasn't moving. Was he already dead? Kess rounded on Konrad, clawing at his fingers in a bid for freedom. "Let me go," she shouted, beating at his upper body with her free hand. "Damn you. Let. Me. *Go*."

Without warning he morphed into someone else. This wasn't her friend, Dr. Konrad Straus. This stranger was a foot taller, pale-skinned, his long golden-red hair dead straight and hanging down his chest and back. He had the coldest eyes Kess had ever seen. A white shirt was tucked into black leather pants, he wore high black boots, and he was covered from shoulders to ankles in a black leather coat. He looked like Death.

He opened his hand and she almost fell. Kess stumbled backward, her knees hitting the bed behind her. Mouth dry, heart trip-hammering, she stared up at him feeling like a mongoose watching a snake. "You're a wizard!"

"Smart girl." He was right beside her without warning, yanking her to her feet, his hand manacled around her upper arm. The way he moved defined creepy. Ice flooded Kess's veins as he said flatly, "Let's go."

She knew she didn't stand a snowball's chance in hell of getting free of him, but every instinct demanded that she fight for her life. She went berserk. Kicking. Scratching. Punching at anything she could connect with. Mostly yards of leather jacket.

After what felt like a hellish eternity, and was probably less then a few seconds, he backhanded her. The blow hit just below her left cheekbone, and her eyes immediately teared. "Simon—"

He shot a frowning glance across the room. "Gone. The only reason I let you think you could fight me was because it amused me. I'm done being amused."

Kess couldn't look away from him, she was too terrified to look at Nomis. Too terrified not to. "Let me at least check to see if he's alive."

"Who is he?"

"I don't know what you mean."

"The wizard, Simon. What's his purpose here?"

Oh, dear God. What was the right answer? She didn't know. She didn't *know*. Where had Nomis gone? Back to join with Simon? Was Simon dead? Had he died not hearing that she loved him? Kess's stomach cramped and her heart and brain refused to believe it. "He—he's on vacation."

The wizard backhanded her. "Liar."

She held her throbbing jaw, her face numb, her heart pounding fiercely as anger rose in a black wave. "Hey! Don't ask me questions and then call me a *liar* when I answer, damn you," she shouted, kicking out as he held her at arm's length. "Take the damned SIM card and get out. I have nothing you want."

"*Au contraire,* my dear, you have something I want quite badly."

"What?"

"Information."

"I'm a publicist. The only information I could possibly give you is about the presidential campaign. Is that what you want? Because, buster, that's all I've got."

"You fucked him." He held her up by the throat, his fingers hard and like ice on her skin. "You know who Simon Blackthorne is, *jy hoer.*"

That sounded suspiciously like *you whore.* But a verbal insult was the least of her problems at the moment. In a dizzying switch of location Kess found herself in an unfamiliar room in exactly the same position. The walls, ceiling, and floor were a dense black, so that the wizard's skin, shirt, and pale hair floated eerily in the blackness. *Oh, God, oh, God. Simon, please* . . . If he was alive, if he knew where she was and who she was with, Kess knew Simon would come. If he didn't come, it was because he couldn't. *Stop calling him,* she told herself as a tide of terror seeped into her brain like slow-acting poison.

"All I know is that he's a friend of Mr. Bongani. That's it." Did he want to know if Simon was a wizard? Or that he was a T-FLAC operative? Kess didn't know the right answer and she wasn't going to give this cold-as-ice bastard any information that could harm Simon. If Simon wasn't dead already.

"What did you do to Konrad?" she asked hoarsely, tasting blood. She tentatively touched her tongue along the cut inside her lower lip. Her eye was already half swollen shut. The strain on her neck was pulling at her entire body. How long could she swing from his hand like this before he snapped her neck?

"Oh, I was Dr. Straus all along. I like to keep in touch with my pet projects."

"*What* pet projects?" *Simon, where are you? You were right. God, you were absolutely freaking right.*

"Who'd you think contaminated the water?"

"I wouldn't look so freaking proud of yourself. You killed millions of innocent people!"

"Collateral damage. They would have died sooner than later anyway. Lousy nutrition. No incentive to feed themselves. They breed like rabbits . . . You look horrified, Miss Goodall. You've been here over two months. Do you think Africans can take care of themselves? Of course not. Here they sit, on one of the richest continents on the planet. And what good is a fucking diamond to some *kaffir* who can't even feed his own family? The entire population of the African continent needs to be allowed to go as extinct as dinosaurs."

"You're insane," Kess whispered, appalled, horrified, and completely terrified by how a madman could say this calmly, sound this rational while he casually discussed the unthinkable. And, God help her, while he easily held her by the throat several feet off the ground.

"My dear, if your eyes get any wider they'll fall right out of their sockets." He laughed and he had very large, very white teeth that creeped her out even more. "Abioyne Bongani is going to make a fine puppet king when the countries of Africa are united into one large, lucrative continent. Mr. Bongani will rule, and I will reap what I've sowed in the last three years. A brilliant plan, really."

"Feel free to pat yourself on the back. I'm not interested in your rhetoric." And she wasn't going anywhere. She wondered fatalistically when he was going to kill her. This conversation was so bizarre, so insane, that Kess had a fleeting thought that she might be having a horrible nightmare.

"Oh, do stay, Miss Goodall. In a few days the people will be told that their president will now be their king. After all, he saved them from a terrible plague, didn't he?"

"I can't believe he would be involved in this." It was getting incrementally harder to breathe through her constricted throat. So her death was going to come sooner than later. *Simon, I love you.* "I don't believe it."

"How naive you are, my dear. Who do you think suggested it? Oh, dear, you've gone very pale. Are you about to faint?"

"No. Nobody is going to elect Bongani king. Certainly not anyone outside Mallaruza!" *But they might,* Kess thought, heart racing and mouth dry. Everyone thought the current president of Mallaruza was a humanitarian and that he loved his people. He'd offered them aid, supplied them with food, medical care, and a military presence. They very well might elect him and join their fate with Mallaruza.

"You think not?" He produced a stack of newspapers and glossy magazines three feet high and dropped them, and Kess, to the hard floor. Kess rubbed her throat. He seemed twenty feet tall from her position on the ground. She tried to stand, but her hand slipped on several glossy magazines.

"There. *That's* what an excellent publicist does, Miss Goodall. Look at the headlines and stories *I* placed."

The publications were spread in a jumble around her. Kess tried to focus on the headlines through blurred vision.

THE MAN WHO WOULD BE KING, *USA Today's* cover proclaimed. *Fortune* magazine's cover read AFRICA SEES NEW POSSIBILITIES IN A FUTURE WITH BONGANI AS MONARCH. *The New York Times,* above the fold, screamed AFRICAN COUNTRIES TALK UNITY UNDER A MONARCHY. KING ABIOYNE BONGANI NAMED 1ST KING OF AFRICA.

They were all dated the next day. The day before the election.

"No one in their right mind will believe this,"

she whispered through the constriction in her
throat.

He laughed. "I have my arm so far up Bongani's
arse I can wipe his nose when he sneezes. I'm the
brilliant ventriloquist, and he's nothing more than
an ignorant puppet."

Simon, are you okay? "What's on the film?"

"My employees contaminating the water. I for-
got Little Miss Sunshine was snapping pictures as
we worked so hard to heal all those stupid blacks."

"You're going to go to hell," Kess said, sick to
her stomach.

He laughed. "What the fuck do you think Africa
is, Sunshine? *Hell.* A place where people die because
of their own ignorance and ineptitude. Africa is the
world's poorest inhabited continent, or didn't you
know? Poorest inhabited continent, and has the most
resources of any continent on the planet. Think
about it. Gold. Diamonds. Petroleum. Copper—
the list goes on. Give *that* a moment's thought,
Pollyanna. I'm just helping them along to the in-
evitable."

"What you are is a bigot, a racist, and a megalo-
maniac. Not to mention stupid. Mallaruzis are
kind, caring, smart, and many of them well educated. They'll see through this scam in a heartbeat."

His teeth flashed. "Smart and educated at say . . .
MIT? Just like their new king?"

"You'll never get away with this."

"You think not? Trust me, Miss Goodall. Within ninety days every black man, woman, and child on the African continent will be happily working for Noek Joubert. There are over a thousand languages spoken. I can converse in all of them. Offer these people education, food, and work, and they'll follow wherever I lead them."

Was he powerful enough to really make this happen? Kess had no idea. What terrified her was that *he* believed it. "Are you going to kill me?"

"Impatient, my dear? No. Not yet. I still have a few choice appearances for you to make."

He had impersonated a caring, kind doctor. Kess had to ask, "What did you do with Judy? Was she part of your scam?"

"Oh, no. I'm holding her somewhere safe until you get there."

"Whe—" She sucked in the rest of the word as everything tilted and went black. A second later she was standing in the brilliant sunshine. Outside.

When Simon teleported her, Kess thoroughly enjoyed it. When *this* guy did it, it left her feeling sick and cold to her marrow. They were standing in the middle of a parking lot outside a row of broken-down warehouses. Kess recognized the area immediately. She and Simon had stopped close by here just a few days ago so he could kiss her. It felt like a different place, and was certainly a completely different atmosphere.

He indicated a rusted-out heap across the weedy cement. "In the car."

As Kess ran she heard his laugh behind her. "Judy?!" Her heart raced as she tried to pry open the rusted trunk. "Judy, are you all right?" Even as she screamed the words she knew how insane they were. If this man had Judy, she was not all right.

The trunk suddenly popped open a few inches. Kess staggered back at the smell. Whirling around, she searched for the wizard. "Where are you, you cowardly son of a bitch? What was the point of killing her? *What?*" She was screaming like a mad-woman. Enraged and more terrified than she had ever been in her life.

"Because I enjoy playing to the death. Is it my fault she broke so easily?"

"Then pick on someone your own fighting weight, asshole. Or are you too scared to fight someone who could hurt you worse than you could hurt them? Too weak to match yourself against an opponent who might beat *you* to death?"

He waved a hand and Kess levitated, her feet three feet off the ground. "Want to take me on, lit-tle girl?" He laughed as he flung her like a rag doll against a corrugated iron fence fifty feet away. The impact ripped the breath from her lungs.

Kess wheezed and gasped like a landed fish as she slid down to the ground, her vision dim. She didn't know which was worse. Being unconscious when he did to her what he'd done to her friend, or wide awake so she could feel everything.

One moment he was across the parking lot, the next he was crouched beside her, the black leather coat pooled around his feet. His long strawberry-blond hair floated around Kess's face and the front of her T-shirt, feeling sticky as it clung. She couldn't move, her entire body numb from the force of the blow. She couldn't even drag in a small sip of air. Terror turned her brain to oatmeal as she stared into the eyes of a monster.

"Here," he said gently. "Let me help you."

No. *Don't want your help. Oh, please, don't touch me.* She didn't want his help. God help her, she didn't want this . . . this *thing* anywhere near her. But her body was still stunned, and she could merely observe as he placed a long-fingered, pale hand on her chest and rubbed gently. Bile rose in the back of her throat as he smiled at her, his hand moving with an obscene familiarity over the upper swell of her breasts as he massaged air into her lungs.

"After I deal with you, I'll kill your boyfriend."

Kess tried to press her bruised back deeply into the corrugated fence to get away from the hand on her chest. Air seeped with agonizing slowness into her collapsed lungs. "W-why. What di-id we do t-to y—"

"Oh, it's not personal, my dear. Killing or skeet

shooting have the same level of entertainment to me."

"S-si . . . ck." Panic, dark and insidious, filled her mind like black ink dropping into clear water as his eyes went opaque.

"I only need you partially alive to entice Mr. Blackthorne to rush to your fucking side. Piss me off and the percentage will decline rapidly."

There was a smell about him. Something that, as the air seeped back into Kess's lungs, made her want to *hold* her breath. It was the smell of death. She turned her head away from him, but the sticky strands of his hair bound them together, freaking Kess out even more. It was like being a fly stuck in a monstrous spider's web. She shuddered, feeling the skin on her face tighten and stretch over her bones.

"You have . . ." She sucked in more air, filling her lungs, "have what you want. The film. Why don't you just be a man and let me g—"

The hand still massaging her chest twisted violently in the front of her T-shirt. He yanked her to her feet, making her head flop painfully as he angrily shook her. What chilled Kess to the core was that he had no anger on his face. *He's going to break my neck* was all she could think. *He's going to shake me long enough and hard enough to break me.*

Once again he held her several feet off the ground so that she had no purchase. Clawing and kicking out she tried to break free, but he just extended his arm and continued shaking her until bile rose to the back of her throat. There was no swallowing the nausea down, and she vomited, her stomach cramping.

Tossing her up in the air like a tennis ball, he punched her in her midriff with his full body weight behind his fist. Kess lost consciousness before she was airborne.

Sixteen

Simon wanted answers, and the best course of action was to get them directly from Bongani. Time had run out and he was done with the bullshit. But it was almost eight P.M., and Abi was neither in his offices nor was he at his luxurious penthouse apartment overlooking the marina.

Simon scried the entire city of Quinisela for wizard power hot spots. He found three: The docks, the church/palace, and a warehouse on the northeastern edge of town. Since the docks and the church were in close proximity to not only each other but the hotel where Kess waited for him, Simon went to the warehouse first.

A quick inspection of the contents and he'd be on his way. He suspected Abi was wandering through the basilica praying for some divine intervention for tomorrow's election/coronation. Or admiring all the gold and marble he'd imported for the enormous white elephant while his people starved or died of a cocktail of spliced genetics.

He had to drive to the warehouse because trying to teleport from the hotel proved impossible. As he drove, he put in another call to Mason Knight.

Knight was unavailable, but Simon left a terse message. This power outage crap was bullshit. He pulled up at the warehouse. Ironically close to where he and Kess had parked like a couple of teenagers a few days before. The series of complicated locks were no problem, but the powerful protection shield around the entire building was.

He finally managed to break through by removing Nomis's corporeal presence from the hotel room across town for a few minutes. He needed all his power to make a crack wide enough in the shield to squeeze through. Thank God he was able to generate enough juice to do so.

No easy task. It had been cast by a wizard a hell of a lot more powerful than Abi.

Only Noek Joubert had power this strong.

What was in here, and why such tight security? He tried checking on Kess. But he couldn't see anything through Nomis's eyes. The protective spell had shut around the warehouse again, cutting him off from outside contact. Well, hell. Unquestionably Joubert's doing. A chill of foreboding slithered up Simon's spine.

Fortunately Nomis was capable of independent thought and action. Simon trusted that part of himself to take excellent care of Kess. Nomis wouldn't let any harm come to her.

Windows up near the roof of the cavernous space let in the gray-tinged half-light of dusk. The air was cool, the temperature kept reasonable by enormous industrial metal fans high in the ceiling. The dull hum of the turning blades masked his quiet footsteps as he crossed a wide expanse of empty concrete floor. Everything there was to see was in deep shadow.

While the front third of the giant space was empty, row upon row of floor-to-ceiling shelving was packed with crates and boxes.

Simon unclipped the powerful flashlight and shone it on the labels at eye level. RED CROSS. MÉDECINS SANS FRONTIÈRES.

Here were Dr. Phillips's missing supplies. He ran a finger across the top of one of the crates, not surprised to find a thick layer of reddish dust there. How long had the doctors begged for these supplies and been told they were on their way? Months? Fury made Simon grit his teeth as he ran the bright beam of the mag light across the face of the shelved containers.

Medicines. Food. Water. Seeds and small farming equipment. Clothing and toys—millions of dollars of aid that would have gone a long way in helping Abi's people, sitting in a gloomy warehouse gathering dust. What had Abi been giving to his relief workers as medicine? Because here it was, ton after ton of medicines sitting right fucking here.

No wonder it hadn't worked. Even on the non-gene-spliced strain. The doctors had been administering nothing more than a placebo for months.

Abi was doling out help *piecemeal*. Simon

guessed these goods had been sitting here for at least four or five months. Help had been right here in a locked, seemingly abandoned warehouse *before* the outbreak of Abi's designer virus.

With his three-sixty vision he watched Abi creep up behind him. Shit. He didn't need to see the man, Simon had heard him cross the cement floor minutes before.

He turned to watch Bongani walking toward him.

"It's not what it looks like," Abi said from the shadows. He held a semiautomatic.

Clicking off the light, Simon faced him in the semidarkness. "It's exactly what it looks like." He didn't reach for his Taurus. He was faster and trained to face an armed man. Abi wasn't. For now he kept his weapon holstered.

"For over twenty years Mallaruza has had civil war." Abi kept walking toward him. "There's been no end in sight. And for those twenty years or more, Mallaruza and most other African nations have been given billions of US dollars in aid. *Charity.* Two-thirds of the poorest countries in the world are right here on this continent. Money, for Europeans, is the solution to our problems. We don't *need* their fucking money. We need to feed our children, we need our crops to grow and our cattle to become fat! We need *not* to be fucking *beggars,* don't you get that?" He leveled the semi-auto at Simon's chest.

"Forty-two out of fifty-two states in Africa have no hope of development. We are a raft at sea at night," he said bitterly. "Africa is sinking despite the billions in aid groups send us. We have to learn to stand up for ourselves. To manage our own destiny. Without aid."

"Great speech," Simon said sarcastically. "Go for it. But not this way. What the fuck are you *thinking*, Abi? *Destiny?* You've sold your soul to the devil and given carte blanche to a terrorist group like the Phoenix, and to a wizard as corrupt and powerful as Joubert."

"I'm going to unite Africa, Blackthorne. Sixty-two percent of the countries on this continent are having their soldiers trained here. Mallaruza is supplying food and aid to them. They *need* a strong, powerful, well-educated leader with vision."

"No one man is strong or smart enough to lead countless millions of people who are already on the brink of destruction."

"I've proven that I can do it."

"How? By poisoning their drinking water so that half of them die a gruesome death from hemorrhagic fever? By stealing and stalling aid from around the world?"

The whites of Abi's eyes showed around the dark pupils, and his face went gray. "You know—"

"That you had the hemorrhagic dengue fever gene-spliced with leptospirosis? Your version of

Munchausen by proxy? Killing with one hand and offering swift and compassionate aid with the other? Millions of people *died,* while you came off looking like a fucking saint."

"But when I'm king, millions more will be saved. I will bring wealth and prosperity to my country."

"Then fix the reasons development aid disappears down a black hole. *Fix* the priorities and the incompetence. Fix the corruption and greed and fucking arbitrary use of government power in the recipient countries themselves. Don't proclaim yourself king and become the puppet of a madman."

"He's not—"

"While you rule with a misguided but benevolent hand, Joubert will be raping all of Africa's resources without anyone being any the wiser. Yeah, I can see your face, you stupid son of a bitch. You think Joubert and the Phoenix are going to allow you to do whatever the fuck you like? Not on a bet. They're going to continue manipulating you just as they've been doing all along. Manipulate you, and the people who trust you."

Simon stepped away from the shelves and spread his feet, anger vibrating through him like a tuning fork. "Joubert is one of the most powerful wizards I've ever encountered. He's going to strip every fucking resource out of the country. Strip them, suck them dry, and leave you with a country unable to sustain its own economy in any way. Every country that throws their lot in with the god-damned King of Africa is going to be ten times— hell—a hundred times worse off than they are now.

"Look around you. It's already started. This warehouse is filled to the rafters with medicines, food, and fresh drinking water. The aid you told your people hadn't arrived. And what are those ships out there filled with? Let me guess? Gold? Emeralds? Weapons? In fact, you're already skimming off the resources as fast as the poor bastards you're killing off can supply them to you."

Abi grabbed his arm. "Join with me, Simon. Together we could make more money than you could ever imagine."

"Blood money." Simon shook him off. "No thanks. I work for the good guys."

Stepping back, Abi threw up his hands. "You're an idealist. Not everything is black or white."

"You're either one of the bad guys, or one of the good guys, and I'm afraid you and your partner are the bad guys."

"What are you going to do, old friend?" Abi asked. "Kill me?"

"No one is killing my asset," Joubert's familiar silky voice inserted as he materialized beside Abi.

In his arms he carried Kess's limp form.

Christ. The protective spell he'd cast around her had failed. Failure hadn't been a fucking option.

Bongani quickly stepped between them. "Do not

do anything . . . foolish," he pleaded, eyes wild as he looked from one man to the other.

Simon shoved him out of the way. Kess was close enough to touch, but he forced himself to focus on Joubert. He could see her well enough in his three-sixty vision, and what he saw made his heart clench. She'd clearly been beaten. Rage roared through Simon's blood as he saw her pale, battered face. He refused to allow himself to panic over the amount of blood on her skin and clothing. He couldn't afford to drop his guard. Couldn't afford to be careless.

Instead of yanking her into his own arms to check her pulse and make sure she was alive, he leveled Joubert with a murderous look, and said with icy calm, "Put her down. Do it carefully and do it *now.*"

"Ooo. I'm sooo scared," Joubert mocked in a falsetto. He opened his arms, his black leather coat looking like bat wings as Kess floated limply in the charged air between them. Long, pale strands of Joubert's hair tethered him to Kess's slack body. A malevolent spider with an innocent butterfly caught in his sinister web.

The mock humor slid off the wizard's face. "You're an amusing diversion, Blackthorne, but not much of an adversary."

"Well, hell. I *hate* to disappoint," Simon said sarcastically as he attempted to throw Joubert back, away from Kess and out of range of whatever the fuck was going to happen next. Didn't work. And if he didn't have enough power for even *that* . . .

Joubert's laugh echoed in the cavernous warehouse. "I doubt you're even a Half wizard, Blackthorne. Maybe a quarter? Possibly not a wizard at all. An amateur magician perhaps? Perform at any kids' birthday parties lately?"

Simon's blood chilled as he tried to figure out how to overcome his power limitations now. When it really counted. The last time he'd confronted Joubert he'd at least had *some* power. Now, apparently he had none.

Zip. Nada. Fucked.

A T-FLAC operative versus a dozen or more armed tangos was part of his training, and doable. But even a team of operatives against a wizard with Joubert's level of power was suicide.

In other words, he was up shit's creek without the proverbial paddle. Unless he could find a way to harness Joubert's powers. All he'd need was a small gap, a few seconds to pummel the guy for what he'd done to Kess, then he'd kill him for what he'd done to the people of Mallaruza.

Then he flashed back on what Kess had said the other day. *"You wouldn't be less than who you are now. You wouldn't lose your job, would you? You wouldn't lose your friends, or your T-FLACy skills, or your good looks."*

Adrenaline jolted through him. If he was going

to pull this off, he had to get close to Joubert. Not just close but practically glued to the bastard. A power steal, assuming he could do it at all in his present, weakened state, required up close and personal. "Scared to fuck with someone with my limited capabilities, Joubert?"

The other wizard flicked a finger. Simon went head over heels backward through the air, slamming with a reverberating *thwack!* into a pile of crates thirty yards away. Half a dozen half-ton containers toppled to the floor, spilling their contents in a jumble of shattering glass bottles, papers, and pills. Joubert was instantly there watching him slide to the floor. Exactly what Simon had wanted. Joubert away from Kess.

Did Joubert have any other superpower other than multiplication? Simon wondered. Could he get the other man to multiply his wizard footprint to disperse his power between a dozen or more mirror images of himself? If so, that would weaken the effect of his powers. Maybe.

Simon picked himself up off the hard cement floor, dusting himself off. "Learned that one in wizard nursery school—" He suddenly felt a weak surge of his own power kick in. *That'll work.*

Teleporting instantly behind Joubert, Simon cupped his hands, fingers and thumbs bent and close together. He struck Joubert simultaneously over both ears. The ten-pound force made Joubert scream in agony as both eardrums burst.

The mild concussion the action caused gave Simon just enough time to jettison Joubert to the ceiling sixty feet over his head, then hold him there. His power didn't waver, but it wasn't nearly strong enough to finish the son of a bitch off. How long could he sustain this? A minute? An hour? Another second? Simon had no choice but to act. Fast.

He shot up to the ceiling, hovering in front of Joubert, whose yard-long hair haloed around his head, waving beneath the slowly rotating fan blades as if he were underwater. "I didn't want you getting lonely up here," Simon taunted.

With his three-sixty vision he observed that far below, Abi had pulled Kess to the floor and was helping her stand. He'd deal with Abi's complicity later. For now, he had to focus his full attention on the task at hand. Killing Joubert.

Taurus in hand, Simon got off a round of shots that had Joubert dancing like a puppet on a string. He slammed in another clip and kept the bastard moving.

It was hot near the ceiling, despite the fans. Joubert was sweating, weighed down by his heavy leather coat.

Simon racked the slide mechanism, the trigger pull cocked the striker, releasing to fire a cartridge in one continuous motion. The barrage of bullets forced Joubert higher and higher, his leather coat swirling around his legs as he tried to get away. Fuck. Joubert had a protection spell. The bullets weren't doing anything more than keeping him moving. Bullets ricocheted off, darting around the room, recoiling off the walls.

Ping. Ping. Ping.

If he was too busy to fight back, that would definitely work to Simon's advantage. He was putting his faith in Joubert's mammoth ego, certain the powerful wizard wouldn't keep dancing around, dodging bullets.

He wiped sweat out of his eyes without releasing the trigger.

He had enough juice to sustain levitation but not much else. As he continued to fire, he was angling the other wizard toward the rotating fans ten feet above his head.

"Lonely?" Joubert asked with a sneer. "Hardly. I'm growing bored." Joubert did a perfectly executed somersault as if from a diving board and cannonballed into Simon from above with the speed of a bullet. Simon vaguely heard Kess's scream as he and Joubert went end over end locked in mortal combat midair.

For those few minutes Simon used their hold on each other and Joubert's powers instead of his own to levitate. He'd breeched Joubert's protection shield. The two of them were skin to skin. In roughly the same fashion he transferred power to Nomis, Simon sucked as much of Joubert's abilities from his vile core as he could and sent them to the only vessel he knew he could trust.

He heard Kess give a little yelp. Grabbing up more spare power for himself, Simon smashed the butt of the Taurus into the other man's cheekbone with a satisfying crunch of bone. Joubert's eyes grew wide and his face turned bright red as he realized what Simon had done.

"Fucker," he seethed, retaliating by pulling a knife and slicing Simon's upper arm almost to the bone. The cut felt ice cold. The blood hot.

"Even after your mugging, I still have more power in my little finger than you have in your whole body." Joubert jettisoned himself away, leaving Simon to free-fall forty feet, then at the last possible second, when Simon could smell the dust on the floor, swooped him up and propelled him in a dizzying spiral, back to the ceiling.

Simon latched onto a steel beam, and swung there, dizzy. *Shitfuckdamn.*

Joubert angled his body and swooped back to the ground, heading directly toward Kess.

The air was thick with a medicinal smell of the supplies upended earlier, and it was dark enough now that visibility was compromised. "Kess!" Simon called. "Shoot the bastard!"

"With what?" she yelled back, clearly panicked.

"Close your eyes and imagine Joubert slamming into those boxes at the other end of the warehouse."

"Why?"

"For chrissake, just do it. *Soon would be good.*"

"I told you I'd handle everything. You were just supposed to get elected. That was your *only* fucking job," Joubert shouted at Abi.

"I know. I know. I thought the Hureni had brought in a Half to help them . . ."

"My boys were having a bit of sport. That's all."

Simon watched Kess falter as she tried to walk. There wasn't enough light to see her face, but he could picture her fury and indignation. Christ, he loved her courage and convictions, but not now. Not when Joubert was moving in her direction.

"You consider the murder of millions of people *sport*?" she demanded.

"*Not now, Kess,* sweetheart. Focus." He tested his powers as one would a tongue against an aching tooth. Bargaining. Praying . . . *Nothing.* His powers were—gone. Completely gone as he swung from a steel beam sixty feet above the floor.

Not a spark. Not a hint. He had to get to her. *Now.*

"*Shazam!*" Kess yelled.

She was wide-eyed as she watched Joubert fly past Simon, hit the wall, and then slide limply to the floor.

Simon smiled as Kess lowered him in a jerky descent to stand beside her. "Shazam?" he asked.

She shrugged. "I'm new at this wizard thing. I thought maybe you had to say something when you were wizarding. It's not like I know the rules."

"The only rule you need to know is," Simon said

as he slammed a new clip in his weapon while jogging toward Joubert's disoriented form. "Do not let Joubert lay so much as a finger on you. One touch and he can reclaim his powers."

"I don't need full powers to beat you, Blackthorne," Joubert sneered as he stood, shrugging to adjust his coat.

Simon trained the gun on Joubert at the same time the other man tossed a fireball in his direction. When bullet met fire there was a loud, bright explosion, followed by a shower of white-hot sparkles as the fireball disintegrated.

"Son of a bitch," Joubert growled, twisting his hand in preparation to toss another one in Simon's direction.

Before he could manage to launch a second fireball, Simon fired another shot. This one went right through Joubert's palm.

He looked down at his hand, then back at Simon. "I'm going to enjoy killing you, Blackthorne!"

"Ditto, dickhead."

Simon spun around, hitting Joubert squarely on the side of the head with his heel, knocking him to his knees. Joubert retaliated by thrusting out his leg and kicking Simon's feet out from under him. He hit the ground with a jarring thud.

Rolling onto his side to avoid the glinting blade as Joubert's knife sliced through the air, Simon trained the Taurus on the other man and prepared for the kill shot.

Before he could squeeze the trigger, the gun grew hot, burning his palms. Hell. He tossed the weapon aside as Joubert turned the black metal to a glowing, molten red.

"Didn't your mother teach you it can be dangerous to play with guns?" Joubert taunted.

Simon used what little power he had left in an attempt to fling the knife from Joubert's hand. The attempt failed. He'd have to do this the old-fashioned way.

Arching his back, Simon snapped up on his heels, then rose to his full height. Shoulders lowered, he rushed Joubert, managing to grab the other man's wrists before bashing him into the wall. Digging his thumb into the open wound in Joubert's palm, he pounded the knife hand against the rough cement until he heard the knife fall to the ground.

He was going to enjoy every second of killing this bastard. He wanted to watch as life drained out of Joubert's body. Simon lifted his arm to press it against Joubert's throat, but instead, he found himself falling forward into the wall. Joubert was gone.

In his three-sixty vision, Simon watched as a snarling, smug Joubert materialized on the opposite side of the warehouse and pulled Kess against his chest, imprisoning her against his body with one arm.

"You lose," he yelled, his head tilted back as a string of electricity passed from Kess to Joubert. A reverse power trail.

Damn.

"I think I'll fuck her before I kill her slowly," Joubert said as he placed a quick kiss on the top of Kess's head.

"Think again," Kess said, lifting her foot and stomping on the wizard's instep.

Joubert didn't react. His lifeless stare was fixed on Simon as, Kess clutched in his arms, he ran balls out across the warehouse, leaping and levitating over the spilled contents and overturned boxes.

Not winded, he spun around in the air. "How about my lovely designer dengue? Want to see this pretty thing bleed from every orifice? Want to hear her beg to be put out of misery? I'm a generous guy. You're welcome to fight for her, pussy-boy."

Simon's body felt like ice. Yanking the Ka-Bar from the holster on his thigh, he ran. Without the power to levitate, he had to push his burning muscles to the limit. Sweat poured from his face. Blood runneled down his left arm, dripping through his clenched fingers. But the knife in his right hand was dry and steady.

He'd never been in the same time and place with Nomis, but there wasn't time to anticipate what the fuck could or would happen if they were. He didn't need power to call him. Nomis appeared far ahead, his corporeal body between Kess and Joubert.

"Want her?" Joubert threw Kess at Nomis, and they both stumbled. Nomis didn't pause as he raised his weapon and pulled the trigger and the double action pumped out bullets faster than the eye could see. It was so dark now that Simon could barely make out the four figures ahead. But Joubert's laughter was clear as a fucking bell. He hung on, willing his power to return.

"Stop shooting. Stop shooting! He's going to save my people," Abi shouted, raising the S&W .45 auto to return fire.

Kess did a quarter turn, but she wasn't nearly fast enough. Nomis swooped in, grabbed her arm, and swung her violently out of the way. She landed several yards across the floor on her belly as Nomis's weapon discharged. Abi crumpled to the floor. Simon couldn't tell if he was dead or alive.

"You have no powers. How the fuck did you get here?" Joubert demanded, as he materialized a weapon and returned fire. Nomis was corporeal, but the bullets went right through him. He fired a succession of rounds directly into the wizard, but Joubert's renewed protective spell surrounded him, and nothing penetrated. Bullets dropped off his coat like marbles from a bag.

In a swirl of leather, Joubert yanked Kess off the

floor, pulling her against him, and rose in a rush to the ceiling.

Simon followed.

"She's gonna make a big mess when she lands," he said with a rough laugh. He held Kess's body suspended over the abyss with one hand. Simon saw the terrified glint in her eyes the second before Joubert opened his hand and let go.

Seventeen

Kess squeezed her eyes shut. All she could think was that it was going to hurt like hell when she splattered on that cement any second.

Love you, Simon.

Her entire body jolted as someone plucked her out of thin air. A second later her eyes jolted open as she found herself squeezed against a hard chest. Automatically she struggled. Bucking and kicking, lashing out with hands and elbows, and trying to bite.

"Shh. Shh," Simon whispered against her hair. "I've got you."

Thank you, thank you. For a moment she was overwhelmed with visceral relief. Then she realized what it meant that Simon had caught her in her free fall. "You have your powers back! Quick. Put me down right now and go and *kill* that bastard," Kess instructed breathlessly. Her heart was pounding so hard she could barely speak.

Simon chuckled. "On my way. Here." He handed her off to Nomis. "Protective spell locked and loaded. This time it'll hold. Take good care of he—Holy shit!—did you feel that?"

Hard to miss the enormous surge of electricity passing between Simon and Nomis; the air around the three of them lit up like the Fourth of July.

"Go!" she urged as Nomis gently set her on her feet. "Oh, wait—Here." She shoved the gun she'd grabbed from Bongani's body at Simon.

He pressed a fleeting kiss to her mouth, then soared away. "That is amazingly fabulous," she said, watching him—*fly*. "And amazingly—well, creepy."

Nomis was holding her against his body. She could feel him. It almost felt like Simon. But not. He was neither warm nor responsive. All his power was pouring into Simon.

"Good. That's the way we all like it. Keep focused, okay?"

She stayed where she was, Nomis's arms securely around her waist, his chest supporting her back. Weird. Very weird. But it didn't frighten her at all. Which was just as weird, she thought as Simon and Joubert crashed into each other in a tangle of arms and legs and black leather high over her head.

She winced at the incredibly loud noises of the sparks and flares coming off their bodies. Every blow, every kick, every shot fired caused a different color explosion until the cavernous warehouse was filled with swirling smoke and the smell of . . . rotten eggs?

A blinding flash of light forced her to squeeze her eyes shut. It was followed by an enormous explosion. The percussion rocked the building hard enough to knock Kess and Nomis off their feet.

Dear God. Were they all going to die tonight?

Nomis's body covered hers as debris and huge chunks of steel and building material rained down on them. It sounded like the end of the world.

One moment Kess was being smothered under Nomis's rock-hard body, the next she . . . wasn't.

Someone slapped her face. "Ow!" she yelled, opening her eyes.

Simon chuckled, his face filling her vision. She loved his face, scratches, dirt, and all. He grinned. "Only you would say 'ow' to a wake-up tap, and laugh as a building was falling on you."

"Is he dead?" Kess asked weakly. She'd used up about twenty years' worth of adrenaline, and it had left her a little disoriented and woozy.

"You still had some of his power banked in you. The combo of that, coupled with touching Nomis for the first time, magnified my power. Noek Joubert . . . disintegrated."

"That means totally-never-to-come-back-dead, right?"

"Right." When he brushed her hair off her forehead, his fingers seemed a little shaky to her.

Kess grabbed his hand, although *grabbed* was hardly the word for her ridiculously feeble grip on his fingers. "Are you okay?"

He smiled. "I don't have broken ribs and lacerations and bruises."

"They'll heal," she assured him.

"Sooner than later," he assured her flatly. "Close your eyes and take a little nap, sweetheart, I've gotta get back to work."

Her heart, which was still jumping around in her chest like Mexican jumping beans, took up a ponderous beat. "Of course. I'll be fine." She looked past him and frowned. "Are we . . ."

"Medical floor of HQ." He looked beyond her and beckoned someone over. "This is Beth. She's going to take good care of you while I'm gone."

Kess looked at the woman through her good eye, the other being almost swollen shut. Great. *She* looked like shit. *Again.* And here was a pretty brunette to "take care" of her. "My lucky day," she mumbled.

Simon, still holding her hand, said to the doctor, "Caleb Edge will be in in about five minutes to fix all this. Give her something for the pain if she needs it." He squeezed her hand. "Be good until I get back."

"Who's Caleb Edge, and does that mean I can be *naughty* when you get back?"

"When can I get out of here?" Kess demanded belligerently as the door opened to admit Simon the next morning. Her heart did a triple axel as he came into the room wearing dark pants and a black T-shirt that outlined his rock-hard body. Kess looked at him, getting her fill. Once again she looked like crap while Simon was spit and polished and looking as though he'd just stepped out of *GQ*'s "Soldier of Fortune" issue.

He'd teleported her to T-FLAC HQ in Montana the day before and she hadn't seen him since they'd put her on a gurney and wheeled her into a room. She'd gone to sleep beaten to a pulp, and woken to find herself bathed with not a mark on her.

These spy types had all sorts of extra-cool advantages.

"I'm sick and tired of being prodded and checked and stared at." She sounded like a sulky teenager, and adjusted her tone because she was already annoyed at herself. Plucking at the starched sheet over her legs, she scowled at him. "The bruises already healed, and the cracks in my ribs are—gone, apparently. They certainly feel fine. I met Caleb Edge last night. Not only is he extremely good-looking, he did a laying-of-hands thing on me, and twenty seconds later I was well enough to dance a jig. If I knew how to dance a jig."

"Glad Caleb made it. I didn't want you in pain for a second more than necessary."

"Is he a healer or something?"

Simon nodded. "One of his powers."

"A handy one to have in your line of work. Now can I leave?"

His lips, his firm, clever attentive lips, almost—almost, tilted in a smile, as his eyes tracked her from the waist up; the rest of her was under the sheet. "Not loving T-FLAC's fabulous hospitality, I see."

"Not much to see in a twelve-by-twelve room for twelve *hours*. I'd like to take a tour of the place," she told him, searching for a sign of his mood. He should have his photograph under *inscrutable* in Webster's.

"You can leave whenever you like," he told her, his big scarred hands holding the foot rail of the bed.

"I can?" Kess threw the covers back and leapt off the bed. Simon was by her side gripping her elbow a nanosecond later as she faltered, unsteady on her feet.

"Whoa! You're bound to be dizzy."

She was. A little. Not enough to stay in bed though. "Where are my clothes?"

"Incinerated. They're getting you something now."

Kess looked up at him, her eyes narrowed. "I hope it's something red and slinky. No. Make that *black* and slinky. *Really* slinky. And FM heels too. And a push-up bra. I'm sick of you seeing me when I look like I've never seen a comb in my life."

"You don't need a push-up bra. You're—"

Trust a man to pick on the push-up bra! "But I do need a *comb,* is that what you're telling me?"

His eyes turned the color of the forest. "In a fighting mood, are we?"

"Don't patronize me, Blackthorne," she told

him, glaring up at him. He was so damn tall, and she was barefoot. He'd been in the room for several minutes and in those eternal several minutes he'd made no attempt to kiss her, or touch her, or— Damn it, he wasn't doing any of the things she wanted him to do, damn him. "I am *so* not in the mood."

"Are you in the mood for some good news?"

That didn't sound very lover-like. "What?"

"Once McKay got Angela Sidel's testimony, he managed to get your case thrown out."

"Oh, Simon—" *You are the most amazing man I will ever meet in a hundred lifetimes.*

"There's more. Not only are you in the clear, Wexler was arrested for the rape of Ms. Sidel as well as three other women. *And* assault charges have been filed by half a dozen former employees for rape or assault. He's going to be on the receiving end of assault himself for a long time."

Relief washed over her. "*Thank you* hardly seems adequate. But thank you for doing this. For me. For Angela. For the other women."

His hand rose as if he was going to touch her, then dropped away. "Talked to Phillips earlier," he told her, his voice a little choked. "We've created an antidote to the virus. Instead of administering it, we're going to do an aerial spraying in about two hours. Should eradicate the virus. They also came up with an antiviral for those already infected. The shot won't be one hundred percent effective, but we're doing our best to save as many as we can."

Kess closed her eyes for a second. "Thank God." When she opened her eyes Simon seemed to be standing a little closer. "The election was today, right?"

"Mr. and Mr. Jungo Kamau were elected president and first gentleman in a landslide election late last night."

He was looking at her so oddly. Was he trying to figure out how to say "Thanks for a lovely interlude"? Was he waiting for her to let him off the hook?

All Kess could manage was "Oh."

"Went out to my place last night. Was building it by hand, but I decided to put a little magic in it and get it ready."

"Oh, so your magic's working at full throttle *now*? Great. Really great."

"Had to get the house finished so I can bring my lady home. It's snowing out there, you know."

Kess used the heels of both hands to smack him in the solar plexus, knocking him back two steps. "Shut up about your *stupid* damn One Day Woman!" She hurt deep inside and her eyes stung. "She's here. Right in front of your idiotic, 'too blind to see me right in front of your face'... um ... eyes. Damn it. *I'm* her. I'm your One Day Woman. I've always been your One Day Woman. Do I have to dye my blasted hair brown for you to recognize me? Do I have to have a boob enlargement? A brain reduction? What the hell do I have to do short of tattooing Simon Blackthorne's One Day Damn Woman on my *forehead* to get you to see what's right in front of you. Me.

"I want to be the center of your universe. Just as you're the center of mine. I'm your woman. You're my man. I don't care if that sounds like a bad country-western lyric. We *belong* together, damn it."

Simon's expression lightened and he cupped her cheek with a gentle hand. "Marry me, Kess."

I love you, Kess, would have been the right freaking words, blast the man. She shoved at his chest again. "Now see? You're just saying that to make me crazy. You can't possibly love me as much as I love you, and I'm *damned* if I'll settle for being a stand-in. I refuse to have to look over my shoulder for the next fifty years in case your One Day Woman is behind me, closer than she appears in my rearview mirror."

His eyes crinkled at the corners, and he shook his head slightly, as if to say, poor woman. What a nut job. Kess could swear he could read her soul and probably her mind as his mouth quirked up in the beginnings of a smile.

"This isn't funny, you know," she said crossly. "I'm once again unemployed. Or possibly unemployable. And frankly I'm not sure that a tame PR job would suit me anymore anyway. I think I've been ruined."

His mouth quirked, but he said quite seriously, "Quite understandable given the last few weeks. Private armies get a bum rap, you know."

She narrowed her eyes suspiciously. "Um . . . Okay."

"What do you think about kids?"

Her heart did a little skip. "Whose?"

"Ours."

"I think ours would be perfect, but given that we don't *have* any, the question is moot."

Simon laughed. "I hope they'll be imperfect, and amazing, just like their mother." He picked her up and deposited her on the bed. With a click the door locked. He stretched out beside her, pulling her into his arms. "Fortunately the job I have in mind is fairly close to home, and I think I have enough pull to get you part-time work if you chose to stay home with the kids."

Kess stroked his face. He needed a shave, but he smelled clean and fresh and larger than life, and her heart filled with joy just being in his arms. She kissed his chin. "I have no freaking idea what you're talking about." Too scared to build a castle on a pipe dream, she finger-combed his hair off his forehead.

"T-FLAC is going to offer you a job in our information dissemination department."

She let out the breath she'd been holding. "Holy shit!" Her entire being lit up with a thousand-watt smile. "You mean I get to work in this cool building with all these amazingly cool people?"

"*I'm* the coolest."

"Without a doubt—Will I be issued a gun?"

He tilted her head up and kissed her. It was an extremely effective way to shut her up. She hoped he used it for the next fifty or sixty years.

Finally he let her up for air.

Kess blinked. They were no longer in the pale green hospital room.

"I love you, Katie Scarlett Goodall," Simon said thickly, slipping her out of the open-backed hospital gown very carefully and pushing her back against the plush cushions of a sofa in front of a crackling fire. "Who knew I'd been waiting for a feisty, sassy, beautiful redhead my entire life?"

"Will you conjure up a slinky black dress and FM heels for me, and take me out to dinner tomorrow? I want a first date. With wine and flowers and flirting and music. I want to look beautiful for you."

"You're beautiful to me just as you are, right now—" He smiled when she frowned mockingly, tucking her hair behind her ear. "I'll conjure anything you want."

"You, I just want you."

"That's going to be a constant," he said nibbling her throat. "No magic necessary."

Everything about him was magic to Kess, and it had nothing to do with Simon being a wizard. He started kissing his way down her body, his lips warm and damp as he murmured soft, sexy words against her skin.

For a moment before she closed her eyes in sheer bliss, she looked at the room behind him. Even though she'd never been there, she recognized the rock fireplace, and the snow-covered view outside the enormous wood-clad windows.

Kess knew exactly where she was.

She was home.

If you enjoyed

Night Fall,

get ready to jump into
Cherry Adair's next romantic suspense,

Night Secrets

He was screwed.

Face pressed to the gritty sand, Lucas Fox attempted to unscramble his brain.

Think, damn it.

Unfortunately he'd fallen forty feet to land on his head. It wasn't nearly as hard as his friends claimed it to be. And speaking of friends—he could use a little help right about now.

The night sky was bright with the light cones of five military choppers illuminating a crosshatch pattern over both the choppy ocean and the narrow strip of beachfront where he lay. They *whop-whop-whopped* back and forth, stirring up sand and causing palm fronds to dance wildly. Down the entire sugary length of the beach, the rows of bright pastel-colored beach houses were strung like gaudy beads and the violently swaying palms were lit up as if it were high noon.

If he were visible, he'd be . . . fucking *visible*. He
was a sitting duck out in the open. A ruffled wave
lapped up to dance playfully against his foot. A fu-
tile attempt to move out of the surf made his head
swim.

Acknowledging concussion—been there, done
that—Lucas focused on cataloging his injuries
while his lungs automatically fought for air. Everything hurt like hell. By some miracle he hadn't broken his neck, a definite plus. He'd been shot, but
only once, and in the fleshy part of his shoulder.
Been there, done that, too. He'd live.

Maybe. Right now he was hanging onto invisibility by willpower alone. He'd been at the tail end
of a Trace Teleport, following Mica Esar, a Half
wizard, when his powers had fizzled out midair.
He'd dropped like a rock. The sand wasn't nearly
as goddamned soft as it looked.

Obviously he'd been unconscious long enough
to hear the distant echo of his window of opportu-
nity slam shut. A chopper flew directly overhead,
making the inside of his eyelids burn red.

Lucas managed to stay out of sight until it
passed. Sustaining invisibility was like holding
your breath underwater for too long. Eventually
you had to come up for air.

He *had* to teleport off the beach.

He gave it his best shot. Visualizing the hidden
end of the long white beach, the sheltered, grassy
section of land, he thought himself there.

Sand still pressed into his cheek. Damn it to hell. Nothing.

He faded in and out of consciousness. A bad thing. Apparently, it was impossible for him to use two powers at once.

He could maintain invisibility for only minutes at a time, but he couldn't maintain invisibility and attempt teleportation. One or the other apparently. Fuckit.

He needed cover, and he needed it fast.

Move.

Too dizzy to think, let alone stand, he fought to hold onto iffy invisibility, his only protection against the searchers. The vibrating ground, thanks to the heavy rotors on the low-flying Hueys, made his brain hurt, and swirling sand stuck like fire ants to his abraded skin. The shouts of the soldiers gathered south of his position let him know they were forming a grid to search the beach and surrounding area. His shoulder ached like a bitch. The bullet had gone through and through, and sand adhered to the bloody wound.

Well and truly screwed.

It took everything in him to remain cognizant. His stomach pitched again and his vision blurred. Great. Just frigging great.

Sucking in a hard-won breath, he considered his options before he passed out again.

* * *

Wearing a bikini and carrying a glass of chilled wine in defense against the lingering heat of the day, Sydney McBride stood to one side of the picture window and widened the gap between the slats of the wood shutters with her fingers to get a better look outside.

She'd been typing up the day's notes and contemplating a swim by moonlight when she'd heard the incredibly loud noise of helicopters overhead. She'd raced to switch off the lights in the bungalow so she could watch the action on the beach unobserved.

The night sky was artificially bright as searchlights strafed the white-capped surface of the water. The illumination also showed at least twenty gun-wielding, uniformed men searching the beach and surrounding area. "Who or what are you guys looking for?" she murmured, intrigued. Clearly someone, or many someones, dangerous.

Sydney's heart did a little tap dance. Woohoo! *Excitement.*

Thank God.

After five weeks of doing nothing more thrilling than compensating for her surgically enhanced boobs, interviewing fellow plastic surgery patients, writing and walking the beach, she was ready to scream with boredom. This was the longest she'd stayed in one place in *years*.

Why all the guns? Was someone stealing penile implants? The thought amused her. A chapter in her new book *Skin Deep* on *that* subject would be entertaining to write if nothing else.

There was much yelling and talking as the soldiers moved with purpose toward her middle-of-the-row bungalow. Whoever they were looking for didn't stand a snowball's chance in hell. She felt a twinge of sympathy for their hapless prey. A *mouse* couldn't escape detection faced with such determination and manpower.

She observed several men knocking on doors far down the line of bungalows to her right. It wouldn't take them long to get to hers. The bungalows were all but empty. At least she thought they were. Sometimes when she'd been walking the beach late at night, she'd seen lights go on or off, and thought she heard voices. But she'd never seen anyone coming or going. As far as she knew, only nine of the twenty-five of the small, luxury beach houses still housed patients. Sydney knew them all.

Polly Straus, nose and boobs; Stan Simpson, chin. There was Karen with her enhanced butt and higher cheekbones, and Denise with her face bandaged after her skin resurfacing and full lift. There was flirty, movie mega star Tony Maxim who'd looked better *before* he was "done." And Kandy Kane, a porn star whose new double Fs made her look as though she were a Macy's hot air balloon ready for lift off. The soldiers might linger at Kandy's door awhile, but they'd be knocking at *her* door soon enough.

Sydney lifted her glass, taking a sip of cold, crisp Casa de Amaro chardonnay and letting the fruity flavor roll on her tongue as the soldiers got closer.

Setting down her glass on the coffee table, she went to find a wrap before they got there. She had a few questions of her own to ask and her new, larger breasts distracted even herself. Crossing back to the window as she tied the belt of a short white robe, Sydney listened to the crunch of gravel as two men approached her front door. Her heart lurched in anticipation. God, she loved drama.

Reaching for the doorknob, she froze in her tracks as a primitive chill of awareness raced up the back of her neck. Exactly the same chill as when she'd been a kid, and frightened to put her feet on the floor because of the monster under her bed. She'd always had a terrific imagination.

The hair on the back of her neck and arms stood up. This was not her imagination.

Someone was in her room.

She started to spin around just as a large hand curved over her mouth. The second he touched her, Sydney's eyes went wide and her teeth snapped together mid-scream as terror rendered her immobile.